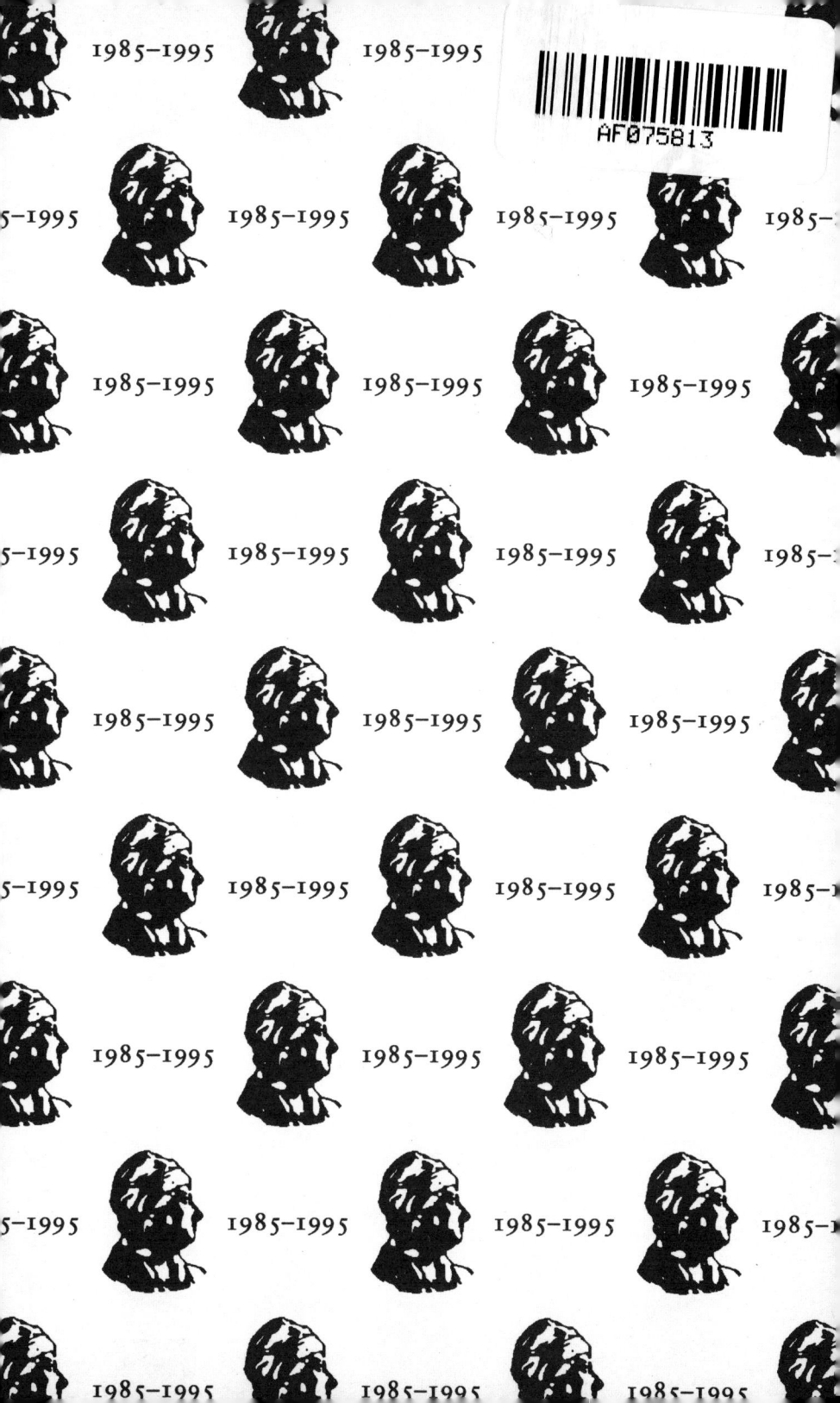

A Night in the Catacombs

For Monika

A Night in
the Catacombs

David M. Kiely

THE LILLIPUT PRESS

Copyright © 1995 David M. Kiely

All rights reserved. No part of this publication
may be reproduced in any form or by any means
without the prior permission of the publisher.

First published in 1995 by
THE LILLIPUT PRESS LTD
4 Rosemount Terrace, Arbour Hill,
Dublin 7, Ireland.

A CIP record for this
title is available from
The British Library.

ISBN 1 874675 61 9, 1 874675 66 X

*Any similarity or apparent connection between
the characters in these stories and actual persons,
whether alive or dead, is purely coincidental.*

*The author wishes to thank the following for
their kind help, support and advice along the way:
Jeroen Huber, Michael Kelleher, Des Kiely,
Mike Maguire, Charles Reede, Fabian Takx,
Jonathan Williams, and the librarians
and staff of the National Library of Ireland.*

*The Lilliput Press receives financial assistance from
An Chomhairle Ealaíon/The Arts Council of Ireland.*

Cover design by Jarlath Hayes
Set in 10.5 on 13 Sabon
by David M. Kiely
Printed in Dublin by ßetaprint

Contents

7	The Day the Rhododendrons Bloom'd
33	To Love a Stranger
56	A Night in the Catacombs
81	A Rhyme to Arabi
90	'Maedeliefje of Eyndhoven' *or* The Travelling Flautist
123	Johnny and the Tall Lady
140	An Hibernian Tale, Taken from Facts
157	Tally Ho and Away We Go!
176	The Drowned Man Fished out of the Drink
191	Hanging

The Day the Rhododendrons Bloom'd

AT ABOUT THREE in the morning in the summer of 1923, two fishing boats met at a point in the Irish Sea, some sixteen miles due east of Dublin. One of the vessels was Welsh and had departed the little fishing town of Rhosneigr that afternoon. It carried the usual complement of captain and crew of three. By the light of the stars (there was no moon that night) one of those crew members was seen to leave the Welsh boat and spring sprightly aboard the Irish vessel. A big leather suitcase was thrown after him. As soon as the transfer was made, both boats turned full rudder. The skipper of the Irish fishing trawler stared uneasily at his passenger.

'Welcome aboard, Professor,' he said without enthusiasm.

'Sank you,' answered the other in a strong Middle-European accent.

He was a thin man and the bulky fisherman's clothing sat awkwardly upon him. Beneath his dark cap a pair of rimless spectacles gleamed and a full beard covered half his face. He looked curiously about him, swaying unsteadily on the rolling deck. The captain cursed behind his own beard and hoped to blazes the coast guardsman in port was drunk by now or, even better, sleeping it off somewhere out of harm's way; he doubted that his passenger would pass muster as a crewman. But twenty-five pound notes bulged in his wallet and there would be twenty-five more waiting when they docked.

'Get that case below,' he told one of the men. 'Stow it where it'll not be noticed.'

'Please be careful', said the passenger, 'zat it is not amongst ze fishes. I do not vish to smell as a fish seller tomorrow.'

The captain grunted.

Sixty minutes later the engine was closed down and the boat glided silently between the arms of the harbour wall at Howth. There was no activity on the wharf at that hour; the other trawlers creaked in their moorings, and the skipper steered his vessel to his own. When it bumped against the dock he leaped onto the stone and made the boat fast on a squat iron capstan; the leather suitcase was thrown to him. The passenger disembarked. He looked about him and the captain saw him fill his nostrils with air. Then he turned his head to the south and muttered some words. The captain was not a well-travelled man and his knowledge of languages was scant; he did not recognize the tongue. He could have sworn it bore some resemblance to his native Gaelic but he put this down to his imagination and his nervousness. The only word he thought he understood was 'rhododendrons'.

'Quiet now,' he said. 'Your man's waitin' down beyond.'

The professor nodded and picked up his suitcase. Together they set off in the direction of the harbour town, keeping as much as possible to the shadow of the wharf buildings. They reached the railway station. A solitary motor car was parked in its forecourt: a Citroën. The driver's door opened and a man wearing a wide-brimmed hat emerged. Money changed hands. The skipper left without a backward glance, one half of his mission completed. The driver turned to the professor and pumped his hand.

'Welcome back, James,' he said.

THE DAY THE RHODODENDRONS BLOOM'D

JAMES JOYCE WOKE later that morning when the first birds sang in the treetops of Donnybrook. It was a beautiful summer morning: the sort of morning you experience in a city that is not built for summer—such a morning takes it by surprise, so to speak. It was just the sort of morning Joyce would have chosen, given the opportunity. It was of good omen, he thought.

He stared at the ceiling, seeing only an expanse of off-white; if there were cracks there (which Joyce doubted, knowing his host) he did not see them. His left eye throbbed, but he was prepared to ignore it. His nose drank in the smells of Dublin: the musty odour of the sheets and the room itself; a smell of Catholicism, of chaste-unchaste bodies that had been in this room at times and had left their auras on the furnishings as surely as a tom-cat marks its territory. He had been in many other rooms in other towns, in other countries, that smelt the same, but knowledge and old prejudices made this room special: Joyce smelt a part of himself.

He closed his eyes again and allowed those post-sleep images to rise: the ones that were important. No Irish Free State, de Valera, civil war, brutality, barbarism, a return to new values. Joyce's images were of an older Ireland, an older race, predating the present one. Finn Mac Cool. Finn of the dark night of Ireland's and the world's past, who stuck his thumb in the roasting salmon and acquired a knowledge of future things.

There was a light tapping on the bedroom door and Joyce said, '*Entrez!*'

Stephen (for we shall call him Stephen) stood in the opening. 'I thought I'd find you awake,' he said, knowing of Joyce's insomnia.

'Time enough for that,' Joyce answered cryptically, but Stephen was used to his friend's sometimes recondite humour. 'A lovely day for it.'

'The water's on, if you'd like a wash. I'm making a bit of breakfast for us.'

Joyce nodded appreciatively to the blur. He heard motor cars pass on Morehampton Road and the sound of a child's laughter. He went to the bathroom; some time later he presented himself in the big kitchen, where the smell of frying eggs and bacon mingled with the smoke of Stephen's Woodbine cigarette.

A NIGHT IN THE CATACOMBS

'Will you be wearing the beard?' Stephen asked.

Joyce rubbed his chin. 'When we go out,' he said. 'You have no idea how much that bloody thing itches when you're not used to one.'

'I would, if I was you,' Stephen cautioned. 'There's enough people in this town'd like to spit in your face or worse if they saw you. Look what happened to Skeffington and Clancy; and Oliver Gogarty was lucky to get away at all.' He filled Joyce's plate from the frying pan. 'It'll be a while more before we've lived *Ulysses* down, I'm sorry to say—especially the Republicans. You were denounced from every Catholic pulpit in the country, you know. As far as most people are concerned, you're the world's most notorious purveyor of pornography.'

'Don't apologize, Stephen,' said Joyce. 'It was to be expected. Besides, the Irish aren't the only ones. Even Paul Claudel returned the copy I sent him. If I hadn't signed the bloody thing already, then I could have given it to someone more appreciative.'

Joyce filled his fork with egg and bacon. He ate two mouthfuls, then lit one of Stephen's cigarettes. Breakfast was over.

'Provincialism', he announced, 'will be the death of this country yet. Look at Yeats and Lady Gregory: their idea of a cultural heritage is the ignorant patois of a toothless farm labourer. Now I know not all of us have had the benefit of classical learning; but they have, and that's why they should know better. I have enormous respect for Yeats as a poet, yet he still seems blinkered by a past that never existed; his mythology is so narrow that it can only turn in on itself in the end—and *vanish* up its end.'

Stephen laughed with his mouth full. 'Enough of slagging Yeats,' he said. 'Tell us about the new book.'

Joyce allowed a plume of smoke to wreathe the remains of his breakfast. He puffed lightly on the cigarette, not inhaling.

'*Work in Progress*,' he said. 'I've started it at long last. Christ knows when I'll finish it.'

'*Work in Progress*', said Stephen, 'is not much of a title.'

'*Work in Pregross*', Joyce smiled, 'was conceived in passion and will be berthed in pain.' His eyes twinkled myopically and hugely behind the thick lenses, the left lens a pale violet in colour. His red-brown hair, still damp from his bath, was brushed forward and parted to one side. 'It will be the dream of a Dubliner but, at the same time, a history of the human race, from preconsciousness to the future, and back again.'

'Will it be anything like *Ulysses*?' Stephen asked, lighting a Woodbine.

'Yes and no,' said Joyce illuminatingly.

LATER, THEY STROLLED down Morehampton Road in the direction of the Grand Canal. Joyce, though his features were unrecognizable behind the false beard, looked the other way whenever a lorry carrying soldiers passed them. Yet it seemed that Dublin had recovered well from the 'Troubles', as the civil war, lately ended, was euphemistically known. Housewives, employed and unemployed men sauntered, walked and hurried. A cart laden with scrap metal overtook the two friends on Leeson Street Bridge, the horse dropping steaming turds in its wake, the carter singing the praises of the Pride of the County Down.

'How long will it take to write?' Stephen asked.

Joyce laughed, showing his gleaming, newly acquired dentures. 'Longer than the last one.' They walked on. 'No, really, Stephen, I honestly don't know. I do believe it may be the last book I'll ever write. ...'

'Always the pessimist.'

'Ah, no,' said Joyce, 'that's not what I meant at all. What I meant was: this book will do things with language that have never been done before—by me or anybody else. And when I've done them, there won't be anything else to do. I'll have used up all that's inside me. I'm at the end of English.'

'I think', said his friend, 'you're too hard on yourself, as usual.'

They came to the south gate to the park known as St Stephen's Green. Its paths and well-tended lawns were already thronged with families and others, out early to avail themselves of the warmth of the bank holiday morning. Beyond the trees rose the façade of University College, founded by Cardinal Newman, where Joyce's literary career had begun, with the publication of an appreciation of Henrik Ibsen's work. James Joyce knew he was seeing this and his native city for the last time. There was no need to return again;

the city was locked in his soul and his memory.

'*Work in Progress*', he told Stephen, 'will be a summation of my writing to date. It will draw upon it like the sea draws on the Liffey for her life. But when Anna Livia and all the great rivers of the world have flowed into the sea, Anna will have died, only to be reborn from the womb of the mother.'

He paused for a moment or two on the humpback bridge that spanned the duck-pond. 'But don't imagine I know how the story ends. I do not. In the same way, I have no idea how the story of Ireland will end: what sort of republic will grow from the madness of the civil war. "There is division hither homeward."

'But I carry the book in my head, and I have carried it there for many years. Everything that I have written to date has been nothing more than a preliminary exercise; a *Fingerübung*: the foundations and the walls and the roof. But this book will be the house within the house, wherein the dream is dreamt.'

'I wish I could follow you,' said Stephen, shaking his head.

The pair left the park and crossed the thoroughfare to Grafton Street, Dublin's most elegant shopping precinct. They arrived presently at Bewley's Oriental Café, whence the aroma of freshly roasted coffee beans drifted out into the street. Stephen ushered Joyce into its wood-panelled interior, where society matrons sipped from fragile cups and sated their mid-morning appetites with little cakes. The place was noisy with the rattle of plates, and smoky with the cigarettes and cigars of reluctant spouses. Stephen ordered two Brazilian coffees. Joyce nodded gravely to a broad woman wearing an even broader hat at the next table. Her answering smile was small, and she resumed remonstrating with her daughter on some vague point of conduct.

'I vill put it more simply, Herr Doktor,' said Joyce, his voice risen to a thin tenor and sounding like that of a Zürich psychoanalyst, much to the amusement of the daughter, a plain girl of sixteen or seventeen with a long nose and prominent teeth. 'HC Earwicker, ze hero, can be compared wiss Fregoli. Ziss man iss ze owner off a public house in Chapelizod. He iss ze father off a girl und two boys, Shem und Shaun, und HCE dreams off zem und his problems. Ziss, my dear Stefan, iss ze story on ze simplest level.'

At the mention of Chapelizod, both mother and daughter had

abandoned their one-sided conversation, and sat sipping tea, ears pricked in Joyce's direction. He had taken a cigarette holder from his waistcoat pocket, and he pressed a lighted Woodbine into it. He grinned mischievously, revelling in his role as visiting academic, secure in the knowledge that few would recognize him. Stephen egged him on.

'I've always been fascinated by dreams,' he said, a little too loudly.

'Ah, dreams,' sighed James Joyce, the 'r' thick and glottal. He waved the cigarette holder in the air. 'Dreams contain vat my *Kollege* Herr Jung calls ze archetypes. He hass established zat all human beinks share ze same vuns. Ziss iss because zese archetypes are rooted deep in ze collective consciousness. Ze man vill dream of ze *Anima*, a female figure zat symbolizes ze repressed bisexual urges of ze dreamer. Ze woman, on ze other hand, vill dream of ze *Animus*, vizz all ze phallic—'

'Sir!' cried the large woman, very red of face. 'I should appreciate it if you did not talk about such disgusting things in public, especially not in front of my daughter!'

Stephen muffled a giggle in his hand. Joyce turned to the woman and puffed on the cigarette, eyes blinking rapidly.

'I do not understand, madam,' he said, his face wearing a hurt expression. 'I am merely discussing a scientific matter vizz my learned friend here. Ze question of dreams is vun of great importance to medicine. Ze penis, you see, plays such a vital role in—'

'I do not want to hear it, sir!' snapped the woman, raising her voice more. Heads turned in the coffee-house. 'Keep your German filth for your own country.'

'I am not Cherman, madam,' Joyce protested. 'I am Sviss!'

The fine distinction was lost on the large woman. 'German, Swiss; it makes little difference,' she told him. 'I think your language most unsuitable. *Most* unsuitable.'

Stephen, on seeing the astonished faces of the café patrons, drained his coffee-cup, picked up the bill, and led his friend by an elbow from the table. Outside in the bright sunlight both broke into loud laughter. They continued arm in arm along the street, beneath the belettered awnings of the stores, smiling and doffing their hats to the more comely ladies. Joyce paused at College

Green, his back to Trinity College. He stared short-sightedly at the roadway and struck the ground with his white, ash-plant cane. He cocked an ear as though listening intently.
'What is it, James?' Stephen asked.
'The water. Do you not hear the water?'
His friend shook his head in mystification.
'We are standing', said James Joyce, 'directly above the river Stein. It flows beneath Clarendon Street and west of Grafton Street, turns at the bank and joins the Liffey almost opposite the Custom House.' The poet grew excited and several heads turned. 'Did you know that', he went on, 'under the streets and pavements of Dublin there are more than eighty miles of watercourses? Rivers! Mile after mile of underground rivers. All flowing darkly to the Liffey and the sea:

> 'In Xenodub did Kubla Khan
> A stately pleasure-dome decree:
> Where ALP the sacred riverran
> Through caverns measureless to man,
> Down to the City Quay.'

'Just think', continued the poet, as they strolled past the Bank of Ireland and along Westmoreland Street, 'of all those underground streams and rivers: the subcutaneous veins and arteries of the metropolis, flowing for generations, yet unseen—and unknown to generations. The lifeblood of Dublin.'
O'Connell Bridge, connecting the two halves of the city, greeted them. Sackville Street stretched beyond: the street that had seen death and destruction during the abortive Rising of Easter Week, 1916. Black gaps still marred it left and right. The poet's poor eyes strained to see the statue that guarded its southern entrance: that of Daniel O'Connell, the great statesman and indefatigable campaigner for the repeal of the Union. Four winged entities at his feet defended the provinces of Ireland.
The River! Joyce leaned over the parapet and looked down with eyes that saw less than his memories. The estuary was at ebb; green and brown slime and weed clung to the stone banks below the high-water mark. Stephen thought that the river smelt evilly.

His friend inhaled deeply, almost in trance.

'Anna Livia Plurabelle,' he said reverently. 'Mother of all waters. Giver of life and Guinness.'

'I take it', said Stephen, 'she figures prominently in the new book?'

Joyce nodded. 'How could she not? The book is about Dublin, and Dublin could not exist without Anna Livia. She gives life to a daughter and two sons, Shem and Shaun, who, being brothers, are naturally rivals.'

'Naturally,' said Stephen, watching two quarrelling gulls skim low over the brown and lazily flowing water, their screeching loud and vicious.

'Have you ever wondered', James Joyce asked almost absently, 'why cities built on rivers have very much in common? Dublin on the Liffey, London on the Thames, Paris on the Seine, Vienna on the Danube, Cologne on the Rhine, Rome on the Tiber. The river gives life, true, but the river also creates division, not infrequently a north-south divide. No one engineers this divide; it seems to occur almost by an act of nature.

'Take Dublin: two universities, the parliament, government offices, the wealthy of the city—all established on her south bank. Why, I ask you?'

Stephen shrugged. 'Birds of a feather, I suppose,' he said. He glanced at Joyce: lean body propped against the bridge, elegant in his well-tailored suit and spats, the full, false beard incongruous under the Borselino hat. His weak eyes were half shut against the harsh light of the noon sun. 'Or have you a better explanation?'

'It is the duality of things,' said Joyce slowly. 'The one becomes the two, of necessity. Two of a kind represent all that kind, in all places and at all times. Names may change, but the principle remains the same. We perceive them as different entities but to history they are the same two entities: Cain and Abel. A further complication arises when Cain strives to become Abel, and Abel Cain. This they will always do, because each seeks, in reality, to become the other. The greater the polarization, the greater the tendency towards union.'

'I think I see what you're getting at, James,' Stephen said. 'One coin, two faces. It's an interesting thought. But what happens when a *third* entity comes along?'

'Ah, then we have genuine movement. The opposites, being of equal strength, have held each other at bay, preventing movement, preventing change. But then comes the daughter, the third castle of Dublin, the river in flux. She is needed to renew the cycle, which goes on to repeat itself in a new guise, in a new era.'

'And this will all be contained in *Work in Progress*?' Stephen asked.

'Oh,' said Joyce with a smile, 'that is only half the story; the story from Anna Livia's point of view. The other is just as important. Perhaps more so.'

Stephen watched a tram cross the bridge. Its open upper deck was a blaze of mothers and children in their Sunday best. A cyclist attempted to cut in front of it; to his consternation, his wheels caught in the tracks, and the tram braked with a jangle of bells and screams from the passengers. Joyce turned at the sounds, not understanding.

'You can tell me all about it presently,' Stephen said to him. 'Over the little surprise I've arranged.'

'WHITE CHIANTI!' EXCLAIMED James Joyce, holding the glass of pale gold liquid to the light and peering into its depths. 'A surprise indeed. You know, I never drink wine until the sun goes down, but today ... today ...'

'Larry', said Stephen, indicating the proprietor of the pub in Middle Abbey Street where they sat at a table by the window, 'got it through a friend of a friend. It won't taste the same as it would in *la bella Italia*, but I hope you enjoy it.' He raised his own glass. 'Here's to the new book.'

Joyce sipped the wine and closed his eyes in satisfaction. 'It certainly makes an improvement on what we have to put up with in Bognor,' he said. 'But anything's better than Bognor. ...'

'What does Nora think of the place?'

'She and Lucia like it well enough,' said Joyce. 'Nora's sister is with her, but I think she misses Paris, all the same. I know I do.'

Stephen topped up the poet's glass from the bottle. 'I'd like to hear more about *Work in Progress*.'

THE DAY THE RHODODENDRONS BLOOM'D

James Joyce stroked his false beard and lit a cigarette. He smoked it leisurely, sipping his wine at frequent intervals. His companion knew better than to rush him, and set himself instead to studying the pub's other occupants. They were a mixed bunch: a hard core of regulars stood shoulder to shoulder with day-trippers, fathers enjoying a respite from their loved ones. Much of the talk concerned the cessation of hostilities that had taken effect in May; the 'Irregular' faction, the IRA, had given up the struggle against those who had signed the infamous treaty, by which the Irish Free State had forfeited sovereignty over six of the counties of Ulster.

The war had been bitter; more bitter even than the fight for independence subsequent to the Rising of 1916. Brother had fought brother, and had murdered almost indiscriminately. More than four thousand people, including many non-combatants, had perished in the conflict. With the approval of the Roman Catholic hierarchy, seventy-seven prisoners of the pro-Treaty forces had been executed.

A short, beefy fellow wearing a straw boater and a handlebar moustache called for a fresh round of drinks, and announced in a Kerry accent: 'My cousin told me that they chained nine prisoners to a pole like kippers, so they did. Then they put a mine under 'em and blew the whole shebang to kingdom come.' Heads were shaken in dismay.

What had the struggle been about? The partitioning of the country was one of the immediate causes; more important was the fact that Dublin's parliamentary representatives were obliged to swear an oath of allegiance to the British monarch. Yet many insisted that civil war, independent of these grievances, was inevitable, owing to the reticence of leaders of both factions to allow the common people of Ireland to decide their own destiny in a democratic way.

The poet had no ears for the recriminatory conversation at the bar. 'There was a farmer in County Wicklow called Michael O'Keeffe,' he began. He sipped some Chianti. 'A small farmer: he kept ten head of cattle, a few pigs and a fairly sizeable flock of sheep. It was from the last-mentioned that he made most of his livelihood.

'Towards the close of a particularly harsh winter, O'Keeffe and his two sons tended the lambing ewes. The farm was situated high against the slope of the Great Sugarloaf, and the snow still lay thickly on the ground. O'Keeffe and his sons delivered sixteen lambs the first day—hard work, as you can imagine, their hands and faces frozen by the cold.

'All went well, up to a point; Michael O'Keeffe himself delivered four bouncing baby lambs, which were licked dry by the mothers before the wet of the afterbirth froze on their little fleeces. The fifth proved more difficult. The ewe, smaller than the rest, lay panting and drooling wide-eyed in the snow, and O'Keeffe knew that she was in considerable pain. One of his sons helped him move the animal into a comfortable position. Her contractions had started, but the uterus had failed to open. Michael O'Keeffe fed her a teaspoonful of poteen, a remedy that is commonly used in such cases. It did not help. The contractions stopped, then started again, with no sign of the lamb. O'Keeffe was afraid that he might lose the mother, so he sent one of his sons to fetch the vet as soon as the man could come, and left the ewe in order to see to the others.

'When the vet arrived some two hours later, there was no change in the little ewe's condition.

'"I can give her something to put her out of her misery," the vet said. "It's plain to see she'll not survive the birth."

'But Michael O'Keeffe was having none of it, and he urged the vet to examine her internally. Inserting his fingers into the uterus, the vet worked them past the mouth of the womb. The little ewe bleated in protest. Presently the vet withdrew his hand and said, "Now I know what the trouble is. There's two of them."'

'"What, twin lambs?" exclaimed Michael. This was a situation he seldom encountered, and certainly not in a ewe of this size.

'"I felt two heads," said the vet. "They've probably got their legs entangled with one another."

'"Isn't there anything we can do?" O'Keeffe asked.

'"I'd say a little prayer, if I were you," answered the vet and the farmer wondered whether he was serious. "In the meantime I'll try to get one of them presentable at least."

'The vet worked his fingers once more into the ewe, and pushed and prodded. All to no avail. Another hour went by and the sky began to darken. Michael was about to give up all hope and allow the ewe to be put down, when suddenly a small black head and a pair of white forelegs appeared.

'"Good girl!" Michael cried. "That's the one anyway."

'Then, to the men's surprise, a second tiny head appeared: a white one.

'"That's it," said the vet ruefully. "They're trying to come out together. It'll be the death of her, Michael, I'm afraid."

'O'Keeffe shook his head sadly, convinced that the vet had spoken the truth. Next moment, the ewe gave a little cry and a single body emerged: a lamb having two heads, one black, one white.'

Joyce, storyteller *par excellence*, had been recounting the tale with complicated movements of his bony hands, each gesture illustrating the parturient struggles of the ewe and the reactions of the men in a manner that rivalled the best mime artists of the Parisian theatre. Stephen was captivated.

'Jayziz!' he gasped. 'A monster!' He refilled their glasses and signalled to the barman for a fresh bottle. 'I saw a picture once of a two-headed dog, but I thought it must have been a hoax; the thing was stuffed anyway.'

'A hoax? Not necessarily,' Joyce told him. 'It happens more often than you'd imagine. But such freaks of nature survive for a couple of hours at the most. This one, however, was different.'

'It was plain and downright stupidity', announced the little man in the straw boater, 'for O'Connor's Irregulars to occupy the Four Courts. Caught like bloody rats in a trap, so they were. Now if that was me, I'd have deployed my men around the city and taken control of the barrackses. Or I'd have attacked Collins in the Castle.'

'Right you are, Brendan,' agreed another. 'Collins had only about three thousand men in Dublin at the time. If O'Connor and Mellowes had attacked, instead of barricading themselves in, they'd have wiped the floor with them.'

The new bottle of white wine arrived. James Joyce lit another cigarette; Stephen filled the poet's glass.

'Glou glou,' said Joyce. 'The sound of sacramental wine being poured at a mass.' He said it without humour: a matter of fact, an observation. A group of youths passed by outside in the bright sunshine, singing surprisingly well in unison. The poet smiled broadly, upon hearing their song.

'Well, go on,' Stephen urged. 'What became of the lamb?'

'Michael O'Keeffe was greatly disturbed,' continued Joyce. 'More than that; he was a highly superstitious man. The ewe died within minutes of giving birth, and this increased his fears. The vet, on the other hand, was intrigued by the whole thing, and he offered to buy the strange creature, perhaps to make a scientific study of it; who can say? O'Keeffe refused. Although he was in awe of the two-headed lamb, it none the less held a certain fascination for him. They argued about it throughout the remainder of the day, the vet insisting that the animal would die anyway and be of no further use to the farmer. He departed the O'Keeffe farm that evening, promising to look in the following day.

'The monster, being motherless, required sustenance from another quarter. Michael O'Keeffe tried to have it suckled by other ewes, but each in turn rejected it. He therefore entrusted it to one of his daughters who, despite her own fear, took pity on the poor, deformed creature. She fed it milk obtained from a ewe, taking care to hold the bottle to each of the little heads in turn.

'Next day, the vet called as promised. The lamb had survived the night, and lay sleeping in the kitchen before the hearth. The vet had brought his notebook with him, and proceeded to make entries, no doubt with the intention of writing a paper at some stage. O'Keeffe's daughter then began to feed the animal, beginning with the left—the white—head. That went well. But when it came to the turn of the black head, the white one cried out in protest, and the lamb sprang from her arms and raced insanely about the kitchen, seeking escape. They caught it, and once more the daughter tried to give the bottle to the black head. The white one protested again and attempted to push the black head to one side. This happened twice more. Finally the vet said: "Never mind. Since they both share the same body, it doesn't make much difference which head you feed; the milk will go into the one stomach."

'Nevertheless, when the vet returned to the farm the following day, he was surprised to find the creature still alive. He examined the monstrous thing and observed that it had grown thinner.

'"I don't understand it neither," said O'Keeffe. "She's been taking the bottle every few hours, but if you ask me, she's only growing weaker. The milk doesn't seem to be doing her any good at all."

'The vet's diagnosis confirmed this. He left to make his calls and returned that evening. The creature lay before the hearth, panting and making small, nervous movements with its legs. All four eyes were closed. It was obvious that the lamb was at death's door.

'"Let me take it with me, Michael," the vet said.

'O'Keeffe shrugged. "What are going to do with it?" he asked.

'"I don't know yet," said the vet. "It's doomed anyway. Maybe I'll have the poor thing stuffed and put on show in the college in Dublin. They'll give you a good price for it, at any rate, so you'll not be out of pocket for the ewe you lost."

'This seemed a sensible idea, so the vet wrapped the lamb carefully in an old coat, and brought it to his practice in Kilternan. His partner was there when he arrived, and he marvelled at the creature, urging the vet to lay it on the table in the surgery. The vet told him of its history.

'"If it's going to die in any event," said the partner, "would you mind if I conducted an experiment on it?"

'"What sort of experiment?" the vet asked, remembering his promise to Michael O'Keeffe.

'"If you ask me," explained the partner, "the body is rejecting all food because the white head refuses to allow the other to be fed. What if we were to remove one head? My guess is that that would save the creature."

'The vet frowned. What the other said made some sense; it was known that the body—both animal and human—could, at times, reject the food given it, leading to starvation and sometimes death. He had never before performed an operation of such complexity. What, he wondered, would the outcome be, should he and his partner be successful? Glory and fame in the veterinary circles of Dublin—and perhaps London—would be theirs. He acceded.

'"Which head do we excise?" he asked.

'"The weaker one," replied his partner without hesitation. "The black one."

'And that is what the surgeons did. Having administered a

weak anaesthetic, they cut off the black head at the shoulder, the operation and the subsequent stitching lasting several hours. They put the severed head in a jar of alcohol, and retired for the night.

'The following morning, the men found the lamb alive and well, and apparently none the worse for the amputation. The creature accepted nourishment and was placed in a basket to convalesce. A week later they removed the bandages, and the lamb, despite its lopsided appearance, was as fit and healthy as any normal specimen of its kind. It had grown considerably, and its snow-white head measured almost one-and-a-half times the size of the black one preserved in the jar.

'The vet was delighted with the success of the venture, and set off to Michael O'Keeffe's farm to inform him of events, taking the lamb with him. But, far from being pleased, O'Keeffe flew into a fit of rage, accusing the vet of dishonesty and treachery.

'"I don't want the bloody lamb!" he roared. "She looks normal enough, except for that piece out of her where the other head used to be. But I haven't a hope of selling her in the market in that state."

'The vet had no option but to pay the farmer for the lamb. When it had grown, he brought it to the slaughterhouse, where he received more than he had paid for it. The paper he wrote together with his partner was turned down by the veterinary college, and all that remained was the little black head in the jar of alcohol.'

Stephen shook his head. 'And that's in the book?' he asked.

'Ah, the book!' said Joyce mischievously. 'I'd quite forgotten about the book. Do you not think', he added, accepting another glass of wine, 'that it's far too nice a day to spoil with talk of writing and philosophy?'

Stephen slapped his knees. 'You're right,' he said. 'And here I was forgetting you deserve a little bit of a holiday, away from your labours. What would you like to do, James? Are you hungry?'

'Just think', said somebody at the bar, 'what might have happened if the Brits hadn't gone and shot Jim Connolly.'

'Would that have made any difference?' asked another.

'I'm damned sure it would've. If Connolly and MacNeill's Volunteers had waited with the Rising—or even if they'd staged another one, later, at the beginning of 1918, when they wanted to introduce conscription—then we'd have caught the English at a bad moment. Our lads at the front—apart from the Unionists, of course—would have mutinied. So would a lot of the ordinary Brits, and the French too. Even the Germans might have laid down their arms, because they were just as sick as everybody else, fighting a rich man's war for him. There'd have been a general rising of the proletariat, so there would.'

'In which case, *you* wouldn't be standing here drinking pints on a bank holiday,' said the man in the straw boater, 'but shovelling shite down at the docks like everybody else.'

'I can ask Larry to do us a couple of pies, if you like,' said Stephen. The poet nodded absently; Stephen gave the order and refilled their glasses. If Joyce had vowed to forget or forgo philosophy, then his promise was short-lived. He turned his eyes to the smoke-browned ceiling and creased his high brow.

'The book', he said 'is about a dream dreamt by Finn Mac Cool, as he lies dying in Dublin, his head at Howth and his feet in the Phoenix Park. Finn is the Adam Cadmon, the celestial being on whom Man is modelled, and to whose state of perfection Man must aspire.'

'Isn't that the Cabbala?'

'In a sense, yes. The Cadmon's journey begins at the feet, in the world of Malkuth, in the Park—'

'Just a minute, James. This is going a bit too fast for me, you know. What in God's name is the world of Malkuth?'

Joyce spread his hands and made circular motions in the air, the turbulences causing the cigarette smoke and dust motes to spiral and dance in the rays of sunlight from the pub window. The beard, spectacles and dark suit lent him a rabbinical appearance. His speech seemed to change accordingly.

'Imagine', he said, 'ten glowing spheres, from here ... to here. They are positioned in such a way that four form a central column, with the remaining six arranged three on each side. This is the Cabbala or Tree of Life.'

'I know of it,' said Stephen.

'Then you will know that these spheres are the *Sephiroth* which make up the plan of the Universe. This one at the top is the *Sephirah* of Kether, the Crown, the head of the Cadmon. Beyond it are the three veils. The *Sephirah* here at the base is called Malkuth, the Kingdom. It is the first rung on the ladder which Finn must climb.'

The publican placed two steaming steak and kidney pies in front of the guests; Stephen pressed two coins into the man's hand. Joyce appeared not to have noticed the publican or the pies.

'So,' he continued, 'in order for Finn to climb to Kether, he must construct pathways between the spheres: twenty-two in all, numbered 11 to 32. At the same time as he constructs his pathways upward, his universal self is engaged in creating a path from Kether to Malkuth. Therefore between them they are building the Temple of the Universe. Do you follow me?'

'With difficulty,' said Stephen, swallowing a mouthful of pie, 'but yes, I believe I follow you.'

'The pathway from Kether, the One, leading to Chokmah, the Two, is path number 11. When Kether becomes Chokmah, unity becomes duality. The fourteenth path, leading from Chokmah to Binah, is called the Path of the Empress. It is ruled by Venus, goddess of love, and Binah is the feminine principle: the Great Sea.

'In the meantime, Finn has constructed the pathway from Malkuth to Yesod. This pathway is numbered 32 and is called the Universe. The first worlds he encounters left and right are Hod and Netzach. He carries Hod to Netzach by means of the pathway known as the Tower. But, once in Netzach, he can return to the Middle Pillar only along the pathway known as Death.'

'So he dies?'

'He does, but he is born again on the gallows tree of the Hanged Man, pathway number 23.'

The poet lit another cigarette, his steak and kidney pie untouched. He stared straight ahead, and his friend knew that his weak eyes were seeing neither the bar nor its occupants.

'Do I take it, then,' Stephen asked, 'that this new book of yours is based on the Cabbala?'

'You could,' Joyce replied. 'It's a feast at which the Cabbala is present. A feast of mankind. "There are rituals of the elements and feasts of the times. A feast for fire and a feast for water; a feast for life and a greater feast for death!"'

'This all sounds a bit morbid to me,' Stephen remarked. Joyce cackled merrily, the high-pitched sound causing some of the other drinkers to turn and stare.

'Not at all! Not at all!' cried the poet. 'It is a joyous book. It celebrates the joys of life.'

'I think you're being punny again, James,' said his friend with a smile.

'Ah, but isn't the pun the highest form of wit?' Joyce replied. 'To play with words is to exploit the analogous nature of both life and language. Is *Leben* not *Nebel* until the poet shows otherwise? "Is a God to live in a dog?" Every word carries the seed of its opposite. And every word is an analogy of every other word, just as every one thing is an analogy of every other thing. That is why my book is a mountain into which I will tunnel from all directions, gathering nuggets as I go.'

'And speaking of going,' he said then, rising somewhat unsteadily to his feet, 'shouldn't you and I be doing that? Here I am doing what I said I would not: philosophizing, while out there Dublin is enjoying herself.'

The poet reached for his cane. 'Give me your arm, good Stephen,' he said, 'and we will disport ourselves amongst the holidaying throng. To sit in a smoke-filled public house on a day like today is little short of sinful.'

'Amen to that,' said his friend, noticing that the second bottle of white wine was now all but empty. He gave Joyce his elbow and they went out into the bustle of Middle Abbey Street. There was indeed a holiday atmosphere in the city. Ragged children hopscotched happily on the pavement. One little boy detached himself from his playmates and waylaid the men.

'Gizza penny, misther,' he ordered.

Joyce reached into his fob and handed the child three copper pieces. The boy was immediately set upon by the other children. They were still fighting over the coins when Joyce and Stephen turned into Sackville Street. Motor cars, omnibuses, trams and horse-drawn vehicles thronged the broad thoroughfare. A rich odour of droppings rose from the roadway and gutter; Joyce sniffed appreciatively. ...

'POETRY', MINNIE POWELL declared, 'is a grand thing, Mr Davoren. I'd love to be able to write a poem—a lovely poem on Ireland an' the men o' ninety-eight.'

Davoren looked up from his typewriter, surprised to hear these words from a simple dweller of the tenement.

'Oh, we've had enough of poems, Minnie,' he told the girl, 'about ninety-eight, and of Ireland, too.'

Minnie's pretty face fell. 'Oh,' she exclaimed, 'there's a thing for a Republican to say!' She moved to the window. 'But I know what you mean: it's time to give up the writing an' take to the gun.'

James Joyce moaned loudly. His friend looked at him in surprise; he was aware of faces staring in their direction.

'Is something the matter, James?' he whispered.

The poet's eyes were shut behind his spectacles. He waved a hand limply.

'It's not the sentiment expressed,' he told Stephen, 'but how she expresses it: the almost childlike naïveté cloaking the bellicosity of the words. What is her name? She will go far.'

'Gertrude Murphy.'

'Gertrude!' repeated James Joyce with feeling. 'Dear Spear, to shake 'neath the beard of the Bard. A worthy foil for Arthur Shields.'

The two friends sat in the front row of the Abbey Theatre, Joyce being unable to follow the action of the play from a greater distance. The house was full, and Stephen had considered himself fortunate to have been able to obtain tickets for the double bill: Lennox Robinson's *Crabbed Youth and Age* and Sean O'Casey's *The Shadow of a Gunman*. Dublin's most famous theatre had braved the rigours of the civil war: in October of the previous year, players and audience had been trapped in the house until early morning, when snipers' bullets clove the air in the street outside. The Republican movement had attempted to shut down all Dublin's cinemas and theatres at the beginning of 1923, but the gallant Abbey had defied the order. They had played under the protection of soldiers of the Free State Army on St Patrick's Day.

Joyce was in his element, delighted to be back in the place where W. B. Yeats, J. M. Synge and Lady Gregory had suckled and weaned the Irish literary theatre movement. He followed every

THE DAY THE RHODODENDRONS BLOOM'D

word, every gesture of the two performances, making noises of appreciation at frequent intervals. When the curtain fell on *The Shadow of a Gunman* and the players had taken their third curtain call, Stephen heard him say, half to himself:

'"Remember all ye that existence is pure joy; that all the sorrows are but as shadows; they pass and are done."'

'DUBLIN', JAMES JOYCE said, 'is the seventh city of Christendom, and the second city of the Empire. It also ranks as third in Europe for the quantity and quality of its brothels. And one of the finest is to be found in Mountjoy Square.'

'I bow to your superior knowledge,' said Stephen coolly, not entirely impressed by the sight of dilapidated Georgian houses, once grand, now filthy tenements housing Dublin's poor, their scalloped fanlights missing panes of glass, and the grime of generations on doors and sills. Mountjoy Square.

'Mountjoy,' said Joyce. 'The joy of the mount.' He stopped and inclined his head, savouring the sounds of the destitute children at play, as they raced in and out of front doors and down steps littered with refuse; the calls of women from one window to another; the wailing of infants from dark interiors.

'There was once a young man,' he began in a slow, decisive voice, 'who came to Dublin in 1906. He was a Welshman named Owen, a sales representative for a firm of haberdashers in the city of Cardiff. Why he came—or was sent—to Dublin is not clear. In any event, he arrived on the packet-boat, which docked at Kingstown in early morning.

'Though he was new to the salesman's trade, it was not Owen's first business trip: he had already visited several Welsh towns and the cities of Bristol and Bath. But it was his first journey overseas, and he was very much excited; not only by the prospect of acquiring new and important business for his firm, but by thoughts of possible debauchery in a foreign country. I should explain that Owen's marriage, whilst sailing on a relatively even keel, lacked warmth and affection, and had done so for many years. Therefore Owen felt that what he missed of love might be compensated for by a copious amount of lust.

'His business completed, Owen treated himself to an excellent dinner in his hotel, and set out in the evening to enjoy the delights of this strange, new city. He decided to sample Dublin's pub life and, to this end, made his first stop at Mulligan's of Poolbeg Street. Having consumed one glass of beer alone, he fell into conversation with two of the bar's regular customers: Francie Hayden, a turf accountant, and John Quigley, a retired national schoolteacher. Presently this motley trio ranged farther afield, visiting several of the city's well-known establishments. After closing time (which in those pre-war days was later than now) they found themselves outside the doors of Mooney's in Parnell Street, very much the worse for drink but determined that the Welshman should not return to his native country without obtaining firsthand knowledge of Dublin's publicly secret night-life. The matter having been put to the vote, Mountjoy Square, partly because of its proximity, became the objective of their carnal quest.

'The three arrived at the bawdy-house of Maggie Crampton at number forty-one, and were admitted by the proprietress herself, a handsome woman of undefinable age who had spent almost half her life—it was said—in Paris. Mr Hayden and Mr Quigley, being familiar with Mrs Crampton's ladies, made their selections quickly and disappeared to private quarters, leaving Owen in the company of another gentleman and four prostitutes. Owen, slightly nervous and unaccustomed to the procedure, accepted a second glass of brandy and attempted to engage those present in conversation, a pursuit in which he was mildly successful, the ladies warming to this callow young man with the unfamiliar accent. The four, in turn, made advances to him, but he seemed unwilling to avail of their services, much to the chagrin of Madam Crampton. Finally, this lady herself took Owen by the hand and led him to her own chamber. She undressed him, divested herself of her own clothing and bade him sit on the bed. Owen, befuddled with drink, made no move towards her.

'"Is there anything special you'd like?" she asked him.

'"I don't know," he said. "I've never done this sort of thing before."

'Maggie Crampton understood at once, and set to work, employing her whole repertoire—which was very considerable, I can tell you. That night, young Owen was initiated into a world whose existence he had hitherto not even suspected: the rites of Venus were celebrated with passion and zeal; no act was deemed too base or perverse for the participants, and Owen was a willing acolyte.

'At dawn the following day, the young Welshman awoke in the unfamiliar bedroom, alone. His head throbbed and his vision was faulty. Yet when he turned his head, an object on the wall caught and held his gaze: it was a small crucifix whose presence he had failed to notice the night before.

'As Owen looked at it, something stirred in his semi-conscious mind. Although brought up in the Catholic faith, Owen had not practised for many years. Now suddenly his thoughts were filled with sentiments of piety and devotion: the true meaning of Christ's passion, death and resurrection became clear to him. He left the bed of debauchery and knelt naked beneath the cross. He prayed with more reverence than he had ever felt before, and it seemed to him that he prayed to a *living* being, a person who heard and acknowledged his prayers, rather than the distant, aloof entity he had learnt of in youth.

'Owen left that house in Mountjoy Square a changed man. When he boarded the mail-boat that evening, he walked with a spring in his step, and when his young wife met him at the railway station in Cardiff they embraced as newly-weds.'

'And I suppose', said Stephen drily, 'they lived happily ever after?'

'Indeed they did,' Joyce answered with a smile. He squinted at the door of the house they stood before. 'Is that number forty-one?'

'It is,' said his friend.

JAMES JOYCE, NOVELIST, poet, playwright and polyglot, caressed the keys of the piano with long white fingers. The middle E flat gave no note. Stephen sat on a sofa, wedged between two heavily made-up lovelies, brandy glass in hand and eyes shining brightly. He raised his glass in a toast.

'To the memory of Maggie Crampton!' he sang. 'May her spirit forever imbue these walls, and her light guide lost seamen to a safe haven. And for God's sake, James, take off that ridiculous beard; you're amongst friends now.'

A buxom girl, wearing only a corset and stockings, leaned on the top of the piano, whose surface was scarred in places by cigarette burns. She cried out when Joyce reached behind his ears and pulled the fake beard from his chin. The face thus revealed was long and thin, the cheeks concave. A small red moustache, sticky with spots of glue, adorned the upper lip, and a trim goatee grew on the chin. Joyce grinned at the girl and stuffed the false beard in his pocket.

'I thought you said you were a rabbi,' she exclaimed. 'You don't look like a rabbi to me, so you don't.'

'He was only codding you,' said Stephen. 'That's the famous Mr James Joyce.'

'You mean the fella who writes the dirty books?' said the girl, wide-eyed. 'My mammy warned me all about him. If she thought I was talking to him she'd be mortified, so she would!'

Joyce eyed the heavy-breasted girl with amusement. He set his glass down on top of the piano, stared at the ceiling for a moment or two, and launched into the introduction to a plaintive ballad. A hush fell upon the room when his clear tenor rose above the music:

> 'Where Lagan stream sings lullaby,
> There blows a lily fair.
> The twilight is in her eye,
> The night is in her hair.
>
> 'And, like a lovesick leananshee,
> She hath my heart in thrall.
> Nor life I own, nor liberty,
> For love is lord of all.
>
> 'And often when the beetle's horn
> Hath lulled the eve to sleep,
> I steal unto her shieling lorn,
> And thro' the dooring peep.

'There in the cricket's singing stone
She stirs the bogwood fire,
And hums in sad sweet undertone,
The song of heart's desire.

'Her welcome, like her love for me,
Is from the heart within;
Her warm kiss is felicity,
That knows no taint or sin.

'When she was only fairy small
Her gentle mother died,
But true love keeps her memory warm
By Lagan's silver side.'

When the final chord of the melody decayed on the air of the smoke-filled room, Joyce remained stiffly seated at the piano. The girl looked at him with red mouth agape. She watched a tear wend its way like a slow-moving stream down the gully of his right cheek. He seemed to sense her compassion because he gazed back at her with eyes whose mournfulness was magnified by the thickness of his lenses. Then he spread his hands wide and swept his fingers across the ivory keys in a double arpeggio. He swivelled on the stool.

'Stephen, me boy,' he called gaily, 'tear yourself away from those motts a mo, and give us something mad and merry!'

He stood up and held out his glass, which was replenished instantly by a girl of dark, almost Spanish, complexion. His place was taken by his friend, who attacked the keyboard with abandon in rapid alla caccia. Joyce drained his glass and set it down. He gave a whoop and, before the startled eyes of the company, pirouetted about the room, left leg extended at an angle of ninety degrees. His angular body spun and contorted, keeping time to the frenetic music and, never making contact with the furniture in the cramped parlour. His eyes were wild as he executed dance steps and passes of his own creation. The onlookers held their breath, expecting him to cannonade at any moment against a chair or table. He did not. Half-blind Joyce had entered the state where the body moves independently of the conscious mind, where learning yields to animal instinct, where the Dervishes had gone and the Gurdijefs had attempted to go: the place where language ends.

Down in Sackville Street, Admiral Horatio Nelson stood atop his Pillar, guarding the General Post Office which had harboured Patrick Pearse's militia. An army lorry, laden with soldiers of another, more powerful calibre, lumbered past. Faint starlight and brighter lamplight sparkled on the gently flowing Liffey. Stephen struck the final chord. James Joyce spun once more in silence, then collapsed on a couch.

"'Ah! Ah! What do I feel?'" he lamented. "'Is the word exhausted?'"

AT ABOUT THREE in the morning, two fishing boats met at a point in the Irish Sea, some sixteen miles due east of Dublin. One of the vessels was Welsh. ...

To Love a Stranger

THE STRANGER CAME in the first week of May. I know that because it was in the same week Coleman John broke his ankle and he jumping the gap between the two big stones in the south cove, the ones that do be exposed clean when the tide is gone. The other children let out their old-laughter at that and Coleman screaming and roaring like a bullock and it after being castrated. Coleman took the best part of an hour to make his way home and got no tea from his mother.

They rowed the stranger over from Big Island in Pat MacDonagh's boat and the four of them making a good walk of it to show off to the visitor. Of course the bulk of the people went down to see what himself looked like, we after being told that it was a man from Dublin. Bridget Conneely said how she'd heard them telling that he was good-looking; I didn't know where she'd heard that at all or if there was any truth in it but, that itself, there were at least twelve of us girls down at the pier when Pat MacDonagh brought the big canoe inside.

'He hasn't got the look of a Protestant on him, so he hasn't,' said Mary O'Flaherty when the boat came up close.

'And who said anything about him being a Protestant in any case?' said Bridget Conneely. 'Just because he's from the east doesn't make him a Protestant. Haven't you any sense inside in your head at all?'

Mary said something terrible but of a low voice that her mother wouldn't catch, she standing there alongside the rest of us. The men were after pulling the oars inside and Pat MacDonagh was already in the water pulling the boat up onto the stones. I got my first good look on the stranger and him resting there in the butt of the boat.

He did have the look on him of one of ourselves when I saw him far from me because of the clothes he had on him but after a bit I could see he wasn't like us at all. He had an old hat on him that came down past his forehead but you could see his eyes right enough and they were a colour that put me in mind of the pools of water below Kilcannagh that do be left to the crabs when the tide is out. He had a big stout head, God bless him, and hair that looked strange as though it was not his own hair and a black moustache turning down at the ends with a bitlet of hair growing too under his lip. His old coat had a patch or two on it and his trouser was damp from the sea. When the men helped him up on the pier you could see that the boots he had on him were poor and in need of mending.

Pat MacDonagh hefted a big leather bag from the arse of the canoe and put it into the stranger's hand. I heard the stranger doing thanks to Pat in Gaelic and it with such a queer sound on it that Bridget and me were taken with a fit of laughing. The stranger turned his big head and looked between the two eyes on me. So direct was that look that it took me all by surprise and I never thought on covering my head with the shawl like Bridget did.

And didn't he smile at me with those fine Protestant lips of his and those light brown eyes laughing of their own! I think I might have smiled right back at him but me being too flustered at the time I don't remember now. But it's no matter because old Mikey Mullin shooed us young girls and fellas away to make room for the men and the stranger, that they could go in peace to Pat MacDonagh's house. Bridget Conneely grabbed me by the arm.

'Is it going up above you'll be too, o Barbara?' she asked and by the way she said it you could see she had eyes for the stranger itself. Bridget was seventeen years of age then in that summer of 1898—bare a year older than me—and not a fella was calling to her father's house yet while her two sisters were married and they less than sixteen each of them.

'It's not going up there I am,' I told her. Now I had every wish to be going up to the MacDonaghs' that day—and every day that would be coming!—in order to look upon the stranger again and the lovely eyes and head of him, but my mother was lying up in her bed since a fortnight after Easter because of the curse someone had placed on her, or so she said. In any case there was nobody but little Mary and myself to make the meals for the men and be in the butt of the house, so I went home to start on the dinner before twilight. I was busy sweeping out the kitchen in the evening when Bridget Conneely came inside and the fall of her eye would have you thinking she was after coming back from a visit to the Pope in Rome itself.

'Do you know what I'm going to tell you?' she asked after making sure first that the men were out of the house—they were away over to Pat MacDonagh's and so were most of the islanders. Little Mary was in her bed and my grandmother was sleeping beside the fire.

'I do not. What is it?'

Bridget pulled a stool up to the hearth and having a care not to wake Granny (who was sleeping most of the day by then, God rest her poor soul).

'His name is Seán,' she said, 'and wasn't the uncle of him over on Big Island in the 'forties.'

'The uncle? I suppose that would be one of the scholars, is it?'

'Indeed it wasn't,' said Bridget. 'The uncle was a Protestant clergyman if you like and Alastar was his name. Some of the older ones are saying it was him they do remember.' Bridget leaned closer and lowered her voice. 'Don't let on,' she whispered, 'but it's saying they are that the uncle was the very Devil himself!'

'Away with you!'

'Isn't it only repeating I am what they are after telling me? The uncle was sent by the Protestant archbishop in Dublin to spread his dirty lies about the Pope and the blessed saints of God. Old Martin John Flaherty had it from the brother that the clergyman went and built a cellar in his big house and it filled with the gold and silver he brought across from Dublin.'

'Gold and silver?'

Bridget blessed herself. 'To put in the hand of any man or woman or child of us who would deny St Peter and the Holy Virgin and turn themselves to a Protestant!'

'That's the work of the Devil all right!' I cried. I shivered and drew my stool up to the turf. 'The villain! Did any man or woman or child of Big Island take his foul silver?'

Bridget laughed and threw a sod on the fire. 'Devil a person,' she said. 'Aren't we no children of last night? To the length and breadth of what old Martin John knows the gold and the silver is there underneath the big house to the day that's in it today.'

'I hope it stays there itself!' I said with anger on me. 'You'd not have a day's luck on this earth nor a peaceful day in heaven if you so much as let it come near you, that dirty Protestant silver.'

'Right is with yourself,' Bridget agreed. She turned her face to the glow in the hearth and I could see her eyes were shining. 'But it's not to tell you of the uncle Alastar I want but of the nephew Seán and he not like him a bit. It is to learn Gaelic he is here.'

'Is it that he has no Gaelic?'

'There's a couple of words inside of his mouth right enough,' said Bridget, 'but not enough to say his prayers with. I'm after hearing that Martin MacDonagh is teaching him.'

'That would give Martin something to do for newness! If ever I saw Martin MacDonagh lift a hand of him wasn't it only to scratch the dirt off himself.'

Bridget laughed at that and she turned to me with a sly look on her. 'I'm thinking it's yourself, o Barbara, would like to be giving Gaelic to the noble person. Wasn't it me saw you looking on him and he stepping up on the pier and it was a fine thing you were seeing.'

I reddened. Bridget Conneely does be seeing more than she should and she does not be afraid of telling the whole wide world about it.

'Is it me?' I said, getting up from the fire and taking the broom to the floor I was just after sweeping. 'Get along with you, o Bridget Conneely! Is it walking after a Protestant I would be and half the fellas on Big Island and South Island and the Mainland itself calling here in the nights before Lent?'

Just then my mother let a little call out of her inside in the bedroom and Bridget stood up.

'I'll be going now,' she said to me. 'Will you be over tomorrow?'

'Someone has to mind the Mammy, o Bridget,' I told her and I letting her out the door.

'Safety with you,' I called after her.

'Safety with yourself,' said Bridget.

MORE THAN A week after that it was when the doctor brought himself over from Big Island to put an examination on my mother. He gave her medicines and soon she was on her feet again.

When the men were gone one morning I hurried over to the MacDonaghs' with the excuse of asking if there might be a letter in it for us (the MacDonagh house is the post office). There was not a one of course and I went away again but not before I looked about to see if I could catch a sight of the stranger. No sign of him was there.

It being a fine summer morning I went the long way home past Moher Fort and down by the south cliffs. There was a lovely calm on the water and in the air and you could see beyond South Island to the shore of County Clare. Some canoes and two hookers were fishing in the sound and from the top of the cliffs you could hear the calls of men and them halfway outside on the water. So warm was the morning that I took off my moccasins and unhooked my shawl and made a bundle of them on the rock and sat down.

The sun was already hot and I pulled up the hem of my petticoat to let the warmth at my legs. I remember looking on them and thinking what fine sturdy legs they were and without a blemish, except for the scar on my right shin where I tripped and fell the few years before that. I leaned back on my elbows and let the bit of wind blow through my loose hair. It was grand to be out in the sun again after me being in the house all those weeks when my mother was ill. I think I must have closed my eyes after that because the next thing I remember is awaking and a strange voice close by me.

'God with you.'

I knew at once it was the stranger. Who else of us would talk in that queer way? I was shocked I can tell you and turned red and white all at the same time. Don't laugh because it's possible. Don't I myself be doing it all the time?

The stranger was standing there looking down on me, and me with my petticoat half up to my arse and not a shoe on my foot and my hair all in my eyes! I straightened my skirts and jumped up on my feet and I hunted for my moccasins and my shawl. The stranger went on looking on me and him with a little smile on his face.

'God and Mary with you, o noble person,' I said and me not knowing what else to do but return his greeting.

The stranger took his pipe from out of his mouth and stretched it at me. 'You,' he began, 'you are ...?' and I swear by the saints of God I never heard Gaelic so poor from anybody in the walk of my days, not even from little John Bartley Conneely and him not four.

By and by I understood it was my name the stranger was asking me.

'Barbara is my name, o noble person.'

'Ah ... Bairbre!' said the stranger.

By the sacred power of the Blessed Mother he couldn't even get that right!

'That's not it,' I said. 'It's Barbara, Bar-ba-ra!' It really was like talking to little John Bartley. I'm thinking the stranger took it under his notice the way I looked on him because then he reddened too. He stuck the pipe of his back in his mouth and let on to pull on it even though a child and it in its cot could see there was devil a bitlet of smoke coming out of the thing in any case.

'I saw ... I saw you last week by the ... by the ... *cé*,' said the stranger in his slow and awkward way.

'Pier.'

'Pier?'

I stretched my finger in the direction of the place I thought he must be meaning. He slanted that big head of his.

'Have you English, o Barbara?' he asked.

'*Tá Béarla agamsa*,' I answered proud. '*Cúpla focail*.'

This brought pleasure to the stranger but I hoped he would not ask me to say too much in English. My father had English and my three brothers had a bit but my mother and my sister Mary and me haven't much at all. So I stayed in my silence and waited until he would say something else. And that was grand because I had the chance now to go and have a better look on himself from Dublin, the Protestant.

He had lovely hands I saw and lovely long fingers on them and a big brown thumb that kept on pushing the tobacco inside in his pipe even if it wasn't burning itself. The skin on his face was brown from the sun and from the wind and the bones in his cheeks were sitting higher than the bones of the men of the islands. The cheeks themselves were thin enough and there were lines on them, the way you'd think the stranger was after lying in his bed a long time with some kind of sickness. When he moved the pipe around in his mouth I could see some of his teeth and it put a surprise on me to see they were just as bad as any islander's teeth and me thinking all the time before this that the Protestants of Dublin had teeth the colour of white marble.

The stranger saw me looking on him so I turned my eyes down to the ground and I saw he had on him a pair of moccasins that were new. They were not stained at all from the water or from the turf. There was happiness on me when I saw the moccasins because there was pity with me for the stranger on that first day and him with the old worn boots that wouldn't keep out a spit if it was to save his soul itself.

'*An bhfuil fear céile agat?*' he asked me of a sudden. I turned the foreign words around inside in my head. I knew *fear* was 'man' but what did *fear céile* mean at all? It put wonder on me if it would be meaning 'husband'. I turned red again.

'I have not,' I answered quickly in Gaelic. 'But if you were there and you seeing the power of young fellas who called at my father's door in the nights before Lent. I sent each man of them away again about his business and they can all of them come back next year again and it's the same answer I'll be giving them! When Barbara O'Flaherty goes to the altar it is to be with a rich farmer from the Mainland or a rich farmer from Dublin, or a handsome American soldier and him back from the war with the Spanish king!'

Well the stranger looked on me with that mouth of his open and the moustache that was turning down even more. I knew that he hadn't got a word of what I told him and it did me much pleasure to see him standing there with his mouth open and I had to laugh. I flung my shawl around my head and took up my moccasins in my hand and skipped away down along the head of the cliff.

'Barbara!'

I turned my face and the stranger was there and he coming with strides after me and the man not used at all to walking on the moccasins. It is not like walking on boots at all for there is no heel to them. I looked on the stranger's face and it was very sad and very serious and I knew I was after putting offence on him. I stopped.

'Talk might not we ... some bit more?' he said in his queer Gaelic and him saying half of the words in the wrong way and putting them in the wrong places too. He was so serious and so shy and those brown eyes in his head and those long eyelashes they gave me a queer feeling. I turned away and I looked out beyond over the water. I heard the breath of the stranger beside me and I knew at the sound of it that he was looking on me. I did not look on him.

We walked on and on along the cliff and side by side and us not saying another word. Now and again I saw out of the corner of my eye the way he looked on me. It was a new feeling I had inside in my heart and it beginning to go faster than it ever did before—and it was not for the length we walked either and me being a girl who can run the width of the island and back again in her bare feet and not catch for her breath. This feeling was different from any feeling at all that I ever had. We don't go walking out with fellas on the island (though I heard of some and I won't say names who do walk out). We don't know a fella until the day he marries us and takes us to his father's house for us to be his wife.

And yet I knew the stories from what the storytellers do be telling in the long nights of winter. I knew of the women—the fine handsome women of the gentry with jewels on them—with love in them for the foreign sea-captains and the soldiers and the other men of the world. I knew them also from the things Bridget did be saying and she after coming back that time from the city of Galway where the girls and the fellas do be walking out together even in the light of day and they not caring a beggar's curse about the way a priest might think on it. Love of the heart! But what is love of the heart if only stories?

'*Muc mhara!*' said the stranger after a while and he standing without moving and his finger stretched in the direction of the sea. I saw the creature.

'A dolphin it is that's in it,' I told him and I saw the way he moved his lips around the words: dolphin, dolphin, dolphin. 'They are the ghosts of men the sea took.'

'Ghosts …?'

I gathered my eyebrows and thought hard and I searching for simple words the way you'd talk to a child, God help us. 'When a man is after getting his death,' I said slowly, 'and the spirit of him can't go up to heaven … when his body is lost … he is put into the shape of a dolphin and he swims across the wide ocean and him crying and groaning … and him breaking the nets of the fishermen of the whole world in his great grief.'

The stranger slanted his head very slow as an answer. 'I understand,' he said. He looked on the sea where the dolphin was swimming and jumping up sometimes out of the water with great leaps the like of a salmon. 'When can the man go to … saint?'

'*Hea*ven,' I said again. Even little John Bartley Conneely knows there is a difference between 'heaven' and 'saint' but I suppose the sounds of the words are close enough together. 'The man can go to heaven when one of the fishermen puts the dolphin to death.'

I blessed myself then and I looking on the dolphin out there beyond in the sound and me thinking a wild thought. Thinking I was that the creature might be the ghost of my brother Michael who got his death the winter before that. My father and my other brother and some men rowed and sailed north and south and east and west but no body did they bring home for burial. There was a body washed inside in the next week but my mother said it was not Michael and it too long a-floating in the sea. But we buried it in any case even if it was without a Christian coffin and my grandmother and my mother and my sister and me keened as loud and as long as if it was Michael himself that was in it. I was thinking the keening was good for my mother then.

'*Tá sé imithe arís*,' said the stranger and there was not a sign more of the dolphin. I hoped it would go swimming over in the direction of the place where the men were fishing in the sound and I put a quick prayer to God that He'd take the creature that day.

Then the stranger took a little book out of a pocket of his old coat and a pencil to follow it. He sat down on the rock and I sat down too beside him. He opened the book and turned pages that were filled with writing in a lovely small hand until he found a white page. I saw him write down some words and I tried to take a story of what it was he was writing but I could not of course. He smiled and put one of his slender fingers under two words.

'Dull fin,' he said. And another: 'sayint'. I thought should I tell him of how stupid he was to still not know the difference between heaven and a saint but then suddenly the truth bared itself to me. Protestants have no saints at all and to the length and breadth of my knowledge they don't believe in heaven either, God forgive them! In any case Father Farragher says that Protestants are not allowed into heaven or Jews or Mussulmen or Turks.

I was sad then and me thinking this handsome man from Dublin would not ever see Our Lord and sit at His right hand for all eternity. I was sad and that is when I put my hand on the hand of the stranger.

I swear to Almighty God it was like a wasp or some other creature was after stinging him, so quick did he pull his hand away from under mine. His face was white and his light brown eyes were open wide as a door.

I reddened again something fierce, I can tell you. But then his face was normal again and I saw a look that came into his eyes and that look made me afraid and cold in the heat of that day in summer. The stranger stretched out his hand and he caught a hold on mine. I felt those soft fingers of his and they softer than the fingers of my little sister Mary and the stranger pressing the calluses on my own hand. I breathed fast and deep and I not sure what was happening at all. I squeezed the stranger's hand and he squeezed my hand again. I thought then: this is love of the heart. Only why was I feeling the love in places that were not even *close* to my heart?

I MET THE stranger again in that lonely spot. Nobody in the world came there. It was only a place where there does be a nest of hooded crows every year and they not liking at all for people to be there, the creatures caw-cawing the way a host of demons would be gloating over a murderer and they at his wake itself. The place is far out on the cliff above Foul Sound where the wind does be sweeping down over the water from the north and the white surf does be crashing below you and gurgling in and out of the caves where the brave young fellas sometimes dare each other to go.

I found the stranger there the day after the one I'm just after telling you about. We hadn't said a word to each other about meeting again but I know my feet just carried me to that spot and I imagine the stranger's feet just carried him there too.

I didn't see him in it itself but when I was close to the edge of the cliff didn't I think someone was after starting a fire because I saw a bit of smoke going up from behind a rock. Only when I got closer did I smell the smoke itself and then I knew it was the tobacco of the stranger that was in it.

'Is that yourself, o noble person?' I called out in a shy way and sure enough the big head with the fine black moustache came up from behind the rock and the pipe stuck between the teeth of him.

'It is better if you stop calling me that,' he said, 'for I am not noble at all. A poor poet is all I am.'

I knew by the way he said the words that he was saying them to himself before that and he trying to get the words right. (Did Martin MacDonagh teach them to him?) I threw the shawl from my head and placed it on the rock beside him. Then I took the canlet of sweet milk from the fold of my petticoat and put that down on the shawl.

'A poet do you say? Are they poems then that's in it when you do be writing in the little book of yours?' The book was in his hand.

He smiled. 'Them are. Hear you one, perhaps?' I laughed again at his Gaelic.

He opened the book and held it from him and his three fingers behind it and his little finger resting against the butt of one page and his thumb resting against the butt of the other. He pulled a big breath inside of him and began speaking. His voice was loud and sweet and him speaking the English words. I put an ear of listening on me and me not understanding at all but feeling that the things he was saying were things from the heart of him. When he was done he closed the book and he looked out beyond on the sea and not a word from him. I put the canlet of milk in his hand and he drank some of it.

'It is a girl that is in it,' I said. He slanted his head as an answer.

'Has she a name?'

'Silín.'

Silín, Silín. ... The sound of the name was like a poem itself.

'Is she pretty at all?' I asked.

He reached into the pocket of his old coat and he took out of it a wallet made of fine leather. I drew myself closer to him. He opened the wallet and I could see there were photographs in it the like of the photographs Father Farragher did have on the walls of his big room over in Kilronan, only smaller.

'This is Silín,' said the stranger and he placed a photograph in my hand.

Never in the walk of my days did I see a girl as beautiful as Silín. She had more meat on her face than has any island woman and her lips were full and round. Her eyes were black as the night itself and her hair was light and spun as fine as the clouds in the sky. The cloth of her clothes was woven on looms I could not imagine and it was ... silk—it must have been silk that was in it I'm sure. Silín was looking for me like I think a queen would be looking and she ruling over all the people of the east.

There was a lump in my throat. I felt my eyes and the tears inside of them. No queen was I. No love could there ever be in the noble person for me. No love of the heart. I was sitting close beside the stranger as you would not put the width of a hand in the gap between us but he could have been sitting on the shore of America for all that. With a sure certainty did I know that no fine poem would the stranger be writing for me.

And yet ... and yet I would find the stranger and him in that spot on most days that were fine. These were days when I could get away from the work in the house and the bringing up of the weed from the sea for the kelp and the feeding of the calves and the sewing and the spinning and the mending of shirts and stockings. I would find him writing things down in his little book or him just lying with the back of him against the rock and him looking out beyond over the sound.

I never spoke of Silín again and the stranger spoke not of her either. Yet she stayed for me the queen the stranger carried with himself. I heard from Bridget Conneely who heard it from my mother who heard it from Mrs MacDonagh who heard it from Pat MacDonagh that the stranger was unwed. Well now, perhaps *not then* he wasn't but I felt that soon or late he would return to the east and he would marry his queen and he would be writing poems to her until the day of his death.

But halfway through the month of June the stranger said something to me that I couldn't understand at all.

'Marry men from the east island girls ever?' he asked. My heart jumped. I knew I was after hearing him aright because since that first day his Gaelic had grown so much better that we could talk for a good while and the stranger hardly needing to be changing into English at all.

'Sometimes,' I said and me trying to keep my voice calm. 'Sometimes there does come a fella from the east and he marries a girl from the islands and he might take her back over there to his farm or to America.'

'You ... marry would you a man from the east ever?' he asked and I blushed the colour of my petticoat.

'I might,' I said. 'I might if it was rich he was.'

A week later and the stranger was gone.

NO FELLA CAME a-calling to our house in the nights before Lent in the year that came after. My father looked on me with anger on him one morning and I knew the thing he must be thinking. No fella was there *ever* who came a-calling for me and now my father was thinking no fella would there be ever.

Bridget was married by Father Farragher along with six other girls. She and her husband with her went back across to his father's house on Big Island. I saw her only one time after that during that summer and I was very lonely. But there was plenty to do for us girls if we were single or married itself and the summer passed as it always did. No evictions were there that year and all was quiet on the island. There was only one man taken by the sea in the months of summer and it was only a man from Claddagh. They found the body and it battered and naked on the stones below Kilbally.

On some days I would go to the MacDonaghs' and sit beside the fire with the women and we working and talking. If any news came from Kilronan or beyond then wasn't it in the MacDonaghs' house where a person would hear it first?

It must have been close by the end of August when I was helping two of the women pluck some geese and the creatures screeching and flapping around so much you'd think they were being murdered, when we heard Pat MacDonagh and three other men coming in at the door. We stopped our work because it was clear that Pat had news. News from his son Martin it was and Martin was after getting a letter on the Mainland where he was working then.

'He is coming next week … Seán, the noble person!' Pat told his wife. 'Is that not a grand thing?'

Well the fuss that was made of the stranger in that year! I had so much work on me that I couldn't go down to the slip but I finished everything as quick as I could and I ran to the MacDonagh's at twilight.

All of the village of Moher it seemed was packed tight inside in the house and people were still going in there at the door when I arrived. I pushed through and I stepped on old Mary Flaherty's toes and I got a whack on the ear for myself and a power of words that would make a fire light by itself on a dark morning.

The stranger was seated in a place of honour near the door of the kitchen and I set myself down on the floor beside his stool. He looked happy. He leaned his head to me and I had that same feeling again in the place that was not near to my heart. He looked healthy and fit. He looked fitter than last year and his hair looked different too. Mrs MacDonagh and the girls were pouring poteen for the men and the stranger was drinking a bit as well. His leather wallet was on his knee and he was pulling photographs out from it and letting the people see them.

That was sport that was in it! I leaned across his knee to see them better—and I think that made the stranger a bitlet shy of me! There were photographs of the men of the island and they after pulling a canoe inside on the beach and Pat MacDonagh was roaring and laughing and saying, 'That's John Folan, so it is, with the face on him, look at that will you!' and John was cursing and his wife was telling him to be looking out for his language in front of the noble person.

But how the stranger could talk Gaelic! He must have been a-practising there in Dublin. I know that Martin MacDonagh wrote to him in Gaelic and even got letters back in Gaelic but to hear the stranger speaking like that was a wonder. And me thinking in the year that was gone there was something wrong with him. ...

There he was showing the photographs and saying, 'This is this house that's in it itself', or 'Do you see yourself, Mr Flaherty?'.

But there was more in it than the islands. The stranger showed us photographs of the Mainland and his own big house with the great windows and his family in the east. And photographs of one of the grand fairs that do be held in the east with the sheep and the pigs as big as cattle and people in their finest clothes for it. We looked at the dresses on the women and the hats and the boots on the men and the carriages they sat inside.

No sign of Queen Silín did I see.

'And this is myself and I in Parás,' said the stranger and he holding the photograph up under the light. (I think it was *Paris* he was meaning but that is what he said.) I was the nearest to it and I looked and looked. The stranger was in it indeed and him dressed in a lovely suit of clothes and a tie of silk or satin maybe and a thin stick in his hand. But when I looked on the other places on the photograph, I turned red in my face and blessed myself.

'Mother of God, help us!' I cried. 'Is it with people in their bare skins you are standing?'

The stranger let out of him such a roar of a laugh I thought he was after getting a seizure.

'It is a garden that is in it, o Barbara,' he said and tears in his eyes from the laughing. 'It is not real people they are but statues of marble!'

There was a great anger on me. The stranger was making a fool of me and all the island there. I stood up and I was shaking and white in the face.

'It is not statues that are in it!' I cried. 'I know statues well enough. Aren't there statues over in the church of Kilronan and haven't they clothes on them too like good Christians!'

Old Mary Flaherty shoved me to one side and took the photograph out of the stranger's hand and let some more light from the kitchen door fall upon it. She put a frown on her face and pulled her old gums together.

'It is statues that are in it right enough, o Barbara,' she said, 'but they are queer dirty ones the like I saw with my own eyes and me serving in the big house in Galway and me a young girl. The French is a queer people and they do have queer unhealthy ways about themselves.' She blessed herself.

There was not a word coming from any person. I walked to the door and the anger on me was making my whole body shake. I turned and wrapped my shawl around me and I spoke loud to the stranger.

'I'm thinking, o noble person,' I cried, 'that it is to hell you will be going by and by.'

I did not wait to see the stranger's face.

THE MONTH THE stranger came back to us was wet and cold and with the wind a-blowing hard every day from the south-west. The men were gone in the dark of the morning every day and they returned in the dark of the night.

It was a bad time for the fishing and the men had little enough fish in the arses of their canoes to feed their families or to sell on the Mainland. The women helped the men bring the weed up from the sea to try and burn it in the rain and helped them in the digging of the potatoes and they wet to their skins. There was great excitement when the wind blew the thatch from the roof of the house of Bridget Conneely's father. Twenty men came and they put on a new roof in the span of a day and the wind blowing.

I saw the stranger but once and him walking wet along the south cliff and the big head of him bent down against the rain. If he saw me then he did not call out a greeting. I did not call out either for I was thinking dark thoughts about the blackness of his soul, God forgive him. I saw him twice more in the MacDonagh house and him sitting up before the fire and him with a book in his hand and a pipe in his mouth. He smiled on me in that way of his. I gave him greeting as you would give to a noble person like himself and he returned it the way he returned the greeting of the older people of the island.

I went to the place on the south cliff two times when I was lonely and I wanted to hear his voice speaking. I was thinking to find him there but of him there was no sign.

And then the news came at the end of September. My mother met Margaret Flaherty at the door and she knew from the wild look on her that the news would be bad. I was taking the dirt from out of the pigsty in the kitchen when I heard the screaming and wailing of my mother. Margaret Flaherty helped me bring her inside to the fire and my grandmother made room for her. By and by Patch and Red Bartley Conneely came to our house and they told my mother how it happened.

'It was out beyond Straw Island,' said Red Bartley and his voice quiet with sorrow. 'We were beating against of a white sea and the sky was so dark then that I could hardly see the bit of a sail we had put up to bring us with safety into Gregory's Sound. My oars were no good on their own because the wind from the south-west was blowing us back over in the direction of Connemara. Patch was doing nothing at all except to turn the sail this way and then that way when the wind would shift and try to knock us over.'

'It did not last at all,' said Patch. 'And it was a queer thing.'

'It did not last,' said Red Bartley. 'Just as we were after passing Straw Island a great calm came down and settled on the water. It was a thing like I never saw before. One minute you had a sea that was as high as the church steeple beyond in the city of Galway and the next minute there was nothing at all except the gusts of wind that were blowing on the head of the water and it with hardly a wave in it.'

'I shouted your husband's name, o Mary,' Red Bartley told my mother, 'thinking him and John must be safe and I heard his answer as clear as if he was there just beyond that door.' He shook his head. 'But devil a hair of him or the boat could I see, so black was it.'

Red Bartley looked on me and then on my mother again. 'Yet it was a queer thing surely that was in it, o Mary. For the words I heard and them coming across the water were these: "There's the north star now, o Red Bartley. There's the north star now and a moon that will light the way for us all!"'

My mother just sat there looking into the flames of the turf with not a tear in her eyes nor a look on her face you would recognize. She was knowing as good as myself was knowing that the first curl of the moon would not be in the sky for two days or three.

'I told Patch to take the sail down,' said Red Bartley, 'for I was sure the storm was gone north and it would not return this night. And wasn't it right I had? Only when we dragged our canoe inside on the beach we saw that your husband and your son John were not there at all and them leading!'

My mother turned her face to Red Bartley then and I swear to Almighty God and his hosts of angels and saints in heaven that the face of her was looking as old as the face of my grandmother.

'That was a star I know all right,' she said. 'That was a star that is not of this place, but of a foreign place.'

While Red Bartley and Patch were telling the story more people came in at the door and the stranger was among them.

THREE BIG CANOES were rowed over from Kilronan in the middle of the day after. Father Farragher and two boys were in the one in front and the bodies of my father and my brother John were in the one behind that. Father Farragher had a grim look on him and he wet to his skin from the rain on the water that day.

The men of Big Island found my father and my brother that morning and them not a perch from each other on the rocks of Straw Island where the water threw them. The sea was good to them. There was scarce a mark on them and only one of John's moccasins was gone.

The men carried the bodies up to the house and each was in a sail of its own and the people came after them. I saw the stranger too.

Father Farragher and the two boys from Big Island said mass in our kitchen for the souls of my father and my brother. My mother made for them a meal of mackerel and potatoes and some smoked bacon she was saving.

God forgive me but I had a wicked thought. I thought that Father Farragher was fat and healthy enough and the boys too and what would we do with only women in the house now and the men all dead or away in America like my oldest brother Coleman? I was not correct or just about Father Farragher. Poor Father Farragher who had to take care of the souls of the people and we giving him no rest at all with our masses and confessions and marriages and christenings and funerals. A hard life it was that Father Farragher had.

Red Bartley came and made coffins with the boards that I went around the village of Moher and asked people for. There were not enough boards in it, so Red Bartley said he would put an old bit of sail on top of John's coffin to hide the face of him when the time would come that he would be buried.

We had to wake the both of them of course and we did that on the same evening. Red Bartley and his brother Patch brought the porter and the whiskey because I think they believed their fault it was for the drowning.

'It was a calm sea, a calm sea I am telling you,' Red Bartley said over and over that evening when he was filled with whiskey. 'We should have gone and looked for them, by God, but instead we went away home.'

My mother told him that the fault was neither his nor his brother's but Red Bartley was not brought comfort. His brother Patch had so much anger on himself and he got so drunk that he picked a fight with Michael O'Donnell when Michael was doing nobody any harm at all. The pair of them went outside and all the men after them to watch the sport, so me and the women and the girls had a bit of peace for a while. Only three old men and little John Bartley were there—and the stranger. He sat with himself alone and his book in his hand. He was writing. Mother of God, to be writing poetry on that evening in the house where a wake was! Protestants are queer folk.

The stranger was looking on me from the beginning of the wake but I let on not to see him at all. He was giving great sport to the fellas with some magic of his and every person was scratching his head and saying, 'Jesus, Mary and Joseph, that is not a natural thing!' when he would cut a length of string and it would be mended again all on its own. I couldn't see all the time what it was that was going on because the stranger was sitting over in the part of the kitchen where the men were sitting and a-drinking. When the men went out to look on Patch Conneely and Michael O'Donnell, the stranger stayed where he was seated and sipped his glass of porter and rolled a cigarette, then another to follow, and another after that.

I did not see the little box he brought with him and him coming inside in the evening. When some of the older men were returned he took it from its place beside the hearth and opened it. It was a fiddle that was in it! The stranger took a long bow out of the box and rubbed the string on it with some powder. He put the fiddle under his chin and he began to play.

Strange and foreign was the music he was making. It was not like the music I knew at all for it was slow and it had so many changes to it that I couldn't remember the start of a tune at all. I began to think the stranger was making them up in his own head, or that he could not remember the starts himself when he would be in the middle of a tune. It was a wonder to see the long fingers of the stranger and they moving up and down on the fiddle. I was in a mind not to look but I had not the strength on me. But then the roaring and shouting that was outside stopped and all the men came back with Patch and Michael and them all red with the blood of the two of them.

'Ah, I see you are after paying court to the women, o Seán,' said Pat MacDonagh and him seeing the fiddle in the hands of the stranger. 'Will you not play a tune now and let the men dance? A dance is better than a fight and it gives hurt to no person at all.'

'I will,' said the stranger and to my great wonder he began the playing of a jig I knew. One of the men who was a powerful dancer rushed out onto the floor and began his dance. Then the stranger played another tune and the men were shouting at him: 'Have you this one, o noble person?' and 'Will you not play that one again, o Seán?'

Soon it was that the stranger grew tired and the men grew so full of whiskey and of porter that they could not dance their jigs and reels and the stranger put his fiddle down. Some of the men went to sleep and others of them began to talk and to tell stories. My mother gave me a poke in the ribs.

'Do you not see, o Barbara,' she said and she stretching her finger to the place where the stranger was sitting, 'that the glass of himself is empty? What will he think of us? Go you and fill it now for him.'

I took the jug of whiskey and went to the stranger's side. He was looking on the men and smoking a cigarette and he smiled when he saw me in it. But his face grew sad then.

'There is sorrow on me for you, o Barbara,' he said.

'What is the reason?' I asked and me not knowing why there was sorrow on him at all. He had a look of surprise on him.

'Because of the reason of your father and your brother of course,' he said. 'What things will your mother do now? How are ye to live?'

I did not understand at all.

'We will live less well, o noble person,' I told him. 'It will be a hard winter. My grandmother will die now maybe, God willing. That would surely be a good thing for the rest of us.'

His eyes opened wide and I could see all the white around the light brown of them.

'A good thing?!' he said. 'But it is your grandmother that is in it!'

I laughed. 'It is that. And tell me, o noble person: has she right with her to live and her an old woman and a long life behind her and the young men to die? It is her who should be dying now and not my brother John or my brother Michael who was taken by the sea in the year that's gone.'

The stranger was quiet and a look on him that was a puzzle. He pulled at his cigarette.

'I understand that, o Barbara,' he said, 'but do you not have love in you for your grandmother?'

I said no word more. I was seventeen years of age in that September in 1899 and that is the age my youngest daughter is now. I was a woman though I was not yet married and I had no house and husband of my own. There was talk (I heard it some years after from Bridget Conneely) that the fellas thought I was too stupid to marry. And yet I married the year after that one and went with my husband to the Mainland.

But the man we called the noble person, now what good was he at all and him surely ten years or more older than me? What did he know of the sorrows of earth? His Gaelic was better than it was when he came to us in that first year, but little John Bartley—and him but five—could speak it better than the stranger. What could the stranger do, except it was to play queer tunes on his fiddle and to do magic tricks and to write things down in his little book? Nothing did he know of our life on the island. Nothing did he understand of work and fishing and putting food in the pot. Nothing did he know of life and—may God forgive him—nothing did he know of death!

Once I thought I had love in my heart for him. He himself had love only for an old woman and her my grandmother.

FATHER FARRAGHER AND the two boys led us to the little cemetery that looks over on Kilcannagh. He put the prayers to God for the dead men and they put my father and my brother John down inside in the earth.

When the first bit of dirt was thrown on them we all of us men and women and children started to keen right away and us frightening the crows off. My mother almost had the piece of sail torn away from the coffin of John but Father Farragher stopped her and she fell on the ground and her face was black with dirt and blood coming from her cheek where the stones were after cutting her. By the time the dirt was on the grave and the rain was falling too much, we were all worn out in any case and we went back to our house again.

I think the stranger left on the day after that but I can't remember now. I wish him well and good fortune, God help him, him and his queen.

Queen Silín. She was only a photograph made of paper and so were the fine words the stranger was writing down. Paper is all it was and it no use to anyone in the wide world at all.

A Night in the Catacombs

LET'S SEE: THERE was Blade Macken and his half-brother Jack; they had been there since Tuesday night, each with a girl in tow. There was Esme Pheasey and some derelict poetaster she had picked up in Nearys (we never did find out his name—not that we really cared, one way or another). Murph Ryan was there too, I remember, but he passed out around nine o'clock so, strictly speaking, he does not count as one of the participants.

Donald Kissane, Raymond O'Rourke, P.J. Slater, Dan Freyne and Noel Molloy were at 'high table', bedecked as it was with five bottles of Irish, three of Scotch, a great many bottles of porter and plain, and the pint of milk that Raymond invariably insisted on bringing but seldom remembered to take before the serious drinking began. Oliver Quill, Desmond Coyle and Lucy Moran were arguing together on a bench in one corner of the vast kitchen, and Mr and Mrs Chambers (we knew them by no other names) were occupying their bedroom somewhere in the labyrinth.

There were four or five women I did not know. They seemed to be friends of Dessy Coyle and Lucy Moran, but when I came in some time after seven, they were sitting by themselves, drinking quietly from what looked like glasses of gin and tonic. I found out later that the women were artists' models, but that is neither here nor there because they do not, as Peadar Cummiskey used to say, figure permanently in the story.

Lastly there was mein host, looking as elegant as ever in a three-piece plum-coloured suit of his own making, and a gorgeous black messaline cravat, as out of place in his own home as a Derby winner in a brewery stable-yard.

Blade Macken, enjoying a state of alcoholic lucidity induced by a drinking marathon that had begun in the Palace Bar at ten that morning, moving to the Pearl at noon and to McDaids some thirsty hours later, started the ball of harmless insanity rolling.

'Do any of ye know why Moses told the Children of Israel that they couldn't eat pork?' he asked the ceiling, his face wearing that expression of benign seriousness which many tried to emulate, but rarely with success.

'I'm not so sure it was Moses,' said P.J. Slater after about a minute's concentrated thought and silent sipping all round. 'More like King Solomon. Seems to me I recall reading—'

'No no, it was Moses all right,' said Blade, a bit irritated that P.J.—a known atheist, and a *foreign* atheist to boot—should challenge his knowledge of the Holy Book. 'Moses, when he came down from the mount.'

One of the G&T girls, a rather pretty one who looked about seventeen and just fresh from the convent, said 'Ehh ...', licked her lips and fixed Blade with a serious look. Mein host leaned against the wall beside the big range, bell of Scotch jiggling in his palm, eyes half shut, regarding this newcomer with amusement.

'Ehh,' she said again, and ears pricked up, 'was it because pigs were, eh, unclean ... and that you couldn't keep pork for any length of time in that climate without it, eh, going off?' The girl looked to her companions for support, noticing that all the attention in the room was upon her, and regretting that she had opened her mouth. Drinking had come to a temporary standstill.

Blade threw the girl a little smile that was probably meant to be encouraging but which actually came across as a leer.

'A fair answer,' he told her, 'and an answer that follows the conventional wisdom. But not, I'm afraid, the right answer.'

'Which we shall undoubtedly be hearing from your own rose-petal lips?' said mein host, inspecting the contents of his glass.

'The reason', began Blade Macken, 'that Moses forbade the eating of pork had nothing to do with hygiene, the pig—*pace* the erroneous assumption of city-born jackeens like yourselves—being as clean an animal as you'd find anywhere.'

'Present company excepted,' P.J. put in.

'Present company excepted,' Blade agreed.

By this time the convent girl's elbows were resting on the table, her chin was propped up by her little fists, and she was gazing a touch glassy-eyed and admiringly at Macken.

'No, my friends,' he informed us, 'the answer lies in anatomy! You see, internally speaking, the pig is near enough to the human being as makes no difference. All its organs—heart, lungs, stomach, bladder, kidneys, ex-e-tera—and its tissues and muscles and so on, are almost identical to yours and mine.'

'I thought that was monkeys,' said Esme Pheasey, and her derelict companion nodded knowledgeably before tilting once more to his mouth his bottle of Mountjoy Nourishing Stout.

'No, the pig wins hands down,' said Blade. 'Skinned and boned, you couldn't tell a young porker from an altar boy.'

'Would you ever go and fuck yourself,' Noel Molloy muttered at Macken's elbow. Macken ignored him.

'You see, the thing about the Israelites', he said to the girl, 'is that they used to be a cannibalistic race of people before Moses brought them out of the land of Egypt, and Jehovah, in order to discourage them from this filthy and genocidal habit, wanted them to avoid the flesh of swine because' (pause for maximum effect) 'it's the closest you'll come to the taste of human flesh!'

'Ah, Jayziz,' someone said. 'That's disgusting, Macken,' said another.

'And totally untrue,' said mein host.

The convent girl had already risen, and was making her way—none too steadily—through the smoke-filled kitchen, and heading in the direction of the lavatory. Macken drained his glass and refilled it from a half-pint bottle.

'I speak the truth, laddie,' he said.

'Yeah, through your arse, as usual,' Noel muttered.

'In medical circles,' Blade continued evenly, 'it is a well-known and established fact. Naturally enough, the medical men are loath to make such facts known to the general public. Think what a commotion it would cause! Rashers and sausages and black and white pudding would disappear from our breakfast tables. Every pork butcher in the country would be ruined overnight. Look', he added, 'at what happened to the haypney. ...'

The row between Oliver Quill and Desmond Coyle had, by then, assumed serious proportions. Wisely, Lucy Moran had chosen silence, and was observing the fun from the sidelines. You will appreciate that, at this remove in time, I am unable to reproduce the argument in *ipsissima verba*. It went something like this:

Q(uill): 'You stupid cunt. Can't you see that there is no such fucking thing as a common language—or, rather, there is no such thing any longer. The constitution of madness as a mental illness, at the end of the eighteenth century, affords the evidence of a broken dialogue, posits the separation as already effected, and thrusts into fucking oblivion all those who stammered imperfect words without fixed syntax in which the exchange between reason and madness was made. The language of psychiatry, which is a monologue of reason about madness, has been established only on the basis of such a silence.'

C(oyle): 'Oh, really? How in the name of Jayziz can we read the silence of madness through the language of reason, using the very signs that are borrowed, without exception, from the juridical province of interdiction? And besides, you pathetic, posturing prole, you're asking me to accept, firstly, that madness is akin to silence and, secondly, that madness is a language that speaks by and to itself. I wish you'd make up your bleeding mind.'

Q: 'I said no such fucking thing, you ignorant gobshite. I am postulating a point in history at which reason and unreason were sundered. I am saying that there's a higher form of reason which is more magnanimous than that which we now call reason; a reason that transcends the division between western reason and madness.'

C: 'All right. Let's assume that this transcendent reason of yours —and mind you it sounds suspiciously Cartesian to me—really exists. In that highly unlikely event, this reason must only conclude that madness is a product of malfunction.'

Q: 'Total shite!' Quill lashed out suddenly and his fist caught Coyle squarely on the chin. Coyle collapsed on the dirty, red tiles of the floor and lay there groaning.

'What haypney?' Esme Pheasey asked.

'Ah, before your time, Esme,' said Macken. 'It was a few years after the founding of the Free State—nineteen twenty-five or thereabouts—and W.B. Yeats was the chairman of a commission that was set up to design our coinage.'

'Funny how they didn't ask the brother, Jack B.,' said Raymond O'Rourke. Raymond was a great admirer of the ageing Jack, who still had his studio a few doors away from where we sat. O'Rourke was a frequent visitor and—some said—copied the master's new style of palette-knife work to an extent that was considered dangerously close to being plagiaristic. 'You'd think now that he'd have been the more natural choice.'

'Well, they didn't,' said Blade, 'because Jack wasn't in the Senate and the brother was. Now someone—I can't remember who—had done a design for the haypney piece, which showed a brood sow with a litter of little piglets swarming around her ankles. Only it didn't satisfy the Department of Agriculture because the cheeks were wrong.'

'Badly done?' O'Rourke asked.

'Not at all. But he'd made the cheeks too fat and there was a run on pigs' cheeks then, instead of the more lucrative sides of bacon that would make more of a profit for the pig farming community. So the design had to be changed.' Macken pulled a handful of coins from his pocket and tossed a copper one to the painter. 'In the words of W.B.: "We have instead querulous and harassed animals—better merchandise but less living."'

Halfpennies were produced throughout the room and studied at some length.

'Same principle applies', Macken informed us, 'in the case of the taste of pork and the medical profession: the general public are kept in the dark as regards the true facts of the matter. But you ask any pig farmer with a bit of experience and he'll tell you that a big boar will strip the meat off you if he gets half a chance.' He dropped his voice. 'There are dark tales told of tinkers who were foolish—or drunk—enough to doss down in some haggard that was too close to the pig trough, only to wake up the following morning gnawed to death by the brutes. Pigs are cannibals, you see; if you don't feed them enough they'll eat each other and come back grunting for more. Indeed, you'll often come across a sow having to defend her brood from the father, who wouldn't think twice about devouring his own children.' Blade spread his hands. 'Human flesh or the flesh of its own kind, it's all the same to a pig; they can't tell the difference.'

'Ah, bollocks!' said Noel Molloy. 'I don't believe a word of it.'

'I agree,' said mein host, topping up his glass from his own personal decanter. 'That young lady was quite correct. The fact of the matter is that, from biblical times up until a couple of centuries ago, a parasitic worm, trading under the name of *Trichinella spiralis*, infested the intestines of the human, the rat and the pig. And that, my dear Blade, you lovely man, is why pork is still taboo in hot climates, not just among Jews but among Mohammedans as well.'

Blade looked sullen. 'Well now, I've said my piece and I'm sticking to it. In fact, I'd go ten bob with anyone who could prove me wrong.'

My God, the recklessness and flamboyance of it! In those times, ten shillings would buy you (ah, dear, dead days!) a solid evening's drinking. You could, depending on your taste, choose from the following:

1. Nine pints of porter;
2. Eleven glasses of whiskey;
3. Seventeen bottles of Guinness;
4. Twenty bottles of Mountjoy Nourishing Stout.

The sheer, mad *Tollkühnheit* of it! Mental calculations were made and lips wetted. We were poor, the majority of us—students, unpublished literati, unhung painters and general layabouts. Slater was among the most affluent, having come to Dublin by courtesy of the G.I. Bill that allowed war veterans to study abroad.

He had enrolled at Trinity in Eng. Lit. and had, to his credit, actually attended a lecture or two during his first Michaelmas term. Alas, the twin lures of drink and splendid conversation in McDaids cheated the literary world of the definitive American novel that would—we were assured almost nightly—emerge one day from his pen. The rest of us were no better, and some of us were worse.

Macken was the scion of an Anglo-Irish family whose once sizeable fortune, compounded of extensive estates in Cork and Kerry, had been dissipated by two generations of fornicators and racing men, viz. those of Macken's father and grandfather. This near-destitute heir was supported in his drinking habits by an English sculptress in Foxrock, who worked in bicycle tubes and beeswax.

Noel Molloy, known to consume anything potable, led the life of an urban nomad. It was not difficult to follow his trail of temporary lodgings: one simply looked for the sheets of dirty foolscap, with which he littered the rooms of friends and one-night-stands; foolscap scrawled with the most appalling and offensive doggerel imaginable. Molloy, too, would remain unpublished for the rest of his life.

Lucy Moran was perhaps the most promising of the Catacombs crowd. Her postgraduate thesis, 'The Substantiation of Wittgenstein's Universal Model in the Ideoglossia of pre-Medieval Narragansett', submitted when Lucy was twenty-two, had both astonished and enraged her tutor, who never forgave her. Poor Lucy: a motor accident in the south of France in 1950 was to nip a glorious philological career in the bud.

And then there was little Donald Kissane ... but no, why go on? We were young and bright, thirsty for drink, knowledge and experience—and most of us seldom had two half-crowns to rub together. Ten shillings!

But there was no time for any of us to take Macken up on the bet just yet, because at that moment there was a bellowing outside the front door, followed by a series of heavy blows on the timber panels. Mein host went to the pantry, opened the curtain a crack, and squinted out. We heard the sound of a motor car making a U-turn above on the roadway, before heading off again in the direction of Leeson Street.

'Brendan B.', said mein host, returning with a grave smile, 'and an accomplice.' Lucy was already opening the front door and those of us who knew the form grinned upon hearing a loud, familiar voice:

'Give'iz a quick feel o' dem, Lucy, while we're under cover o' darkness! Now, now, don't be bashful.' A little scream. 'Jayziz, dere's atin' and dhrinkin' for a whole family includin' d'in-laws on dem lads!'

Brendan Behan entered the Catacombs, the basement warren of debauchery in Fitzwilliam Street, Dublin, early on the evening of 1 November 1947.

He seemed smaller in those days, perhaps because of the leanness of his physique; diabetes and a phenomenal consumption of alcohol would transform his body to a flabby ruin within ten more years. In 1947 his skin was without a blemish and his blue eyes sparkled. His teeth were perfect, white. There was not a female in that room who did not alter her posture or facial expression when he came in; he had a strong, if not to say overpowering, effect on women. The ones who knew him knew what to expect of him (no, let me rephrase that; they knew they could expect *anything* of him); those who did not, felt themselves none the less in the presence of a most unusual young man. At twenty-four he was already an IRA veteran who had spent two years at Borstal in England, four years in Irish jails, and he could not set foot in Britain because of a deportation order that was still in force.

As a writer, he had not yet made his mark; the novel *Borstal Boy* and the plays, *The Quare Fellow* and *The Hostage*, would come later. As far as I knew, all he had written by 1947 were one or two poems in Irish. For us, Brendan Behan was not a writer but an entertainer, a one-man-show of astonishing versatility and wit.

I could tell by his demeanour that evening that Behan was bent on devilry. He deposited his entrance fee—an armful of clinking, grey paper bags—on the kitchen table, grinned to the 'audience', and did up the buttons of his soiled, white shirt which was, in strict conformity with the fashion dictates of the set to which he belonged, open almost to the navel, displaying his florid torso and dark chest-hair. Then he turned the shirt collar up and fastened all three buttons on the jacket of his filthy, crumpled, black suit.

Something extraordinary occurred during the next few seconds.

I was there, I was near-sober, I saw it; and yet I have difficulty putting it into words. Others who knew Brendan Behan as well—if not better—as I did, will have the same story to tell: of his innate ability to play any part he chose at a moment's notice, the ability to climb at will inside the character and personality of the famous.

I do not think that he rehearsed the roles he played; it was, as I said, an innate talent, something passed on to him by his parents, both of whom had a bent for literature and music. If Behan had not become a writer, then the Dublin stage could have gained a formidable actor, comedian, showman and impersonator. And one, moreover, whose rich baritone was considered to be among the city's finest and most sensitive. That, too, would go in later years.

But impersonations, not song, were to introduce the programme of entertainment that night in the Catacombs. Like some genial, true-life version of Dr Jekyll and Mr Hyde, Behan dropped the mask of the north-side ruffian and took on what amounted to its antipode. And this, seemingly, without any effort at all. By some trick involving the muscles of his face, by a tilt of the shoulders, by the motions of his small hands and feet, Brendan caused himself to disappear. The boy from the Dublin slums (he wasn't, actually, but he liked to give the impression he was; it was part of the image, even then), the hard-drinking, rumbustious, foul-mouthed, part-time house painter and part-time poet was gone. In his place stood a figure from the late nineteenth century, a London dandy; all that was lacking were the cane and gloves. Brendan's personality supplied the details; I could almost see the white flower in the buttonhole and the large diamond in the shirt-front, smell the lavender or rose scented handkerchief and the costly toilet water. Oscar Wilde stood resurrected among us.

'My dear, dear friends!' Behan gushed, advancing on the room with hands to the fore, fingers splayed. 'You cannot possibly know what a privilege it is ...' (he danced to where Murph Ryan sat, scooped up his bottle, drained it, dabbed his pouting lips with a filthy, brown-flecked rag as if it was the daintiest silk, and bowed) '... for your exquisite selves.' There was a smattering of applause. Behan turned to mein host.

'And my dear young sir,' he said, 'to share your good wine—and your meat—is a pleasure which keeps me returning to your door, if not always to your house itself.' Mein host acknowledged the dubious compliment with his usual patrician, almost sacerdotal, gravity. 'To sin for pleasure is a social grace; to sin from necessity is a social indiscretion.'

While Behan was spouting this nonsense, a bottle sailed through the air and shattered against a whitewashed and peeling wall. Coyle had risen once more, and Quill was ready for him.

Q: 'Look, Coyle, you twisted little pedagogic prick, the breakdown of philosophical subjectivity and its dispersion in a language that dispossesses it, while multiplying it within a space created by its absence, is probably one of the most fundamental fucking structures of contemporary thought. Even an arsehole like you should be able to understand that.'

C: 'You mindless turd! There can be no language other than the language of our own reason.'

And more abuse in like vein. ...

'Allow me to introduce an associate of mine,' Behan continued unperturbed, and we were suddenly made aware of the stranger, the visitor who up until that moment had escaped our attention, so dominant was the character that Behan had conjured up in our company. Now I saw that the man standing with Lucy by the door was one of the most strikingly handsome youths I had ever laid eyes on. He could not have been more than twenty-one, and his clothes set him apart from that group—mein host excepted—by the refinement of their quality and cut. The hat was, well, *sculpture*; the overcoat was artistry in warp and weft; the suit beneath it could have been bespoken by a duke.

The wearer was blond and pale-complexioned in the manner of heroic English youth of the Rupert Brooke school: vigorous, romantic and innocent, as opposed to weak and effeminate—if you see what I mean. His moustache was hardly more than a line above his upper lip. He carried his small and wiry frame like a boxer—like an athlete, anyway. I wondered where Behan had found him; he was not of the type that frequented McDaids, Behan's favourite pub and poetry platform. Where the young visitor came from, though, was immaterial at that moment, for Behan could not have chosen a better 'straight man' for his present charade.

'Ladies and gentlemen,' he said, gripping the youth's arm and ushering him forward, 'I give you ... Lord Alfred Douglas, the incomparable Bosie!'

Strange to say, the newcomer was not at all perturbed to find himself cast in this supporting role. In fact, he seemed to revel in it. It was flattering, to be sure, to be a favourite of Behan. Behan had that effect on people, both male and female; the man was charismatic to the point at which his followers and cronies were indistinguishable from the acolytes of the leader of some new sect. To be with Brendan Behan, even in those early days, was to know and to share the full vigour of life.

'Bosie and I', Behan announced, 'find ourselves in something of a stew.' 'Bosie' smiled. 'The matter involves the father of my young companion, to wit, the most infamous brute in London!'

At this point, Behan turned his back on us and ran his fingers through his greasy, black curls, tousling them. When he faced us once more, Oscar Wilde had vanished. I swear, it was uncanny: there stood John Sholto Douglas, ninth Marquess of Queensberry, looking daggers at us, brows meeting in a fierce, Neanderthal-like grimace.

'Alfred!' he roared in a voice that chilled. 'What the devil's this I hear about you and that posturing, white slug, Wilde? As if one arse-bandit of a son weren't enough! Bad blood, bad blood, that's what it is. I give your mother the blame for that; all on her side.' He reached into a pocket, produced what looked like a grocery list and slapped it backhandedly with his fingers. 'Can you explain this disgusting letter, boy? Well, *can* you?'

'Bosie' looked suitably startled; Behan addressed to us his reading of the letter:

'"My own boy, when you speak your verse, your sweet, full lips put me in mind of a chubby red earthworm doing push-ups on a mirror. When we kiss, the mellifluous sound is that of a toothless old biddy drinking up at closing time. When your firm, white bottom—"'

'Enough!' cried the magically re-manifested 'Wilde', ripping the grocery list into four pieces and tossing them in the air. 'For you to speak my delicate lines is an affront to art. You are a monster, sir, and there is only one way in which a gentleman can deal with a monster. Put 'em up, I say!'

Behan assumed a boxing stance that would have shamed Jack Doyle, his handsome head with the dark curls held tall and proud, fists raised shoulder-high and threatening.

Then abruptly he was gone—and a maniacal figure took centre stage. In one bound, 'Queensberry' sprang up onto the table, upsetting drink and drinkers, bottles flying and smashing on the floor, porter foaming. His ugly eyes were slits in a furious, ruddy face, and his lower lip was thrust out and salivating. His body was apelike, legs bent at impossible angles, hairy fists swinging wildly.

'Now, you dirty, Irish sodomite! I'll give you a taste of the Queensberry rules, damn you!'

Behan began to hop up and down on the table, growing ever more simian before our eyes. He yelled and whooped and grunted, until the dividing wall between man and ape was breached; his hands dangled progressively lower at his sides, his legs grew squatter and his feet angled ever outwards. The atavistic performance was complete.

The real Brendan Behan stepped lightly from the table, opened his jacket and shirt, and beamed his disarming schoolboy smile.

We clapped and stamped our feet and shouted our approval, not caring a curse for the respectable inhabitants of the neighbouring Georgian buildings. They housed the cream of the professional classes and some of Dublin's rich. But we were the Chosen, the bohemians; their rules of conduct did not apply to us. I think they, and others like them, turned a blind eye to our excesses simply because we provided an antidote to the poison that was Irish public morality in the years before the war, before the 'Emergency'.

The Emergency. It was possibly the Nürnberg war crimes tribunal that finally brought home to me the enormity of our treason. None expected Switzerland to go to war; Europe's banker hedged her bets as always with the blood-money that kept her economy sound. But what was *our* excuse, and that of Portugal, when between us we might have given the Allies supremacy in the Atlantic, and saved I don't know how many lives? How many lives of the more than forty million that were lost between 1939 and 1945? Those insane statistics; they meant so little to the designators of our Emergency.

Here is an analogy: we, the Catacombs crowd, were the little

Neros, feasting and fiddling while the world burned.

Here is another: we were the scruffy jesters who were allowed to insult and amuse the king, while his courtiers and barons—the clergy, the bureaucrats and the politicians—made of Ireland what John Ryan called a 'stifling greenhouse'. The country was, he said, a 'green density of gombeen-man, crawling hack, bogus patriot and pietist profiteer'. Poor Ireland needed us, this I truly believe; she needed us that she might, through us, sin vicariously and thereby restore some equilibrium to a land gone mad. She needed our bohemian *laissez-aller*, our intellectual insanity, our depravity; she needed the inspired devilry of sons like Brendan Behan.

'A song, Brendan!' Blade's half-brother Jack called. 'You'll have to give us a song now, so you will.'

'I will when I'm good and fuckin' ready,' Brendan assured us, and accepted an uncorked and foaming bottle of stout from his young companion. He took a huge swig which had some of the brown liquid coursing down his chin and adding to the stains already present on the shirt. When he had finished the bottle, he unleashed a great, sonorous belch, threw his head back and began the song.

By this time, the young artist's model had found her way back from the lavatory, back through the long, black hall that stank of things unmentionable. Her make-up was a little smudged but her cheeks were rosy again, and she had rejoined her friends.

The women were astonished to hear the voice that had so recently shunted effortlessly between the affected speech of London's *fin-de-siècle* aestheticism on the one hand and near-animalization on the other, quiver now in beautiful, fragile song. The air was one I knew—'Come, Stranger, tell to Me'—though I had never heard it sung before in its entirety.

I did now. Brendan's falsetto, clear and flawless, interpreted the words of a girl in Penal times, a girl whose lover refused to obey a law that dictated how his hair should be worn: in the English, rather than the Irish, style. As each verse unfolded a fresh episode of the story, I was struck by the intensity of this sweet excursion into yet another region of the landscape of Behan's complex personality. I was struck by his ability to effect yet another transformation, seemingly with so little effort. Once more, if I closed my eyes, the coarse and unwashed bowsey in filthy clothes that reeked of porter receded. There appeared in his place a sad and beautiful girl, standing on some lonely shore in the west of Ireland, singing her lament to the waves. I could visualize her clearly: her dark hair was caught up and pinned in the mode of the early eighteenth century; she wore no make-up or jewellery and her clothes were of hand-spun tweed and wool; her feet were bare. She raised her noble chin to the sky, and told me movingly of her love for that young man who must face the gallows on so trivial and preposterous a charge. Her voice held the fire of defiance. I think I may have shivered.

'Jayziz!' Lucy broke the quiet when the song ended. 'I swear to God, Brendan, you're a powerful singer. Fair play to you.'

'Like a choirboy,' said Blade Macken.

'More like Maria fuckin' Callas,' offered Noel Molloy.

'That thought had occurred to me too,' said mein host slowly. 'Isn't it a curious thing how the male voice can sound so uncannily similar to a female one, in tenor and falsetto. Yet one seldom hears the converse. I mean, a woman singing like a man. ...'

'Dat depends on ... wh-where you dhrink,' said Brendan Behan, with the hesitation in speech, the slight stammer that was to remain with him for the duration of his short life. 'I could show you a couple o' pubs in Moore Street at seven in de mornin' where d'oul' wans do be beltin' dem out like navvies on de quays. And dare you cross one o' dem biddies; dey'd have you talkin' outta de s-s-side of your f-fuckin' cheek as soon as look at you!' Behan scooped a broken bottle from the floor and made a movement that left us in no doubt about his meaning.

Mein host went a bit white. 'I'll take your word for it, Brendan,' he said. 'But really what I'm getting at is—how shall I put it—the sheer *versatility* of the male animal. I mean to say: look at your own performance just now. You can go from being the next best thing to an orang-utan all the way to becoming a sensitive girl singing about her doomed lover. Almost instantly. And the point about it is: it's so damned convincing!'

'That's what I thought too,' I said.

Lucy was not taking any of this. 'What makes you fellas think', she said, 'that ye've got the monopoly on impersonation? Have ye never seen Phillo Dempsey doing Adolf Hitler?'

'It's not the same thing,' mein host countered. 'She does it well of course, I'm not denying that, but she hasn't got what Brendan has. It's down to a question of physicality, I'm afraid. Men can be women but women simply can't be men. It's a matter of, well, adaptability. We're just built differently, and that's all there is to it.'

Coyle roared at Quill, and Quill hit him again.

Q: 'You fucking moron, Coyle! What more proof do you want? It's enough to look at Dürer's 'Horsemen of the Apocalypse', sent by God Himself. These are no angels of triumph and reconciliation; these are no fucking heralds of serene justice, but the dishevelled fucking warriors of a mad vengeance. The world sinks into a universal fury. Victory is neither God's nor the Devil's. It belongs to fucking madness.'

C: 'And who's saying it doesn't? But you still don't fucking understand what madness *is*. Madness is, in every sense of the fucking word, only one case of thought *within* thought. *That's* what Descartes was getting at!'

The pair moved to the pantry, accompanied by blows and curses, each to continue his own *reductio ad absurdum*.

'No, no, I won't accept that,' said Lucy. 'You make it sound as though women are a different species from men. And that's not true. No offence, but it may seem like that to *you*—you being, well, you know. ...'

'No offence taken,' said mein host, but we knew he did not mean it.

'Look at the facts,' Lucy continued, really getting into her stride. 'We're not built so very differently as you seem to think we are. I mean, compared to the male and female of other animals. Take the peacock and the peahen or, better still, a queen bee and a drone; the one can weigh about a hundred times more than the other. And those are just two examples. But with humans? Maybe men have a bit more hair on their chests, but essentially there's little difference between male and female, apart from the obvious appendages.'

'God bless 'em!' Behan roared, and uncorked another bottle.

'But when all's said and done,' Lucy said, 'those are basically the same thing in varying degrees. Why do men have nipples? Now there's a good one for you.'

'Or why do we have a coccyx?' asked Behan's companion.

These were the first words he had spoken since his arrival, and we all turned our attention on him. His exquisitely made hat and coat were discarded and he had loosened his tie. Four emptied bottles of stout stood before him on the table; he was clearly at home in our eccentric company.

'A what?' someone asked.

'A coccyx.'

'Watch your fuckin' language, Philip,' said Behan.

'I'm sorry,' said the young man. 'I'm referring to the final bone of the spine, the bone appended to the sacrum.'

'Jayziz, Mary and Joseph,' said Behan.

'Sorry,' Philip said again. 'The coccyx is the triangular bone at the base of the spine. It serves no purpose whatsoever, and there are some who think it may be a vestigial tail.' The young man's expression was one of deadly seriousness. 'It may well represent a verification of Darwin's theory. If it can be proven that it is indeed the vestige of a tail, then there can be no doubt that we're descended from the apes.'

The tumult in the pantry grew.

C: 'You and your bloody seventeenth century! What are you saying: that an entire history of reason began in the seventeenth century? Bollocks!'

Q: 'Bollocks to you, too! It's what I've always suspected: important works like *Discours de la Méthode* or *Meditationes de Primâ Philosophiâ* mean about as much to a silly cunt like you as the fucking *Beano* or the *Dandy*.'

'Or even from the pigs,' said Dan Freyne from the corner. Behan opened his mouth to say something. 'Oh, I was forgetting that, Brendan: you weren't here when Blade was trying to convince us that we all taste the same as a side of bacon.'

'We *what?!*' Behan yelled. Blade explained.

'You're a stupid bollix, Macken; I've always said it.'

'Would you go ten shillings to prove it, though?' said Blade.

Behan turned to Philip. 'Would you give's de lend of a loan of—?'

'No, I would not,' said the young man, 'because you might well lose. Mr Macken is probably correct.'

'Jayziz, I need a fuckin' dhrink.'

'It's a rhetorical question, of course, because there isn't a way of proving it. You'd have to carry out an experiment, and where do you find someone who's prepared to eat human flesh?'

We agreed that this posed a problem.

'And where would you get it anyway?' asked Noel Molloy.

Philip brightened. 'Oh, that shouldn't be difficult. We have any number of cadavers at the College.'

'Cadavers?' said Noel.

'Bodies, corpses ... donated for medical purposes ... dissection, that sort of thing.'

'Philip is a student at de College o' Surgeons on de Green,' Behan explained.

'I see. ...' said mein host, slowly and thoughtfully.

Noel stared at him and voiced our thoughts. 'Jayziz, you're not seriously suggesting that ...'

'Oh, my God,' said one of the G&T girls. 'I think I'm leaving. This is sick.'

Brendan Behan bellowed. 'By Christ, dat'd be fuckin' great crack!' He did a little dance and put an arm around Philip's waist. 'Could you get us in dere at dis time o' night?'

'Certainly. There's a night-porter on duty. It's quite common for someone to want to work late on gross anatomy—especially now the academic year has just started.'

Behan's face was a picture of animal glee. 'Who's here that I don't know about?' he asked mein host.

'Er, well, there's Mr and Mrs Chambers, I suppose. ...'

Behan drank deeply from the bottle in his hand. His eyes were wild. 'Jayziz, why not?! Can you see de pair o' dem? Fuck me!' He drained the bottle. 'Get your coat, Philip,' he ordered. 'You and me's payin' a visit to de Royal College o' Surgeons—an' de Bailey, in dat order.'

'The Bailey?' I asked, as the pair headed for the door.

'For de pork o' course,' said Behan. 'Where else would you get some at dis time o' de night?'

A NIGHT IN THE CATACOMBS

(IT OCCURS TO me just now, while I am writing this, that the first of November is All Souls' Day. It is the day after Hallowe'en, the night when witches and ghouls and demons and what-have-you are supposed to be 'abroad'. That date, I think, would have been more fitting for the macabre mission upon which Brendan Behan and his companion embarked.

Looking back on it, it is probably one of the most distasteful episodes I remember of those wild days. And yet, it seemed innocuous at the time. Drink, as we know, is a terrible thing, and there is no denying that the Catacombs crowd that night had indulged in drink in their usual way, viz. to splendid excess. We could laugh then at the excesses—Brendan's especially—believing, as we did, that we were harming no one. We were, after all, the Chosen; we were immortal.)

THIS TIME IT was a horse-drawn cab that stopped up on the street. Even with the windows shut we could none the less hear Behan roaring something irreverent at the driver before the vehicle clattered away.

A little over two and a half hours had elapsed since the duo had left; in that time a great deal more alcohol had been drunk and the troops were showing signs of it. Blade's half-brother Jack had lifted his girlfriend bodily, and carried her off to a damp room somewhere in the labyrinth. Quill and Coyle had patched up their differences and were once again the best of friends, toasting noisily each other's health with someone else's Scotch. Murph Ryan, as I mentioned earlier, had passed out some time around nine o'clock. Mr and Mrs Chambers were still absent when Behan and his friend returned.

We heard them opening the iron gate, and their footsteps rang on the steep, black steps. Lucy, in deference to the neighbours, went to the door again before Behan had a chance to hammer on it. He entered the kitchen like a Cheshire cat that has got the cream.

'We don't want to hear the details,' said Blade Macken, 'but was the expedition a success?'

'It was,' said Behan, and he drew from a pocket two items: a brown paper bag, the bottom of which was stained a dark red, and something wrapped in newspaper. With a great show of gravity, he cleared a space for his spoils on the kitchen table. By this time, all drinking and conversation in the big room had stopped.

'Which is which?' Blade Macken asked, and there was a touch of dread in his voice.

'Dis is de pork,' said Behan, tapping the paper bag. All eyes were drawn to the newsprint.

'It isn't ... it isn't *really* ... is it?' Macken's girlfriend asked hopefully.

'De genuine article,' said Behan. 'Do you want to see it?' He began to unwrap the parcel.

'Christ, no,' said the girl. 'I'll take your word for it. Merciful hour!'

Behan grinned and called for a bottle of stout and a ball of malt. When both had been drunk, he looked at each of us in turn. His eyes were bloodshot and maniacal. Something in his expression made me think suddenly of a predator scenting blood. This was unfair to Behan; it owed more to my state of mind at the time, and less to Behan as I knew him to be.

The truth about Brendan Behan is that he was one of the gentlest, most sensitive souls I have ever known. This must sound like a ludicrous statement, given his reputation and the carnage that he made of his life. Yet that reputation is one which Behan himself nurtured like a delicate bloom. He needed it—or thought he did—and, when matters got out of hand, he could no longer turn back the clock. The world saw him as the archetypal stage-Irishman: the hard drinker, the bum, the brawler, the rebel, the iconoclast. When the media of Ireland, Britain, and the United States wished him to perform, Behan was delighted to oblige. The reputation was cemented in outrage after outrage, to the amusement of the world.

At the height of his fame, Behan would insist that he was not a poet. I knew better. The success he achieved with the novel and the plays eclipsed the poems in Irish he was writing in the 'forties; only the *gaelgeoirí*, the Gaelic speakers among us, could appreciate the extent of the passion, love and feeling that are contained in those lovely verses. More than anything he wrote in later years, the poems reveal the soul of the man whom Flann O'Brien was to call 'the proprietor of the biggest heart that has beaten in Ireland for the past forty years'. Behan seemed determined to conceal from the world the gentleness I remember, the gentleness that he drowned in days and nights of drunken revelry.

And insane practical jokes.

'All right,' he said. 'Now who's goin' to do de cookin'?' I saw Lucy and most of the others pale. 'Or do I have to do every fuckin' ting meself? A great fuckin' lot yooze are.'

'I'll do it,' said Philip, somewhat to our surprise. 'I don't mind,' he explained. 'After all, it's nothing to me. ... I mean, being a medical student, one becomes used to such things. A body's a body, if you follow me. It's only dead meat. ...'

There was a scurrying and a flurry of many feet and muttered farewells as the artists' models left hurriedly.

'Right!' said Behan, 'I'll get de fryin'-pan,' and he hunted through the debris of cupboards and shelves. Eventually he located a big cast-iron pan beneath an assortment of dirty plates, cups, cutlery, green bread and putrid meat that had been laying siege to the sink for many days. He found a cake of soap somewhere and, with the help of water from the cold tap and a knife, soon had the frying-pan in a reasonable state. He discovered a tub of lard on a shelf and cut off a wedge; the larded pan was placed on the range (which was never allowed to go out during the cold months). Philip, in the meantime, had unwrapped the two portions of meat; he laid them side by side in the frying-pan.

Dear God, they really were going through with it!

'This is the time', said Blade Macken, 'for the faint-hearted left among us to withdraw.' No one budged. He took from his pocket an orange-coloured banknote emblazoned with a stylized portrait of Kathleen ni Houlihan, kissed it like a celebrant would the host at the consecration, and spread it flat on the table. 'There,' he said. 'There's my ten bob. Any takers?'

Of course there were, as Blade well knew there would be. We were all sporting men—and women—fond of a flutter, either within or without the turf accountant's shop. Quite a few of us seemed to be in funds that evening because within seconds there were other orange notes, small piles of nickel and copper, and even one of those large white English five pound notes which we seldom saw, covering Blade's wager.

This would not do, I need hardly say, so Brendan Behan very

gallantly offered to hold a book on the Pork Sweepstakes. By the time the betting had closed, the odds were these:

>Can tell the difference: 10-7
>Can't tell the difference: 3-4

'Right,' said Behan. 'Dere are two pieces o' meat. What we do now is dis: we halve de pair and give a half of each to de two tasters. Dat way, we get a fair test.'

This seemed a reasonable suggestion, and Philip sliced the meat accordingly. He returned the frying-pan to the range. A hush fell as the sound of bubbling grease was heard. A sweet odour began to intrude upon the smells of mildew, body sweat, cigarette smoke and stale porter which were characteristic of the Catacombs's kitchen on any chosen evening. It was, to my nose at any rate, the aroma of frying pork.

'Someone g-give dem a shout,' said Behan presently. 'Dey're nearly done.'

Mr and Mrs Chambers came into the kitchen. They were an odd couple. I knew very little about them. I never saw them apart in the many months that I knew them—not once. In a den of licentiousness like the Catacombs, where infidelity (even to one's partner of an evening) was the norm, Mr and Mrs Chambers were pillars of propriety. I did not know whether they were even married. Perhaps not; I have never known a married couple to perform the sexual act together so often, so protractedly and so untiringly as they did. They seldom left the Catacombs, except to buy groceries and the occasional bottle of dry gin, which they invariably drank, not in company, but in the privacy of their room, for which they paid mein host a small rent. One had to pass these tiny quarters on one's way to the lavatory, and I cannot remember ever once doing so without hearing, from within, Mr and Mrs Chambers going, as Brendan Behan used to put it, 'like de fuckin' clappers o' hell'.

Now they stood beneath the naked bulb which hung from the ceiling of the kitchen, he with an arm around her waist. They were both pale—which should not surprise, given their lifestyle. They were both in their early twenties; he thin, she given to a slight plumpness. Both had dark brown hair; both dressed in cheap, drab clothing. One met their types serving behind the counters of Dublin's bigger stores in the 'forties. I have often wondered what evil turn of fortune had brought them to permanent tenancy of a room in the Catacombs.

'It's a little experiment,' Behan told them. 'I'm d-doin' it for a friend o' mine who's just after openin' a butcher's shop in Camden Street.'

Mr Chambers was immediately suspicious—and who could blame him?

'What sort of experiment?' he enquired. His accent was a northern one; Louth, possibly. 'What are you up to?'

Behan grinned. 'Ah, now don't be tinkin' I've anyting up me sleeve, because I haven't. I'd do it meself, I would, except de gargle has deadened me taste-buds. You see, de ting is: Gallagher—dat's me friend—is after doin' a deal wi' someone he knows who says he can supply him wi' discount pork.'

'*Dis*count pork?'

Brendan winked. 'Gallagher's not assin' any fuckin' questions. But he w-w-wants a second opinion before he, eh, p-p-places an order.'

'In other words,' said Blade Macken, 'he wants someone to taste the pork for him and give their unbiased opinion.'

Mrs Chambers eyed Behan, the pan, the rest of us, and Behan again, in that order. 'I hope this isn't some kind of foolish joke, Mr Behan. ...'

Macken came to the rescue. 'Fear not, Mrs Chambers. There is nothing whatever wrong with the meat.' He inhaled the odours issuing from the pan. 'In fact, it smells delicious!'

'Then why don't *you* assist Mr Behan?' said Mr Chambers.

Blade showed his palms. 'For the very reason Brendan doesn't trust his own judgement. I'm afraid I wouldn't be a good judge either.' He looked about the kitchen. 'None of us would. Too much to drink.'

'An' we tought', said Behan, 'dat de p-p-pair o' yooze might be hungry.'

This was a shrewd observation of Behan's, born of an awareness that there is nothing quite like *le galop* for working up an appetite. Mrs Chambers ran her fingers through her hair. By now, the juices in the frying-pan were sizzling briskly; I fancied that I saw Mr Chambers's nostrils twitch.

'Well, why not?' he said.

Behan emitted a roar like an ass's bray and beat the smoky air with his little fists. He rushed to the kitchen table, which by then was a shambles of congested ashtrays, broken glass, and bottles in various stages of fullness and depletion. Brendan cleared a space by the simple expedient of brushing the mess aside. Bottles toppled. Mein host rushed in and attempted to save as many as he could from destruction. (This action, I should point out, owed less to fastidiousness than to mein host's ability to subsidize his weekly rent by collecting the empty bottles left over from each evening's drinking, returning them to the public houses with the aid of a wheelbarrow and claiming the deposit.) Lucy Moran wiped the tabletop as best she could, and set two plates, cutlery and all. Philip whipped the frying-pan from the range and bore it to the table.

The sweet aroma of fried pork rose to the vaulted ceiling of the kitchen. Drinking stopped. Philip made a great show of placing the portions of meat on two dinner plates.

'Er, shouldn't we mark them in some way?' I suggested. Mein host nodded. From somewhere in the pantry he produced two toothpicks. These were inserted in two of the four cuts.

'Now,' said Behan. 'Yooze bot' have half of each piece o' pork. Take your time, dere's no hurry, and tell us which tastes de b-best.'

'You're sure you know which is which?' asked Blade Macken. Behan assured him that he did. The test began.

The quiet of the kitchen was disturbed only by the sound of distant motor cars and horse-drawn vehicles, the occasional cloop of a cork being pulled from a porter bottle, and the grating of two sets of knives and forks on porcelain, as Mr and Mrs Chambers settled down to their meal. We waited.

Finally, after what seemed like fifteen minutes, Behan held up a hand. Both plates had been cleared except for two small pieces of meat, each flagged with a toothpick.

'Ladies first,' said Behan. 'What's de verdict, Mrs Chambers?'

She knitted her brows. 'Umm ... the one with the toothpick, I would say. It seemed to be, well, fresher and more—what's the word?—more succulent.'

Behan nodded and looked at Blade Macken.

'I'm not sure,' said Mr Chambers. 'To be honest, I didn't taste much difference between them at all.' Blade grinned. Mr Chambers spoke to Mrs Chambers. 'But I wouldn't go along with you, dear, about the freshness. If anything, the piece *without* the toothpick tasted fresher ... and more tender. To me, at least.' He turned to Behan. 'I'm sorry. This can't be very helpful.'

'Ah, but o' course it is!' Behan shouted. 'You're sure now? You preferred de one wit'out de toot'pick in it?'

'I ... think so, yes.'

'And you, Missus ...? You preferred de one *wit'* de toot'-pick?' She nodded. Behan gave a whoop.

'Dat's fuckin' marvellous! Now I can tell Gallagher dat he can take de discount p-pork. He'll be fuckin' deligh'ed, so he will.'

Mr Chambers yawned. 'Heavens,' he said. 'It was certainly very filling.' He stretched. 'I think I might just go and have a little lie-down.' He turned to his table companion. 'Are you coming, dear?'

She smiled sweetly. They thanked Behan for the meal, bade the rest of us good night, and left for their room. We waited until they were safely out of earshot. Corks popped from porter bottles. Behan drew a folded paper from one pocket, and a wad of banknotes from another, followed by a handful of coins.

'Right!' he said. 'Do we all agree dat de test was conducted fair and square?' We did. 'An' dat de results clearly indicate dat dere's no difference a' tall in de taste o' p-pork and human flesh?' We agreed that this did, indeed, appear to be the case.

'Good. Now dat dat's settled, I suppose I have to pay out to de winners?' We assured him that we expected nothing less. Behan consulted the sheet of paper on which he had noted the book; money changed hands. As the winners toasted their good luck and the losers drowned their sorrows, I saw that Behan had kept back a quite considerable sum of money; I calculated that it must have been in the region of two pounds and ten shillings. Blade whistled in sporting admiration.

'A good night's takings, Brendan,' he said. 'And you wanting to bet against me in the first place.' He shook his head with a smile. 'What made you change your mind?'

'I didn't.'

'You didn't what?'

'Didn't change me fuckin' mind. I *haven't* changed me fuckin' mind.'

We were alert—inasmuch as we could be alert at that hour in the Catacombs. Blade's expression turned to one of anger.

'Wait a minute,' he said. 'You didn't cheat, did you?' He gestured towards the plates on the table. 'That *was* what we thought it was, wasn't it?'

'Course it fuckin' was! What do you tink I am? You have it on me word of honour dat what was eaten here tonight was de genuine article.'

'But you didn't bet against me,' said Blade, puzzled.

'No, I didn't. And will I tell you w-why?'

'Please do.'

'Because me gran'fader always used to say: "Dere's no such ting, Brendan, as a poor b-bookie, only a poor punter". An' dem were wise words.

'You see, Blade, me oul' flower, a b-bookie doesn't really bet against you, even dough he's de one who m-m-makes dee odds. No, de bookie is de cunt who stays neutral, while all de fuckin' eejits like ourselves trow away our good dhrinkin' money by bettin' against each udder, horse against horse. And we're de stupid bastards who always lose.'

Behan, with a grand gesture, swept up his winnings and returned them to his pocket. He raised a bottle to his lips, drank noisily and belched. He pointed a finger at Macken.

'An' I still tink you're f-fuckin' wrong,' he said, accusingly.

> Sure if Eichmann
> Knew that,
> He'd turn
> In his urn,
> So he would.

A Rhyme to Arabi

AUGUSTA: Wilfrid ...?

WILFRID: Yes?

AUGUSTA: I thought that you must surely be asleep.

WILFRID: No, I was thinking ... just thinking.

AUGUSTA: So was I. You must not fall asleep, Wilfrid. It would not do for you to fall asleep.

WILFRID: I know.

AUGUSTA: If any of the servants should find you here. ...

WILFRID: I know.

AUGUSTA: You are smiling, Wilfrid! I believe that you should not mind at all.

WILFRID: I am not smiling. And even if I were, you could not know it.

AUGUSTA: I can see in the dark, you know ... as a cat.

WILFRID: You *are* a cat. I sometimes believe that you are a cat.

AUGUSTA: What things you say, Wilfrid! And it is not quite dark. Look, there is light showing through the curtains.

WILFRID: Augusta! Where are you going?

AUGUSTA: The moon, I wish to see the moon.

WILFRID: Please come back. No, don't do that.

AUGUSTA: It *is* the moon. Look, Wilfrid. The moon has just risen above the stables. Do come and see.

WILFRID: No. And you shall catch your death.

AUGUSTA: I once saw the moon in the desert, Wilfrid. It was a night not so very unlike this one. It was winter, too, and William and I had gone to visit the temples at Luxor. In *extremely* learned company, too, I might add. There were three French professors, and Mr Villiers Stuart—you know him of course. And a wonderful young German scholar whose name I cannot remember. I know that everybody was charmed by him. And such erudition! He and William and I ventured into the desert on that first evening. The stars, Wilfrid! Never before had I seen stars quite like the stars in the Egyptian desert. Countless stars shining so brightly that one was quite in awe of them. And there, too, was the Milky Way, shimmering as a scarf of the most diaphanous gossamer from one horizon to another. It was a night when one could not but believe in the glory of God, and in the majesty of His Creation. I clasped William's hand and I sensed his wonder, too. And then ... and then the moon rose, Wilfrid, just as it has risen tonight above the stables. Yet how unlike our own moon it seemed. It was a sickle moon, but lying perfectly on its side, a single, bright star gathered in its arms. William and I quizzed our German companion about the strange appearance of the moon, for we knew he had knowledge of such things. He explained the phenomenon to our satisfaction, but I have forgotten now. It concerned, I believe, the relative proximity of Egypt to the equator, and the tilt of the earth's axis in winter. I have forgotten now. He was very erudite, our German friend; most handsome too.

WILFRID: I rather think you should return to bed. You shall definitely catch a chill and I shall hold myself responsible.

AUGUSTA: But science, Wilfrid, will never, ever take the place of myth and poetry. When I looked at that moon, I understood how the ancient Egyptians had come to see the sun and moon as celestial sailing vessels. That moon appeared to me as a gleaming ship, having the star above her to light her way through the void. It was a tremendous spiritual experience. Yet more than the ancient Egyptian gods, I thought upon the goddesses of Greece and Rome: Aphrodite and Venus. I knew then why those ancient peoples had pictured their goddess with the horns of the moon upon her head and a single star upon her brow. It must have been thus for them, too, seeing that wondrous moon in the desert night.

WILFRID: Are you quite certain about the single star? And you really must return to bed.

AUGUSTA: I wrote a sonnet then, Wilfrid. To the moon. It was not, I am afraid, a particularly good one. Shall I recite it for you?

WILFRID: If you wish. Yes, yes, please do.

AUGUSTA: Not in its entirety. I cannot remember all of it. ... It begins thus: Had I first chanc'd upon thee in this place,/And not instead in Hyperborean lands,/Then odes I would have writ to thy night face,/As cold thou lit my way on Midian sands;/Obscured by Banba's clouds, thy pagan womb/Was rendered, by a virgin, passion's tomb.

WILFRID: Good heavens! You would do well not to allow that to fall into the wrong hands. It is positively blasphemous.

AUGUSTA: You are the first living being to hear it. I destroyed the manuscript a long time ago.

WILFRID: You did well to do so. Now kindly come to bed.

AUGUSTA: Not yet, Wilfrid. I shall put my robe on, if that should allay your fears for my health. Better?

WILFRID: Hmm.

AUGUSTA: How quiet it is. There is no sound at all. It was just like that, too, in the desert. No, the silence there was even more pronounced than this.

WILFRID: I know. There is no silence on earth quite like the silence of the desert by night.

AUGUSTA: When I was a little girl, I had a dream in which I left my bedroom at Roxborough one night and walked, alone, eastward to Dublin, with only the stars to light my way. I can, even now, recall that dream quite vividly. I was not frightened, in my dream, even though I felt that there was not a soul left in the whole world except me. I walked onward towards the east, knowing with certainty that I would find there something that I had sought. I did not know what it was, but something drew me there. I had this wonderful feeling of expectation, the feeling that children have: that somewhere there is a fabulous place, a country where one shall know no fear, or be a stranger, yet where one has never before set foot. My feet made no sound as I walked. There came no sounds from the countryside around me, no wind in my face, no rain. Only the night and the stars. When I awoke the following morning, it was with a sense of peace and fulfilment—as though I had really and truly visited that magical place. Do you know, Wilfrid, that when I stood in the desert in Luxor, I experienced once again that sense of peace and expectation? I felt that soon I would be in some way fulfilled.

WILFRID: If that is intended as a compliment to me, then I by all means accept it.

AUGUSTA: You are laughing again, Wilfrid. But I do not mind. And yes, you are correct: it is, in some ways, a compliment to you. Yet principally it is a compliment to Arabi.

WILFRID: To Arabi?! Augusta! Must I see him now as a *rival*?

AUGUSTA: Do not tease me, Wilfrid. It is you whom I love, not Arabi. I am saying that Arabi and his cause may have brought me close to ... fulfilment. Do you understand?

WILFRID: Yes. ... Yes, I believe I do.

AUGUSTA: Oh, it sounds so much like a melodrama. I do not wish it to sound like a melodrama. Do you not see it sometimes in that light, Wilfrid?

WILFRID: No, I do not.

AUGUSTA: When I am here, in England, in Crabbet, in your arms, I think of Egypt as something that happened to another person. Or as a dream.

WILFRID: Or as a play?

AUGUSTA: Perhaps a play. What are we, Wilfrid—have you ever considered that? I mean to say: are you and I, and William and Anne, and Mr Gladstone, and Mr Granville, and all the others, not in some way unreal? Look at us, Wilfrid, you and me. We write sonnets for one another. Are they to be the sole contribution that we make to this world? Shall they inscribe my gravestone with the legend 'poetess'? Oh, I know this sounds rather maudlin, but sometimes I believe that it was in Egypt that I made the only contribution to life that I shall ever make. One short hour of glory and, after that, *nothing*. I think about Egypt, about Arabi, about his wife, about their people, and I become aware of the intensity of life there. All those people, all those poor, unfortunate people. Do you know, Wilfrid, that when Anne and I went to visit Arabi's wife, hundreds of people turned out to meet us? They were mostly men, and a few children. I looked upon those dark faces and I saw *life* etched there. There was one old man in particular; he looked to me about eighty, but I suppose he could not have been more than forty—how quickly they age! It was as if the whole history of his race was written in the lines of his face. When I was close to him, close enough to touch—though of course I did not touch him—I felt as though I had come face to face with Egypt, perhaps with the whole of Arabia. I had seen them before, daily, the fellahin, in their thousands, and they had made little impression upon me. Perhaps because there were so many of them, all going about their affairs. Yet when I was so close to that old man, I realized how important was that one, single life. You and I might have passed him in the street every day and not spared even a second's thought for those things which most concerned him. Why *should* we care? What did it matter to us when he was born, and in what circumstances? How many wives and how many children he had? How many summers in his life he had starved, or how many children of his had died of fever or disease? Why should we care, Wilfrid? And yet he cared about *me* that day, and about Anne.

WILFRID: Of course he did. But not, I think, as a person—merely as the representative of a foreign power—forgive me for saying this. Perhaps he mistook you for Queen Victoria. Did you know that some of the waiters at Shepheard's genuinely believed that you were Queen Victoria? It is true. Do you remember that big portrait they have hanging in the dining-room? Well, I chanced upon a couple of the niggers whispering among themselves one afternoon and pointing at the painting, then pointing towards you—you were taking tea with Anne at the time. I was, naturally, curious, and spoke to them about it. D'you know, they were positively convinced that the Queen was visiting incognito. I can't say that I blamed them. It's an early portrait and you do look uncommonly like her, especially your hair.

AUGUSTA: Yes, the Queen quite liked my hair, I am told.

WILFRID: Really? Oh, yes, you were presented to her when you married William, were you not?

AUGUSTA: It does not matter. It is of no importance. I am thinking still of that old man. I am thinking of destiny, of the Fates that set one soul down in the greenhouse of wealth and leisure, and another down in a world of want and danger. It is all so unfair, Wilfrid! Who are we that we are more deserving than they? Why should Arabi's people toil like beasts in the fields in order that they can provide bread for their children? It is so cruel.

WILFRID   At least they have bread now. In Ismail's time they scarcely had even that.

AUGUSTA: Tawfik Pasha is no better. Why should he, a Turk, encumber himself with Egypt's lot? He is quite content to live in the luxury of the Abdin Palace, far from the misery of his subjects. No, Wilfrid, I cannot help but grieve for that old fellah, who saw his country bartered among foreign powers, and could only stand by helplessly and do nothing. Think on it, Wilfrid. How should you feel if England were owned by the merchant banks of Europe? If all Sussex were the property of Rothschild, or if Oppenheim held Cambridgeshire in bond?

WILFRID: I know. I said as much to Arabi. I quoted Byron: Trust not for freedom to the Franks.

AUGUSTA   And now the Franks have Egypt, and the English too. Must this be the lot of small nations, that they must be forever in the debt of Europe? How much of the hardship in the world is caused by foreign interference!

WILFRID   It cannot last. My sonnet is almost done. I am considering calling it 'The Writing on the Wall'.

AUGUSTA   That is a strong title. You simply must come and see the moon, Wilfrid. It is quite, quite breathtaking.

WILFRID   If only I could find a rhyme to Arabi. ...

AUGUSTA   Arabi? I have wrestled with that difficulty, too. He possesses a most unfortunate name.

WILFRID   Yes. Freedom-fighters really ought to have names that can be rhymed easily. Yet they seldom do. Even Byron poses difficulties. Iron is close. Alfred Lord Byron, brave man of iron. Yet it rings false somehow. Siren? There *is* the Greek allusion.

AUGUSTA   Must you place it in a rhyming position, Wilfrid? Can you not place it in the middle, or at the beginning of a line?

WILFRID   I have tried that. It seems to upset the metre. No, I am working on a stanza, which is quite satisfactory so far, with Arabi in the fifth line: To Alexander's city he did go,/And held the height where once the Pharos stood;/A thousand ships were lying stern to bow/At anchor, there beyond the harbour's flood./Egyptians, stand! exhorted Arabi. ... And there you have the problem, d'you see.

AUGUSTA: I understand the difficulty, Wilfrid. Oh, there is a cloud drifting past the face of the moon. How it spoils things!

WILFRID: Now you *must* return to bed. I insist upon it.

AUGUSTA: Very well, Wilfrid. I shall leave the curtains open, otherwise I may not find you in the darkness.

WILFRID: I truly believe that, were I to find a rhyme to Arabi, the sonnet should acquire such power. You are cold.

AUGUSTA: Hold me, Wilfrid. Yes. ...

WILFRID: The power to stir the hearts of men. Such an unfortunate name, though.

AUGUSTA: Some freedom-fighters have very satisfactory names. Wolfe Tone, for one. How easy it is to rhyme Tone ... a soldier to the bone. Or Thomas Davis ... come to save us. O'Neill ... seal, feel, real, England's heel, though these are only single rhymes. O'Donnell ... rhymes happily with Tyrconnell, or Daniel O'Connell. Even Cuchulain has a rhyme or two: sullen, Glencullen. ...

WILFRID: It's the language, of course; that's the difficulty. Now if I were to write it in Arabic ... there are any number of rhymes: *darabi* ... *járrabi*. There! By using the feminine imperative, all manner of things can be addressed to the Queen! But who could read it? Certainly not the people who matter ... Her Majesty, Gladstone, the Cabinet.

AUGUSTA: The wax model we saw yesterday at Madame Tussaud's —it was so lifelike. How clever they are! One could almost shake Arabi's hand. I thought then: if only he could speak, if only his voice could be heard. Yet he must remain forever mute, or speak through the voices of others. How terrible that must be, Wilfrid, to have so much to say and have no voice with which to say it.

WILFRID: Are you thinking still of Arabi?

AUGUSTA: Perhaps. You are so warm, Wilfrid. Yes, I am thinking still of Arabi, but I am entertaining yet another blasphemous thought. You are smiling again! I am thinking of the first verse of John: In the beginning was the Word. I am wondering whether that does not apply to all things: whether it is necessary for us to enunciate a thing before it can become a reality. Or must the reality be there first before we can put a name to it? I am tempted to believe the former. When a people can put a name to that in which they believe, then they can believe so much more in it—even to the extent whereby they can die for it. Perhaps words of power are a prerequisite of all great movements.

WILFRID: There is some truth in that.

AUGUSTA: Perhaps, too, of emotions and passions. The sense of power that grips me, Wilfrid, when I say to you: I love you.

WILFRID: Hmm. I fear I shall simply have to content myself with: Egyptians stand! did Arabi exhort. ... I do not believe that there *is* a rhyme to Arabi.

'Maedeliefje of Eyndhoven'
or The Travelling Flautist

BY THE GRACE of our lord, 'tis a calm, clear Day in the Winter of 1755. The Sky is so tall as only such Skies can be in Brabandt; Clouds have gather'd on the Borders of the Horizon, slipt down from on High, leaving a clear, tho' most pale, Blue, wherein the Orb of the Sun is affixt. The Day is cold; too cold, perhaps, for the Traveller who walks the Road that leads to Eyndhoven.

We may reveal, without further Pre-amble, the Identity of this Traveller, for all the World shall know of him soon enough. He is Oliver Goldsmith, and, at the Age of Six and Twenty, he is quitting the Low Countries, subsequent to an unhappy Period of Learning in the good City of Leyden. Truly unhappy, for Master Goldsmith pored not, when at that *venerable University*, over Books of great Literature, but read, in their Stead, Tomes of medickal Interest. These Last did not *greatly quicken* Master Goldsmith's mind. Nor, alas, did those Masters, whose onerous Task 't was to impart to him their learning in Physick, Anatomy, Chymistry, Chirurgery, and other germaine Sciences. Would that these Masters had been of the Calibre of Mynheer Boerhaave, Scholar of Leyden, and Master of Goldsmith's Masters at Edinburgh; they had not been thus; Goldsmith was put out of Heart.

This Oliver Goldsmith: what Manner of Man is he? Let us look to his Appearance, for Clues to his Character, as he trudges the Road to Eyndhoven. He is by no Means a tall Man; some might term him small; yet his Boddy is thick, and *very broad* across the Shoulders; a fine & manly Chest doth he possess; he does not want for Health and physickal Strength. Is this Master Goldsmith handsom, the Reader might inquire? To which Question, we must answer 'Nay'. This Reply will surely dishearten, for is it not so, that a Hero should, in the best of Tales, be fair of Brow? Alas, this History is not a fabular Tale, but *a fair Telling*. The Countenance of Master Goldsmith is that, which Freind Boswell, in Days to come, shall call *coarse & vulgar*.

The Brow bulgeth outward, and is markt by twin Clefts, which Feature lends the Head the Semblance of *an Infant Head*, wherein the parietal Bones of the Fontanella are not yet knit; this infantile Similitude continues even unto the Form of the Mouth, whose upper Lip o'erhangs, to an alarming Degree, the lower; the Nose of Master Goldsmith is *large & gross*, and the Nostril is equinal in its Flaring. Indeed, the Stranger, who has not yet heard Goldsmith speak, might wonder at the Nature of the Voice: is it to be that of *a whining Infant*, or that of *a whinnying Horse*? Now, lest the Reader imagine that the aforedescrib'd physickal Afflictions be all which beset the unfortunate Traveller, let us look to the Cheeks; they are scarr'd most cruelly with the Evidences of the Small-pox, suffer'd by Master Goldsmith at the Age of Nine; verily here walks a Man whose Beauty shall not carry him with Success through Life; we might venture the Wish that the Grossness of that Forehead conceals *a Brain of lyke Proportion*.

The Hat upon his Head, the Coat upon his Back, the Breeches upon his Arse, the Stockings upon his Calfs, the Shoes upon his Feet: this is the only Raiment that Goldsmith possesses. In Winter, mark you; for 'tis the Month of February in Brabandt; 'tis a Month wherein the Wearing of good & thick Cloth is advis'd. Why, then, is Master Goldsmith so unseasonably attir'd? The Truth is that our Hero is also a *gaming Man*, and, by this Vice, he has render'd himself almost penniless in Leyden, without the Means, by which a Taylor could have made for Goldsmith a warm Coat for his Journey; there is no Rattle in the Purse that dangles from Goldsmith's Belt, for a *lonely Guilder* does not rattle against old Leather.

How, then, will Oliver Goldsmith finance his present Interprise: the Grand Tour of the Kingdoms of Europe? Let us not shew too great a Concern, for, in Goldsmith's Knap-sack, there rests a fine, wooden Flute of German manufacture; its Ventages are blacken'd from much Use; 'tis the Instrument with which Master Goldsmith hopes to acquire Lodgings & Board, during the Course of his Travelling. For does he not have a Model, by which he can measure his future Progress? He does, 'tis certain; that Model is *no One other* than the Danish Baron Holberg, whose good Voice, and a trifling Skill in Musick, were the only Finances he had to support an Undertaking so extensive as the Journeys between Rome, Paris, Copenhagen and Oxford; so he travell'd by Day, and at Night sang at the Doors of Peasant Houses, to get himself a Lodging; this, and more, shall Goldsmith lykewise do.

The Road to Eyndhoven is *narrow & poor*; Goldsmith must tread with Care, for the Rain that fell last Night upon Tilburgh is now froze; it forms Ice upon the Pools of Brown Water; the Wends and Landa's on either Side are those of the Flat Country, belov'd by the Painters Aelbert Cuyp and Salomon van Ruysdael. 'Tis graizing Land; small Knots of Cows wander slowly, in search of Green Grass; Frost is melting quietly in the Sun of Morning. The Dutch Farmer is hard working and resourcefull; Rain falls aplenty upon this Land, and it must be drain'd away, lest Fen form; Goldsmith sees the Multitude of deep *Slooten*, cut by the Farmer, in order to facilitate the Drainage; their Banks are tufted with Willow Trees; their Branches are not suffer'd to grow to full Maturity, but are proon'd each Spring; 'tis their Roots that protect and keep the Soil of the *Sloot*. These Canals are froze, tho' very lightly; Goldsmith espys a solitary Duck upon the smooth Surface of One of them; the Bird hath found a Spot, where the Ice is thin, and it dips its spatulated Bill in the cold Water, in search of Sustenance. Goldsmith, too, is *cold & hungry*; he hath promis'd himself, that he will pause at the next Dwelling he see'th; alas, there are so few between Tilburgh and Eyndhoven.

But what is this? Upon the clear, Winter Air of Brabandt, come *Sounds* at Goldsmith's Back; the one resembles the rhythmick Fall of heavy Dyes; the other is not unlyke the Ring of Species changing Hands; for the Traveller, these are the Sounds of approaching Fortuna.

He pauses in his Stride, turns and looks Westward: there, coming along the Road, is the Shape & Form of a Vehicle, pulled by an Horse; the Cart is one used for the Conveyance of Hay; 'tis no more than a Frame upon an Axle; the Head of the Cart is high, and its Rim is curv'd; the Sides slope down to a Rere, that is, in lyke Manner, curv'd; the Cart is pull'd by a Dutch Draught Horse, whose Breath is White Smoke, thrown out in quick Bursts from each Nostril. Standing in the Cart is a Dutch Farmer, garb'd in the *untoward Clothing* of the Country-men of Brabandt: upon an Head of lank Hair, he wears a half cockt Narrow leaved Hat, laced with Black Ribbon; he wears no Coat, but *Seven Waistcoats and Nine Pairs of Breeches*, so that his Hips reach almost up unto his Arm-pits; his Face is ruddy, his Nose is Purple, and his Eye is moist from the cold Wind; no Hair grows above his upper Lip, yet a full and Yellow hispid Beard covers him from Ear unto Chin. Goldsmith stands, and views the Approaching of the Cart.

The Carter reins his Animal in, and the Beast *snorts & stamps*, as tho' to signal to Goldsmith its Annoyance at this Disruption of its Journey. Oliver Goldsmith doffs his Hat, and bares his unwasht Wig, in deference to the superiour Position of the Carter; for superiour he is, indeed, when *his* are the Means of Conveyance; Goldsmith's Hat, on the other Hand, being once most comely blockt and braided, is *by far the Superiour* of the Head-gear worn by the Carter; the Carter does not see 't thus, for Wind & Weather and Dust & Dirt have made of 't a poor Showing; the Carter does not see a peregrinatious Irish Gentleman; the Carter seeth a poor & soilt Traveller of his own & native Brabandt.

'*Ge wilt seker mede ryden*,' he says, in none too freindly a Fashion. '*Stap er dan in; er is Ruimte genoeg voor ons aller Beyden.*'

Goldsmith blinks in Perplexity, upon hearing this barbarous Tongue; his cleftèd Brow knits the more.

'Na, waar wacht mijn Heerken op? Een Trappe, wel?'

Goldsmith, imploying his best & most lucid French, and 'inunciating' both clearly & slowly, attempts to make known to the Carter, that his Ignorance of the other's Language, whilst being, perhaps, impedient to quotidian Conversation, should not stand in the Way of the Carter's conveying them both to the nearest Domicile, whose Position (Goldsmith makes clear with a pointing Finger) must surely lye in the Direction, in which both he and the Carter are travelling. The Carter spits upon the Road-way.

'Eyndhoven.'

'Yes, yes!' exclaims our Hero. 'Eyndhoven, indeed.' Goldsmith is pleas'd that he and the Yokel can communicate so well. He climbs on Board the *Boerenwaegen*; its Oaken Floor & Staves reek of ancient Cow Droppings, Urine, fœtid Grass and other *malodorous Things*. Goldsmith braces himself against the Side, as the Carter lashes the Horse into Motion. Goldsmith's Feet slip on the slimy Wood; he must steady himself.

Wind gathers. 'Tis a biting, cold Wind, and its Breath causes Master Goldsmith's Teeth to chatter; yet he is making Progress in the Cart; Two Miles, perhaps e'en Three, pass 'neath the Hooves of the Dutch Draught. Is that Smoke which Goldsmith espys ahead? 'Tis Smoke, indeed.

'Here will do nicely, thank you very much,' he tells the Carter.

'Eyndhoven, *ja*.' The Carter urges the Horse to greater Effort, and they pass the thatcht Roof of a Farm-house; the Smoke, issuing from the Chimney, carries a Promise, now to remain unfullfill'd, of *Warmth & Hospitality*. Goldsmith sighs and clenches his Teeth, in order to deter them from chattering. 'Tis well for the Carter: the Man wears *Seven Waistcoats*; Goldsmith's single, thin Coat can not compare, as Protection against the Bite of Winter.

An other Farm-house appears: again, Goldsmith must watch, helplessly, as 't disappears behind him. A Windmill towers upward in the Distance; its Blades hang frozen; no Water turns its great Wheel. An other Mile distant, an other House is seen. Still the mad Carter will not call halt; Goldsmith begs and intreats; he is of Mind to clamber over the Rere, and spring from the moving Cart, but he decides that he will not run this Risk; he is fearfull that his Legs are now so froze, that they may not sustain him in the Leap, and that he may fall and break One, or both, upon the hard, icy Road-way.

'Eyndhoven, *ja*,' his Tormentor says, as Dwelling after Dwelling passeth and recedeth. A Curse upon Eyndhoven! thinks our unhappy Hero.

The Sun of Winter, being pale when Goldsmith started this Morning upon his Journey, hangs now as a Golden Coin, low in the West. Oliver Goldsmith sees it not; he is croucht in a rere Corner of the Cart; his Knees are drawn up to below his Chin, and his Hands move over them briskly, as he attempts to restore the Blood Circulation to Hands & Legs; he is miserable, he is hungry, he is *past Despair*.

'Eyndhoven!' says the Carter. Goldsmith nods glumly.

'Eyndhoven!' says the Carter again.

Oliver Goldsmith hath heard *a new Note* in the Voice of the Brabandter. He arouses himself from his unhappy Crouch, and peers over the Side of the Cart. Ahead, he sees Columns of Smoke ascending: the Presence of many Dwellings; there is a tall Spyre amongst them, then an other.

'Eyndhoven,' says the Carter once more, and displays his blacken'd Teeth. Goldsmith is o'erjoy'd.

Eyndhoven, the Town accurs'd by him, hoves into Sight: 'tis *no Petty Town*; there are Three Churches, each of them Romanist; One such, a Gothic Marvel of soaring Portail, Flying Buttresses & Campanile, stands on the Left Bank of the River Dommel, a Water of fair Importance that, some Distance to the North, pours into the mighty Rhine; the Dommel is the *Artery of Eyndhoven*, used, as it is, by the Merchants of Brabandt, for the Transport of Coals, from Limburgh to the Cities of Holland; the Coals are borne upon Barges, each Barge availing of the Current, on its North bound Journey, and sturdy Horses, on its Return. The Dommel is froze now in Places along its Length; not here in Eyndhoven; there is much Trade upon 't.

Oliver Goldsmith remains mute, as the Cart clatters through the Streets; some are cobbled with the big, rounded Stones, known to the Brabandters as *Kinderkopjes*, or Children's Heads; they are icy, and the Hooves of the Horse slither & slip by times. 'Tis quite fully dark when the Cart, at last, ends its Journey upon a wide

Square, seeming the very Centre of this Brabandtsche Polis. With deft Hand and fleet Movement, the Carter unyoaks his Beast. Nary a Glance does he afford our Hero; he leads the Animal to an Arch-way, and Goldsmith hears the Hooves echo loud against the Walls of a Court-yard.

The Carter re-emerges presently, loosens his *Nine Pairs of Breeches*, finds his Bald Richard, and pisses in the Kennel. By this Time, Goldsmith has descended, *painfully & slowly*, from the Cart; the Carter beckons him with a freindly Gesture, which Signal is accompany'd by unknown Words in that guttural and barbarous Language. The Meaning is clear: a Lamp burns behind a thick Window of the Building that adjoins the Arch-way; coarse *Voices & Laughter* emanate from this Building; Shadows move across the Window; 'tis a Publick House.

Shall Goldsmith join his 'Host'? 'Sbodikins! Oliver Goldsmith hath had enough of the accursèd Carter; he raises his Hand, and calls a polite Refusal, in his most eloquious French; the Carter shrugs, and turns into the Ale-house, without a further Word. Goldsmith is alone; the Square is desertèd.

There sounds the Boom of the Bell in the Campanile of the Church beside the River; 'tis a Single Note, clear & sweet upon the still Air. Goldsmith has no Time-piece; that, too, hath fallen a Victim to the Fall of the Cards. 'Tis now quite dark; there is no Moon; it may be the Hour of Six; it may be the Hour of Seven. A Dog barks, and its Call is answer'd from the other Side of the Dommel. There come the Sounds of a Tumult, or an Altercation, from the Inn. There also come the fainter Sounds of *marching Feet*; these are not to Oliver Goldsmith's Lyking. The Footsteps draw nearer; they are attended by the Notes of Metal striking upon Metal; Goldsmith thinks to divine their Import: the *Night Watch* of Eyndhoven approacheth.

Some Lane-ways and Alley-ways lead away from the Square; Goldsmith chuses One, which must surely carry him far from the Officers of the Peace. In his Choise, he is not mistaken; as he reaches the End of the Alley, he hears the Sounds of the Night Watch fading. He stops and listens. A Dog of some Size passes him in the Darkness, grunting and snuffling as would a Pig. Goldsmith leans against the Gable Wall of an House, and considers his Position.

The Guilder resides still in his Purse. 'Tis certainly tempting to contemplate upon what that Coin might buy: Board & Lodgings for a Week, perhaps; Warmth & plaisant Company; by an other Token, he has been *reckless & unparsimonious*; only the Lord knows what the Future may hold; nay, best to hold that Guilder in Reserve.

But hark, what is this? Upon that chill Evening Air, is borne *a most wonderfull Melody*; Goldsmith is astonisht; for the Melody, made upon a Spinette, and play'd with a gentle (tho', it must be say'd, poorly tutored) Hand is One familiar to our Hero, yet One he has not expected to hear in Brabandt: 'tis no One other than the Hymn, 'Quers of Angels Do Him Adore', penn'd by the English Composer, William Byrd.

Oliver Goldsmith's physickal Discomposition is forgotten; in his Mind's Eye, his Fingers dance upon the Ventages of a *specktral Flute*, as they follow the Holy Ditty that he has play'd so often in Lissoy; Goldsmith's stiff & cold Legs have found a Motion of their own; they carry him towards the Place, whence the Melody issues, just as the Pyper charm'd & enchanted the Children of Hameln; save, in this Instance, 'tis the *very Pyper* who is bewitcht, and the magickal Door in Koppelberg Hill is the Door of a *stately Mansion*, which stands aloof, and flankt by Two tall Lindens.

Lights blaze in Four Windows, in the lowest Storey of the great House. As Goldsmith draws nigh, he sees the Twin Lions of Stone that guard the broad Steps; a Fore-paw of each Beast rests upon a Shield, displaying the Arms of the Province of Brabandt; this is the House of a Person of some *Standing*.

The Melody ends; there is a Pause; an Other takes its Place. Now the Ringing of the Spinette is so resolv'd, as to put to Flight all other Sounds from the darken'd Town; Goldsmith's Joy is great, for this Second Ditty is even less a Stranger to him than was the First: 'tis the sprightly 'Upon One Morn Did I Espy', by the English Poet and Composer, Thomas Campion. Our Hero's Hand moves to his Knap-sack, and draws out the German Flute; he puts it to his Lips.

As the Second Verse tinkles from the Spinette within, Master Goldsmith's Flute finds the contrapuntal Notes, and they rise lyke a Færy Song, to *inwrap & imbrace* their Sisters. Imbolden'd by this magickal, melodickal Inosculation, Master Goldsmith increases the Power of his Breath upon the Reed, making Musick so loud, that the *intire Town* of Eyndhoven must surely hear 't. Behind the lighted Window, the Spinette stops; Goldsmith, without a Thought, compleats the Verse's Thema; this done, he lowereth the Flute from his Lips, and singeth:

> 'Upon one Morn did I espy
> A Maiden, seated near the Place
> Where Swains and Sweethearts oft-times lye,
> Intwinèd in Love's gay Embrace.'

The Double Door of Koppelberg Hill flys open, and, fram'd in the Light, stands a Servant in Livery; Goldsmith decides to discontinue his Song.

'*Wie daar?*' the Servant calls, in that indecorous Tongue of the Low Lands. '*Toont U!*'

Goldsmith conveys to the Man his Inapprehension; the Servant translates to the more mellifluous Language of the Franks.

'Who's there? Pray, show yourself!' Goldsmith obeys.

'I am requested', says the Servant, 'by the Master of this House, to bid you *welcome*, Monsieur, and to escort you to the Withdrawing Room, where he is to receive you.'

'That is indeed *most generous* of your Master,' Goldsmith replys. 'And I will be delighted to comply with his Request, for I am chill'd to the very Marrow!'

'I sympathize, Monsieur; 'tis quite unseasonably cold for the Month of February.'

Goldsmith casts his Eye about him, as he is led through a sizeable Hall, lay'd with square Tyles of Black & White, hung with Portraits, and Sailing Vessels workt in Oils; One of these Latter, a Canvas of *Gargantuan Dimensions*, is a superb Rendering of a Merchantman of the Dutch East Indian Company, in full Sail; the Hall is a Store-house of Treasures taken from those Indies; there are Vases and Urns of great girth & highth; a Throne, whose Legs, Rests, Seat and Back are a *bewild'ring Concinnity* of phantastick Animals & Dæmons & Men, some carv'd from Black Wood, and some from White Ivory; there are Conches, edg'd with Silver, and strange Weapons and Idols, incrusted with Jade and precious Stones. To say Truth, thinks Oliver Goldsmith, Baron Holberg hath met his Master!

The Servant flings open a Pair of High Doors, to reveal a Room, whose Grandeur o'ertrumps that of the Hall. Two Chandeliers, each bearing Four Scores of Candles, throw their Light upon the Chamber and its Three Occupants, Two of whom sit on either Side of a *veritable Furnace* of a Log Fire; the Mantel-piece that incloses it is deckt by exquisite Dutch Tyles, and surmounted by other Treasures from the Orient.

There is a Man seated in an High-backt Chair, whose Upholstery comprizes alternate Stripes of White Satin & water'd Red Silk; he smokes a most elaborate Pype of Meerschaum, ochreous from Use; his Wig is longer and fuller than is the Fashion, and it does not want for Powder; its Wearer is fat; he sits with stout Legs spread wide, these being incas'd in impeccably White Stockings; the Buckles of his Shoes gleam; both his Breeches and Waistcoat are of dark Red Velvet; his Coat has an expansive Collar, trimm'd with Silver; his Shirt is of Brussels Lace; a Pair of tiny Gold Spectacles rests upon his broad Nose; the Eyes behind the Lenzes are *full of good Humour.*

The Mistress of the House sits opposite the Master; she is voluminously clothed, disregardfull of the Heat of the Fire. She is a Deal younger than her Husband; Goldsmith ventures the Age of Eight and Thirty; she differs from the Ladies, whom Goldsmith has incounter'd in Holland, in as much that her Figure is trim, having a fine Waist, and a well rounded Bosom; her Hair is Fair, Golden Locks of 't peeping from beneath her Bonnet; she is *very handsom,* thinketh he.

Had Goldsmith expected to incounter a Room cramm'd full of sumptuous Furniture, then he hath 't amiss, for this Room's Furnishings are spare: besides the Chairs, in which Master and Mistress sit, there are only Two Others in that huge Interior; one has been placed close by the blazing Fire; the Other is set before the Spinette, which stands beneath One of the Chandeliers. As Goldsmith enters the Room, the Occupant of that Chair turns, and our Hero's Heart makes a Leap within his Breast.

The Maiden is surely the Daughter of the Mistress of the House;

they are almost One-of-a-Figure, and the younger of the Two is reveal'd more fully & deliciously by a Gown that leaves the White Shoulders quite bare. *There* is the same trim Waist and splendid Bosom; the Face is the Face of the Mother, lessen'd by a good Twenty Years; 'tis a Countenance, whose Lyke or Semblant Goldsmith hath not seen before; 'tis the Face of an *Angel incarnate*. *Those Lips*: they are so delicate as the Petals of a Rose; *those Eyes*: they are of the Blue of Sapphires; those Cheeks: they are as the Blush of a firey Sunset upon a Skin of White Snow; *that Hair*, imbraided to a Golden Crown, is of the Hue of Honey. Goldsmith, in the Presence of this *rare Vision*, feels the hot Blood course through his chill'd Frame.

'Good evening, young Monsieur,' says the Master, rising to meet his Guest; 'pray, be welcome in this House. You are the Maker of that fine Musick & Song?'

'Aye,' says Goldsmith, 'tho' 'twere but a poor Accompaniment to that which I heard from without.'

The Master bows. 'You are gracious, Monsieur. Our Daughter, Maedeliefje, possesses an high Degree of Inthusiasm, yet I fear, that she has much to learn of Technique. But come, Monsieur, will you not acquaint us with your Name?'

''Tis Goldsmith, Sir; Oliver Goldsmith.'

'And I, Monsieur Goldsmith, am Rogier van Aerdenhoudt, Apothecary of Eyndhoven. My Wife (Goldsmith kisses the Lady's Hand) and my Daughter (Goldsmith bows low in the Direction of *the Vision*). 'Please, Monsieur,' says the Apothecary, indicating the unoccupy'd Chair, 'Do sit near the Fire, and give us Company. I observe that you are cold, and that the Journey has been long. Perhaps a Glass of warm Punch will be comfortable.'

'You are most kind, Sir,' says Oliver Goldsmith, pulling the Chair to the Blaze. The Servant pours and hands a warm Glass to the Guest.

'I hope you'll find 't to your Mind,' the Apothecary says. 'I have prepar'd 't with my own Hands, and I believe you'll own the Ingredients are tolerable.' He raises his own Glass. 'Will you be so good as to pledge me? Here, Monsieur Goldsmith, here is to our better Acquaintance.'

The Pledge being drunk, and Goldsmith having warm'd himself

by the Fire, the Apothecary imbarks upon easy Conversation.

'Your Proficiency with the Flute gives you Credit, Monsieur; its Notes were a fair Complement to my Daughter's Melody. I hear the English Fall of your Words, and they offer the Clue to your Provenance.'

'I beg Leave to correct you, Sir. I am not English, but an Irish Man.'

'Indeed! Then you have stray'd far.'

'I am ingag'd upon a Walking Tour, Sir, and I had hop'd to see the Candle-lit Caverns of Maestricht, before venturing onward to Paris.'

'You are a Scholar?'

'Late of Leyden, Sir.'

'Ah, Leyden! 'Twas there, at that great University, that I study'd Botany, amongst other Sciences. 'Tis ever to my Regret that my Studies ended before the Arrival of the great Linnæus. You know, perhaps, of his Reputation?'

'Of course!' Goldsmith pats his Knap-sack. 'I carry with me always his *Systema Naturæ per Regna Tria*. 'Tis a wonderfull Source of Inspiration to me. I have an abiding Interest in the Natural World, tho' I must own to a Preferrence for the Animal Kingdom; I consider 't far remov'd above the Vegetable Kingdom, and its lowest Denizen is possess'd of very great Privileges, when compar'd with the Plants with which 'tis often surrounded.'

The Apothecary slaps his Velvet-clad Knees. 'But this is astounding, quite astounding! Fortune 'tis indeed, which has brought you to my House this Night. There are few Pass-times, Monsieur, which afford me greater Pleasure than good Intercourse with a learnèd Man, as I note you are. 'Twill give me great Sport to debate with you the Importance of the Denizens of the Vegetable Kingdom, for I consider them to be *of vital Worth*. In truth, Monsieur, my Calling has made me uncommonly aware of the *Life giving Properties* of divers Herbs. I challenge you, Monsieur Goldsmith, to confute the following: The Flesh of a Beast will sustain Life, but an Herb, when scrupulously prepar'd, will *save* a Man's Life, should he be unwell; *ergo*: The Vegetable is possess'd of *greater Privileges* than is the Animal, *verbum sat*.'

'You have a fair Argument in your Cup, Sir,' says Goldsmith.

'I bow to you. Your Punch, too, is fair. Yet I must risk appearing impertinent, by stating that your Talk of the sustaining Properties of Flesh has serv'd to re-mind me of my Hunger, for I have not eaten since the Morn.'

'But Monsieur,' crys the Host, laughingly, 'you insult us! Our Table is your Table, and it can not be otherwise in Eyndhoven. My Butteler will have instructed the Kitchen Servants to prepare an extra Meal.' He consults his Watch. 'Your Visit is timely, for we usually dine *at this very Hour*.' He turns to his Wife. 'Madame, will you be so good as to inform our Guest of the Constituents of Tonight's Repast?'

The Lady's Voice is so comely as her Face; 'tis the first Time that Goldsmith has heard her speak; to our hungry Hero, however, 'tis the *Content of the Speech* that is of prime Importance:

'For the First Course, Monsieur,' she tells him, 'there is a Pork Pye. Next, there is a boil'd Rabbit and Sausages, a Florentine, a shaking Pudding, and a Dish of Taffety Creme.'

Goldsmith is well pleas'd. No sooner has the Lady spoken of these Dishes, than the Butteler enters the Room once again, and announces that *this very Meal* will be serv'd in the Dining Room. Goldsmith, quite gallantly (for his Eye has been upon the *beautifull Daughter*, when ever Opportunity made 't possible) proffers the Mother his Arm, and the Company repairs to Table.

The Dining Room is so sparingly furnisht as the Withdrawing Room, containing little more than a most richly polish'd Table of Mahogany Wood from the Americas, Ten Dining Chairs, and a Mahogany Side-board; a Fire to rival the First burns in the Grate; an old Portrait of Stadholders of the Netherlands hangs upon One Wall; Goldsmith sees that One of these States-men resembles strongly the Mistress of the House; again, Two great Chandeliers blaze from the Ceiling. Goldsmith is placed opposite his Host at a Table's End; the Ladies are seated at its Flanks. Goldsmith is thankfull for the Size of the Board, for the Road hath made him stinking; 'twould not do for Two Ladies so handsom as these, to be in Proximity to his *stale & malodorous* Transudation.

The Meal is brought up. Its Quality & Nouriture exceed Goldsmith's Expectation, and he is well satèd before the Time that the Last Course is serv'd. Throughout, the Conversation is of a learnèd Nature; his Host speaks, at Length, of his own Calling, a Profession that has inabled an high Degree of Prosperity for the van Aerdenhoudt Family; there is much Business for the Apothecary in the Province, Goldsmith learns, owing not to an immoderate Amount of inferiour physickal Health among the Burgers and Country-men, but owing to an high Incidence of Melancholia in the Region.

'To what do you attribute this Melancholia?' Goldsmith asks, wiping his Lips clean of the good Wine. The fair Maedeliefje fixes him with a Look of *great Interest*; indeed, throughout the Course of the Meal, the young Lady's Gaze has *oft* been upon Goldsmith; tho' neither she, nor her Mother, has spoken. Verily, thinks our Hero, the Manner of this Maiden is odd: 'tis as though Goldsmith were *an Intimate of hers*, in the Stead of a Stranger, come but lately to her Father's House and Table!

His Host pauses before giving Answer to Master Goldsmith's Question, summoning his Thoughts. 'To the following,' he says, at last: 'The Earth yields Nouriture to Vegetables; sensible Creatures feed on Vegetables; both are Substitutes to reasonable Souls, and Men are subject amongst themselves, and all to higher Powers; so God would have 't; all Things, then, being rightly examin'd, and duly consider'd, as they ought, there is no such Cause of so general Discontent; 'tis not in the Matter itself, but *in our Mind*, as we moderate our Passions and Esteem of Things. *Nihil aliud necessarium ut sis miser, quam ut te miserum credas*, as Cardan sayeth: Let thy Fortune be what it will, 'tis *thy Mind alone* that makes thee poor or rich, miserable or happy.'

'I know of what you speak, Sir,' says Oliver Goldsmith. 'Is this not the Disease of the Hypochondria, those Viscera—Spleen, Stomach, Liver and Gall Bladder—where Melancholia is oft found?'

'You are knowledgeable, Monsieur; for 'tis those Hypochondria which my Receipts treat; I do not hold with Blood Letting by Horse Leeches, except in Cases where the Patient's Boddy is full of Blood; nay, 'tis generally more efficacious to make use of the Privileges of Vegetables, in Conjunxion with warm Baths. Codronchus, for Example, magnifys the Oil & Salt of Wormwood above all other Remedies, preferring it before all those fullsom Decoctions and Infusions, which must offend by Reason of their Quantity;

Wormwood, taken in a small Measure, expels Wind, and *most forcibly moves Urine*, cleans the Stomach of all gross Humours & Crudities, and helps the Appetite.'

At this Point, Madame van Aerdenhoudt vents a little Cough, design'd to attract the Notice of her Spouse. The Pharmacopolist turns to her, where upon Madame van Aerdenhoudt begs Leave, for her and for her Daughter, Maedeliefje, that they may be excused from the Table. Goldsmith rises & bows to the Two Ladies, regretting that their further charming Company will be denied him this Night; Maedeliefje fixes Goldsmith with a *final & winsom Smile*; 'tis a Smile, thinks he, that betrayeth *more* than maidenly Politeness! Then she casts her Eyes on the Ground, and follows her Mother from the Room. Our Hero has no Time, in which to grieve over the Exit of the comely Maedeliefje, for the Apothecary at once resumes his Discourse:

'Ah, what a *Bounty*, Monsieur Goldsmith, hath the Lord given us in His Garden! For the treatment of Malady in the Hypochondria alone, there is a Plenitude of Alexipharmica: Aniseeds, Dill, Fennel, Germander, ground Pine, *et Cetera*. And for the Expellation of Wind, one can chuse from the most simple Roots & Herbs, or from Compounds of these: Galanga, Gentian, Angelica, Enula, Calamus, Aramaticus, Valerian, Zeodoti, Iris, Condite Ginger, Aristolochy, Cicliminus, China, Dittander, Penny Royal, Rue, Calamint, Bay Berries & Leaves, Betony, Rosemary.

'And the Spyces, Monsieur Goldsmith! Let us not forget the Spyces: Saffron, Cinnamon, Bezoar Stone, Myrrh, Mace, Nutmegs, Pepper, Cloves, Ginger; and Compounds, such as Dianisum, Diagalanga, Diaciminum and Diacalaminth—all wonderfull in the Resolving of Wind. As Bessardus sayeth, Monsieur: *Si non levando, saltem leniendo valent peculiaria benè selecta*; a good Choise of particular Receipts must needs ease, if not quite cure, not One, *but all, or most*, as Occasion arises.'

'To say truth, this is of great Interest, Sir,' says Goldsmith, tho' 't must be own'd that our Hero grows a little weary of the Zeal, by which his Host inumerates his Remedies; the Fire is warm, his Belly is fill'd, and a certain Drowziness steals over him. But the Apothecary is a Brabandter to the Bone, and 'tis his Wish that his young Guest be as comfortable as possible in his House; he therefore summons a Servant, to prepare a Room for Master Goldsmith, compleat with Basin, Soap, and a Change of Linen for the grimy Traveller. An Half Hour later, Goldsmith descends to the Withdrawing Room, where his Host is seated once more in his Chair beside the Fire; there is a new Addition to the Furnishings: 'tis a little Card Table, and a Deck of exquisitely colour'd Tarocchi Cards; Goldsmith observes that the Cards are imblazon'd with the Coat of Arms of the Habsburgs.

'Are they not quite gracious, Monsieur?' says van Aerdenhoudt. 'A small Present from the Kreishauptmann, Conrad Baron Von Trautmannsdorff, given to me upon the Occasion of his last Visit.' The Apothecary's Expression is full of Pride. 'You will, no doubt, have heard of the Baron, Monsieur Goldsmith? He is an Intimate of the Emperour, Joseph II; 'twill be a *great Honour* to welcome him into our humble Family.'

'I do not understand, Sir.'

Van Aerdenhoudt beams with Pleasure. 'Ah, Monsieur, I was forgetting; how could you know? Baron Von Trautmannsdorff and our Daughter, Maedeliefje, are to be wedded, not Three Months hence. Think on 't, Monsieur! The Kreishauptmann is the *most important Representative* of the Austrian Emperour in his Netherlandish Dominion.'

'I congratulate you, Sir,' says Goldsmith. In Truth, his Heart is sore, for Maedeliefje of Eyndhoven hath stolen 't. He is not pleas'd by the News that she has been contracted to an other—more so, when *that other* is clearly a Man of a *far higher* social Position than he, a poor Travelling Flautist; Goldsmith is all too aware that the Differences of Birth, Fortune & Education make an honourable Connexion with Maedeliefje impossible.

But now the Apothecary pulls the Cork Stopper on a Bottle of fine Schnapps, and Host & Guest drink to One and the Other a Pledge; the strong Admixture of Herbs & Spyces settles Goldsmith's Mind, and gives Comfort. He has no Call upon Grievance, having a good Repast in his Belly, and clean Linen upon his Arse; the *Goddesse Fortuna* has been generous.

The Goddesse Fortuna! Can it be that his Host hath read Goldsmith's Thoughts? For he places the Card Table 'tween them, and picks up the gorgeous Playing Cards: They are made of Linnen

Rag, and each is colour'd most exquisitely in oil'd Pigments; the Courts are *Four* in Number: Emperour, Emperesse, Prince and Princesse; the Four Cards of the Emperour have the Lykeness of Joseph II, of the House of Habsburg; the Four Cards of the Emperesse bear the Lykeness of his Spouse; Goldsmith doth not recognize the Personages of the other diminutive Portraits.

'Do you play, Monsieur?' asks van Aerdenhoudt, as he shuffles the elegant Cards with practist Hand.

'I have been known', says Goldsmith, 'to hold an occasional Hand at Whist.'

The Apothecary laughs. 'I knew 't!' he crys. 'When you came to my Door this Night, I said to myself: Here is a *gaming Man*. But Whist, Monsieur, is liefer play'd at a Table of Four; come, I will show you a Game of my own Invention; 'tis quite simple, yet it affords great Sport: I call 't *Seize*.'

Here is *a rare Quandary*, wherein our Hero finds himself: He is, indeed, a Gamester, and few Pass-times are dearer to his Heart than an Evening's Sport at the Tables; but he has no Wager to hazard; Nought, save the solitary Golden Guilder that rattles not in his Purse. Will he hazard All, his *whole & intire Fortune*, the Price of Lodgings & Board for a Week, or longer, on the chance Fall of a Card? A foolish Question, for this is *Oliver Goldsmith*!

'The Game', says van Aerdenhoudt, 'is play'd with the Purpose of obtaining an Hand, telling *Sixteen*. The Dealer deals the Player and himself a single Card; each Card of the Courts tells for Ten, and the plain Cards are told by their own Pips.' He extracts a Card, and lays it, with its Face upward, upon the Baize; 'tis the Nine of Diamonds.

'An high telling Card, Monsieur,' he says. 'Will the Player risk a Second?' He turns up an other: 'tis the Three of Hearts. 'Ah, tell the Pips, for they make up Twelve. Will the Player hold on Twelve? Aye, for a Third Card may burst him.'

The Apothecary reaches into a Pocket of his Coat, and takes out a Silver Snuff Box, most handsomly workt in Filligree; he puts a Pinch of Brown Snuff to his Nose, and sneezes.

'And so to the Dealer,' he says, ''tis his Turn to play. He does not know what Cards the Player holds.' He turns up the Card he has dealt himself: 'tis the Prince of Spades. 'Ten, Monsieur.' He takes an other; this Time, 'tis the Deuce of Spades. 'Twelve! Dealer and Player each hold a lyke Number of Pips! But this the Dealer can not know. What will he do; will he hold, Monsieur? Nay, for the Player may have Thirteen or More.' The Apothecary takes a Third Card: 'tis the Emperour of Hearts.

'Soh! The Dealer loseth, Monsieur Goldsmith. See you, the Risk is great, when this Deck is imploy'd, for 't containeth *Sixteen Courts*, in the Stead of the customary *Twelve*, and therein lyeth the Sport.'

'To say truth, 'tis an agreeable Game, this Seize,' says Oliver Goldsmith, 'and I will risk an Hand. A Question, tho': How will the Winner be decided, when each Man holdeth a lyke telling Hand?'

''Tis simple, Monsieur. In such a Pass, 'tis the Dealer that wins. And so, before each Hand commences, a Dealer is chosen by cutting the Cards; he who draws the lower Card wins.'

The Pharmacopolist takes a Pinch of Snuff one more Time; he returns the dealt Cards to the Deck and shuffles them; Goldsmith is *Planet Struck* by the *Speed & Dexterity* by which he accomplishes this Act; the Movements can scarce be follow'd with the Eye; he passes the Deck of Cards to Goldsmith.

'Pray, cut, Monsieur.'

'We have not yet agreed upon a Wager,' says Our Hero. The Apothecary smiles.

'In Time, in Time, Monsieur. Let us first play an Hand, that you grow accustom'd to the Game; there after, will we say a Guilder upon each Hand, for a Beginning?'

A Guilder; Goldsmith is much reliev'd. He makes the first Cut of the Game, and shews the Card: 'Tis the Ace of Hearts, marvellously limn'd with an Eagle, having Two Heads, and surmounted by a Golden Crown. He returns the Card to the Deck, and deals One Card to van Aerdenhoudt, and One to himself; the Apothecary looks at his Card, and calls for an other; he studys this, and calls upon Goldsmith for a Third; then he places his Hand of Three Cards Face down upon the Table.

Goldsmith looks at the Card that he has dealt himself: 'Tis the Emperour of Clubs; he takes an other from the Top of the Deck: 'tis the Six of Spades; Goldsmith now holdeth Sixteen; he shews his Hand to van Aerdenhoudt. The Apothecary is well pleas'd.

'You see, Monsieur? 'Tis no difficult Game; you have master'd 't all ready. Let us now cut for the next Deal, and here is my Guilder.'

Goldsmith draws his own Guilder from his Purse, lays it next to that of van Aerdenhoudt, and cuts: 'Tis a Princesse; the Apothecary cuts to a Seven; Goldsmith examines the Card he is dealt: 'Tis an Ace, *an auspicious Start*; he begs an other: 'Tis a Four; he begs a Third Card, and Joy!: 'Tis the Prince of Diamonds; he lays the Cards upon the Table; there is a light Rapping upon the Door, and a Footman enters, with Logs held in his Arms; whilst the Fire is fed, the Apothecary draws his own Card.

'The Goddesse Fortuna smiles upon you, Monsieur!' he says. 'For I am burstèd.' The Apothecary hath drawn an Emperour, and this, taken with the Emperesse he hath dealt himself, hath caused him to exceed Sixteen by Four. Oliver Goldsmith hath *doubled* his Fortune.

Again, Goldsmith loseth the Cut; again, Goldsmith winneth the Hand: He is richer by *Three Guilders*.

The Game continues in plaisant Fashion; a Second Bottle of Schnapps is order'd; Goldsmith's Luck wins him many Hands, and, ere long, a *sizeable Pyle* of Golden Guilders stands at his Hand; the Apothecary takes a Pinch of Snuff, and shuffles the Deck.

'If you are agreeable, Monsieur,' he says, 'I will hazard Ten Guilders. Will you match them?'

Goldsmith matches them, loses the Cut, and wins the Hand.

'Double, Monsieur? I will match your Twenty Guilders with mine.'

The Apothecary o'erdraws: He loseth a further Twenty Guilders; he doubles his Wager; Goldsmith wins the Eighty! Now must he surely stop, thinks Goldsmith, for I have won a Fortune, and his Purse can not be so deep that he will risk More. Yet van Aerdenhoudt doth risk *Eighty Guilders more*; Goldsmith loses the Cut, and wins the Hand.

The Pharmacopolist pauses and smiles; he takes an other Pinch of Snuff and sneezes loudly. Goldsmith's Side of the Table gleams with Gold Coin. The Schnapps is strong & heady; perhaps 'tis excessively so, for our Hero feels now a Rush to the Head, an

Experience of Lightness in the Limbs, and a Glow of Happiness; Goldsmith licks his Lips, and savours this rare Feeling. Can it be attributed to the unbounded Luck that has been his Tonight? He dares not tell the Pyle of Coin, for that would not be seemly; but o, 'tis great; Wealth is his. O, *Fortuna!*

The Apothecary lights his Meerschaum Pype; he puffs long upon it, and regards Goldsmith with a Smile; the more van Aerdenhoudt smiles, the more Goldsmith warms to his genial Host; there is Silence in the Room; finally, the Apothecary speaks.

'Monsieur Goldsmith, such Luck as yours I have not seen *in all my Life*. You have wager'd Tonight a single Guilder, and have receiv'd from 't a Return, in excess of *an Hundred-fold*; my Fortune is now your Fortune: I have no Gold more in this House with which to wager.

'And yet, Monsieur, I am a sporting Man, and would welcome a Chance, to retrieve those Guilders of mine that you have won; I have, as stated, no Coin more; if you are agreeable, then, I have *a Proposition*. But first, Monsieur, I will put a Question to you: What is your Estimation of my Daughter, Maedeliefje?'

'I do not understand you, Sir.'

'Come, come! You will agree that she is uncommonly comely?'

Goldsmith is uncertain of the Form his Reply must take. He chuses to answer: 'Most assuredly, Sir; she is most charming.' The longer Goldsmith dwells upon the Thought of Maedeliefje, the more his Amour for her waxes.

'Most charming, you say? She is more than that, Monsieur! There is *not her Lyke* in all Brabandt; a Man must journey far, in order to find a Girl so fair as Maedeliefje; 'tis not because of my Position & Property, that the Baron Von Trautmannsdorff is soon to take her for his Wife, tho' she is educated and most civiliz'd; 'tis on Account of her great Beauty. Since the Day, when she turn'd Fifteen, Suitors have come from *All Parts* of the Netherlands, and Flanders, and France, and Germany, to present their Proposals of Marriage; I have turn'd each Man of them away, Monsieur, and I have awaited the best Offer; my Patience hath been rewarded, for the Kreishauptmann will open the Doors of Europe to me; I will be a welcome Guest at the Court of the Emperour Joseph; I will travel in Chariots of Gold from one sumptuous Palace to an other, and I will be on intimate Terms with crown'd Heads in all Countries; and all this because I have the good Fortune, to have father'd a beautifull Daughter. What a Prize I have, Monsieur! Is that not a Prize?'

'Verily, Sir, your Daughter is a Prize.' *Those Cheeks, those Lips.*

Van Aerdenhoudt beams. 'You agree, then, Monsieur. I am gladden'd, for I feel certain that you will agree also with my Proposition. But before I state 't, I beg Leave to put an other Question to you.'

Goldsmith is troubl'd, for there is *Something not quite aright*; this Talk of Maedeliefje hath made him Wary; he senses a Misschief, and Rogier van Aerdenhoudt's next Words do not allay his Suspicion.

'You must answer briskly & truthfully,' he says. 'The Question is this: What Price, Monsieur, should a Man pay, in order that he might lye with my Daughter?'

'Sir!' Goldsmith blushes mightily. *That Waist, those Titties.*

'Speak true, Monsieur Goldsmith, I beg of you.' He looks about him. 'We are alone here; we will not be o'erhear'd. My good Wife, my Daughter, and my Servants are all abed. That which passeth between us—'

'Sir, I implore you to go no further! 'Tis not seemly that you talk thus about your Daughter. I will hear no more of 't!' Goldsmith feels the Blood rise in his Ears; he is very uneasy.

'Come, come, Monsieur,' says van Aerdenhoudt with steady Voice. 'Are we not *educated & much travell'd Men*? If my Question doth appear unseemly, then I ask you to consider this.' The Apothecary fills their Glasses again. 'My Daughter, Maedeliefje, is contracted to the Austrian Baron, who will wed her in the Month of May. Her Dowry hath been fixt, and, *entre nous*, 'tis a paltry One, for my Daughter is contracted to a Man of *large Fortune*, who, in his Generosity, has elected to waive the Bride Price, to which he is entitled by Custom and Tradition. I need hardly tell you that my Wife and I think ourselves design'd by the Stars to *something exalted*, and all ready we anticipate our future Grandeur, for the Baron, as I have stated, is a Man of exceptional Riches.

'Maedeliefje and the Baron have met upon but *One Occasion*, Monsieur Goldsmith. I must say, with Chagrin, that their Meeting was not a joyous One, for Maedeliefje was not so taken with the Baron as he is with her; she thinks him *rough & uncouth*—as indeed he is! but what Matter?—and of arrogant Disposition. She can not love him, but neither he nor I expect that; she may yet learn to love him, by the Grace of God, and such a Pass would truly make of me an happy & contented Man.

'And yet, Monsieur Goldsmith, I am mistrustfull of Love! We sit here, the Pair of us, in my fine Mansion, repleat with my good Meat & Wines. You will have observ'd that I am a Man of some Wealth—aye, and of Position also. Yet *Love* did not buy these Things, but the generous Dowry, bestow'd upon me, when I wedded Maedeliefje's Mother. The Oils upon the Walls, the gorgeous Objects from the Orient, the Casques & Bottles in my Cellar: All owe their Provenance to my Wife's Father, the Jonkheer Pieter van Gesteren of Rotterdam, whose Ships & Barques ply'd the Routes to the Eastern Indies, and return'd, groning, with the Treasures of those Lands.

'Do I love my Wife, Monsieur? In Truth, I do not, comely tho' she is, as you have noted. Nay, I enter'd into my Marriage Contract for *Commercial Gain*, as hath many a Trades-man before me, that I might exalt my Position; this I have done, and I am happy for 't.

'I am happy, too, that our Union hath produc'd, not an Heir, but a Daughter, whose Beauty will further exalt my Riches & Position. I see your Discomfiture, Monsieur Goldsmith, yet I ask you: Has 't ever been otherwise, that a Man did not look upon his Daughters as a Means by which he could better himself? Would that our Union had been blest with more Daughters the Lyke of Maedeliefje, say I!'

Maedeliefje, Maedeliefje.

'Now, to the Baron: Conrad Von Trautmannsdorff is, lykewise, a Man of the World; the Kreishauptmann knows the Price that must be pay'd, ere he lyeth with Maedeliefje, and he does not shrink from paying 't. So I ask you once again, Monsieur Goldsmith: What Price will a Man pay for my Daughter? Not to wed her, mark you, but to lye with her for *a single Night*?'

'Sblood, all 's out! Oliver Goldsmith listens with Disbelief, but he has heard it aright: The Host, that he thought so gracious & noble, is offering him—the poor, gadding Flautist—his Daughter, for *a Night's Pleasure*. Goldsmith colours once again. *Maedeliefje*.

'I see you hesitate, Monsieur,' says the Apothecary, smiling all the while. 'Then I will help you. Will we say a Guilder?'

'Sirrah, this is monstrous!'

'Aye, you speak Truth: I insult the fair Maedeliefje. Very well, we will say Ten.'

Obstinate Man, thinks Goldsmith, still to persist in his Outrage! He opens his Mouth to speak, but no Words issue forth. *Maedeliefje*.

Van Aerdenhoudt reaches across the Card Table, and counts out Fifty Gold Pieces from the Pyle at Goldsmith's Hand. 'Fifty, Monsieur: is that not a just Price?'

'I ... I ... zounds! Sir, but I am discompos'd, and will be discompos'd. To be treated thus!'

'I vow, Monsieur, you bargain well.' The Apothecary begins to count the Guilders that Goldsmith hath taken from him; he places them in Pyles of Ten; Goldsmith looks upon the Operation in Silence; when the Telling is done, there are *an Hundred and One & Eighty Guilders*, all told.

'Behold, Monsieur, a veritable Fortune. Such a Price hath no Man ever pay'd for a Night's Sport with a Woman, not even at Versailles; I'll be bound and flogg'd if 'tis not so. An Hundred and One & Eighty Guilders, for to lye with Maedeliefje. Monsieur, I accept!'

'I will not pay 't.' Goldsmith's Voice is weak.

The mad Pharmacopolist laughs. 'Nay, Monsieur, you will not. Did you think that I would afford you *so easy a Bargain*?' To our Hero's Amazement & Distress, van Aerdenhoudt takes the Cards, and commences to shuffle them anew. 'We will play One last Hand, Monsieur Goldsmith; One Hand that will decide Maedeliefje's Fate: Should I win, then you are an Hundred and One & Eighty Guilders the poorer, and Maedeliefje is robb'd of her Maidenhead; should I lose, then you quit my House on the Morrow a wealthy Man, and Maedeliefje goes to the Baron a Virgin. Are we agreed?'

Goldsmith licks his Lips. Truly, this is a Bargain more to his Taste, for Oliver Goldsmith is, as we have observ'd, a gaming Man. The Wager (and the strong & heady Schnapps) does cause his Blood to race, and his Palms to grow clammy; mad or no, the Apothecary of Eyndhoven has spurr'd our Hero to accept. *Here*, on the Table, lye the Thirteen Pyles of Golden Coin, if he should win; *yonder*, lying abed, awaiting his amorous Imbraces, is the lovely Maedeliefje of the Golden Hair, if he should lose. Did ever the Fiend tempt a Christian so sorely? *Maedeliefje.*

'I am agreed,' says Goldsmith.

'Huzzah, hurrah!' crys the Apothecary. He fills Goldsmith's Glass and his own, and drinks One more Pledge to our Hero; then he takes an other Pinch of Snuff.

The Wager is fixt; van Aerdenhoudt shuffles the Cards again. It seemeth that an *Hush* falls upon the World: there is no Noise, save the merry Crackling of the Log Fire in the Grate, and the light Sounds of the Cards, as they move lyke a Rillet between the Apothecary's pudgy Fingers. The Shuffle being compleatèd, he cuts the Cards once, twice, thrice, and sets them down aforn Goldsmith. Our Hero heareth the Tolling of the Campanile, giving the Hour of Midnight; from another Quarter of the Town, comes the 'All's well' of the Bell-man.

'Pray, cut, Monsieur,' says van Aerdenhoudt.

An Ace! Goldsmith hath surely lost the Cut again; aye, for van Aerdenhoudt cuts a Princesse; he deals our Hero a Card, and himself, also; Goldsmith does not tremble as he tells the Pips; he is a winter'd Gamester. The Pips are Ten in Number; Goldsmith requests a Second Card.

'Tis a Six: *the Hand is his*; he lays his Cards, Face down, upon the Baize. Van Aerdenhoudt looks intently at his First Card, and frowns; his Eye moves to Goldsmith, and the Golden Rims of his Spectacles shine in the Light of the Chandeliers. Does he suspect; can he know? Goldsmith's Face betrayeth no Emotion.

Van Aerdenhoudt draws a Second Card; he can not conceal *his great Joy*; he flings the Cards upon the Table: he hath drawn an Emperour and a Six.

'*Seize*, Monsieur!' he crys. 'The Hand is surely mine.'

'Not so,' says Goldsmith, shewing his Hand, 'for I hold Sixteen, also.' The Apothecary shakes his Head, and regards Goldsmith with some Mirth.

'You forget, Monsieur, that upon which we agreed before the Commencement of our Play: in the Event of a Tye, 'tis *the Dealer who winneth*.'

Goldsmith *hath lost the Fortune* so lately gain'd. He watches with Dismay, as the Pharmacopolist returns the Golden Guilders to his Purse.

'Do not be disconsolate, Monsieur,' he says, rising, 'for I will honour my Part of the Bargain: I go now to rouse my Daughter, Maedeliefje, that she can prepare herself to receive you. Pray, pour for yourself an other Glass.' And he quits the Room.

Oliver Goldsmith sits alone at the Card Table that has play'd Host to the Game of such *uncommon Sport*. Idly, he picks up the Four Cards and returns them to the Deck. He pauses. What is this? His Eye hath fallen upon the topmost Card, that with which van Aerdenhoudt hath won the final Hand; he takes it up, and looks at it intently.

O, Villany! Can this be true? The Back Side of the Emperour of Diamonds bears a tiny Trace of a Brown Powder, all but invisible to the Eye, where it marks the Escutcheon of the House of the Habsburgs. Goldsmith examines the next Card; it, too, is fucated with Brown Powder, save that the Mark is in a different Place. He inspects the other Two Cards, with which van Aerdenhoudt and he have lately play'd; each shews a Trace of the Powder. Goldsmith had thought to win with a Six of Hearts; *here* is that Six. His Host hath beaten him with an other Six; *here* is that Card, also; both are stained Brown *in One and the same Place*. The Snuff, the accursèd Snuff; the Apothecary has play'd falsely!

O, Woe; what is Goldsmith to do? Can he confront the Trickster with his hainous Crime? He can not, for he is a Guest in his House. That apart, where is the Proof? The chance Fall of Snuff upon a Card? Good Gracious, nay, 'twill never do. And what hath Goldsmith lost Tonight, save *One single Guilder*? And what a paltry Price that is, to pay for the Pleasure that awaits him in Maedeliefje's Bed Chamber: The Vision of Beauty is to be his Bride for a Night; even now, that Angel incarnate awaits him. What Man would not relish such a Prospect? *Maedeliefje*.

MAEDELIEFJE OF EYNDHOVEN

The Doors fly open, and there stands the Apothecary, a Candle Holder with lighted Taper in Hand; he beckons Goldsmith.

They ascend the broad Stair of Marble, by the Light of the Candle, and reach a Landing, upon which stands a stout Dressoir, heavy with Oriental Plate most exquisite. A Corridor leads off, to Left and Right. Van Aerdenhoudt shews the Way to a Door at One End. He stops.

'My Daughter's Bed Chamber, Monsieur Goldsmith,' he says in a Whisper. 'There burns a Light within, so you will have no Need of this One. I therefore bid you *Good Night*, for I go now to my own Bed.'

Goldsmith looks after the Apothecary, as he disappears, silently, back down the Passage, taking the Light with him, and leaving his Guest to the Darkness. Verily, thinketh our Hero, this is a Night that is the Lyke of *no other Night*, and his Host is truly a Man of *few Scruples*, to surrender his own and only Daughter's Honour so lightly! Goldsmith hesitates at the Door before which he stands. He hesitates, tho' 'twould not be just to say that this Hesitation is of long Duration. *Maedeliefje*.

Will he knock? Aye, 'tis better so; he raps lightly upon the Door, turns the Handle, and enters.

The Chamber is lit by a single Oil Lamp that stands upon a Commode with Parquetry Decoration and 'Ormolu' Knobs; there is a Mirror upon the Wall, behind the Commode; its Gilt Frame is wrought in the riotous Rococo Style, and its Glass throws the Light of the Lamp about the Chamber; the Light illumines the Floor, whose Tyles are partly deckt by a most elab'rate Rug, shewing Squares and Lozenges of many Hues; there are gorgeous Prints and Hangings upon the Walls; there is a Screen of Leather that is highly lacquer'd; its Colours & Figures suggest that it comes from far Japan or China.

But Goldsmith's Attention is not upon these Furnishings; 'tis upon a *great Bed*, whose Posts are well turn'd, and whose Legs are Cabrioles of Lions' Paws; the Drapes are not drawn fully, and, thro' their Opening, Goldsmith espys an Head upon the Pillows: 'Tis the Head of the beauteous *Maedeliefje, the Angel incarnate*; she lyeth with her Face turned from the Light, in Modesty, and her Tresses are spread loosely, lyke Tendrils of *spun Gold*.

'Pray, who is there?' she whispers most delicately.

''Tis I, Oliver Goldsmith,' he answers in the same Whisper. His Voice quavers; there is a Tension and a Stillness in the Chamber.

After a Time, Maedeliefje says: 'Monsieur Goldsmith, I ask but this: that you adwesch the Lamp, ere you enter my Bed; 'twill be a Comfort to me.'

'Delicate Creature! your Commands could even controul a Debate at Midnight; to a Power so constitutional, I am all Obedience & Tranquillity.'

Our Hero speaks but Half a Truth: Obedient tho' he be to the Lady's Wish, tranquil he is not, for Passion & Lust are arisen in him. With Motions that are *flutter'd & fever'd*, he extinguishes the Lamp, loosens his Clothing in the Cimmerian Blackness, and creeps unto the Bed, with the nervous & expectant Breath of Maedeliefje to guide his Steps upon the cold Floor. He pulls back the Covers, and slips between them.

The Shirt that Maedeliefje wears is woven of soft Fabrick; it whispers against the Sheets, as she turns to him in the Dark; then he feels her lissom Arms wrap themselves about his Neck, and her warm Lips find his own. O *Joy!* that lovely Mouth parts, and Goldsmith feels the Maiden's hot Breath blow, and hears her deep Moans of Pleasure; his Fingers are intwin'd in those lovely, Golden Tresses, as he places *Kiss after Kiss* upon her Cheeks & Throat; his Yard swells against the Damsel's Loins, as the Fever of Love seizes him; his trembling Fingers find the Hem of the Night Shirt, and he raises it high; his Hands travel o'er the smooth, warm Flesh that quivers 'neath his Touch. O Joy upon Joy! those *firm & round Titties* are in his Hands; Master Goldsmith grones; a single Thrust, the Maiden crys out, and the Two are conjoin'd.

With what Fire do the Pair engage in the *Sport of Sports*! With what Élan do they revel in the *lusty Joust*! With what Ardour do they celebrate the sweet *Union of the Flesh*! The Timbers of the Bed grone & shake, as the Lovers bend their Boddies to the Aphrodisian Task. *O Joy, o Bliss.*

The Deed is done, and the amorous Pair lye spent, Boddies drench'd with the Transpiration of Ecstasy; Goldsmith's Fingers caress the smooth Belly of the Lady, and she murmurs pretty Words of Love in his Ear.

But listen! what Din cometh from without the Chamber? Can this be the *Tread of booted Feet* upon the Stair, and the angry Voices of many Men? Oliver Goldsmith raises himself, all Thoughts of Amour forgotten.

'O, my terrors!' he crys, 'what can this Tumult mean?'

The Door bursts open, and a Boddy of Men enter. They are Seven in Number, and Two bear Oil Lamps: these are Rogier van Aerdenhoudt, Apothecary of Eyndhoven, attir'd in Cap and Night Shirt, and his Butteler, dress'd in his Outdoor Livery. The other Five carry Weapons: Steel & Stave, Pistol & Muskette; Goldsmith is in no Doubt that they are the *Officers of the Night Watch*. The Pharmacopolist's Face is grim; gone is the Masque of Congeniality that he hitherto wore; he holds in his Hand the *same Taper* that led our Hero to this very Chamber; he raiseth it high, so that its Light might better illuminate the great Bed, with its resplendant Drapes and Cabrioles of Lions' Paws; Rogier van Aerdenhoudt points an accusatory Finger at Goldsmith.

'There,' he thunders, '*there* is the Adulterer, the Author of a gross Deception and Villany. Seize him, Captain; he is yours.'

Adultery? thinks our hapless Hero; o, what can this mean? As the Boddy of Men advances upon him, he turns and looks at his Bed Companion.

'Tis *a gross Deception* and Villany indeed! For the Lady, who has lately shared with him the Act of Venery, is *no One other* than the Wife of the Apothecary! Oliver Goldsmith is the Victim of a *dastardly Fall*.

How the Lady in the Bed is now transform'd! Gone is the lusty Creature, who so willingly & avidly accepted his Imbraces; now she weeps & snivels & protests her Innocence: She lay sleeping soundly (she insists), when, to her immense *Horror & Dismay*, Monsieur Goldsmith, a *Stranger* and Guest in her House, enter'd her Bed Chamber, and forc'd his Attentions upon her. What could she do, but acquiess to his *bestial Desires*? He was the stronger, and she had fear'd *for her Life*, against this lustful Dæmon, who had gain'd Entrance to their House under false Pretences, had accepted their Meat & Wine, and had so basely abus'd her Husband's Hospitality; she is sham'd & undone!

'Why, won't you hear me!' crys Goldsmith, as the Night Watch advances. 'By all that's just, I knew not—'

'Hear you, Monsieur!' Rogier van Aerdenhoudt bellows. 'To what Purpose? I now see through your low Arts; your Freindship, as common as a Prostitute's Favours; and as fallacious. Well, Monsieur, a Cell awaits you in the City; aye, and a Gallows, too, I should not wonder. Here are your Clothes, Monsieur. Don them, if you'll have so much Decency left in you, under the Sheets, that my Lady Wife will not be forc'd to look upon the naked Boddy of the Villain who hath conspurcated her, *in her own Bed.*'

Goldsmith's further Protestations fall upon deaf Ears; he is led from the Chamber by the strong Arms of the Officers of the Night Watch; led, in Shame & Disrepute, from the House of the Apothecary; led through the silent Streets of Eyndhoven, to the Quarters of the Watch, and there flung into a Prison Cell, dank & cold: O, *Misery.*

The Hours remaining to the Night pass; a Cock crows a Welcome to the Dawn. Oliver Goldsmith hath slept little in the foul Cell; the Rats and other verminous Creatures have seen to that. His Head aches, and his Throat burns with an unnatural Fire; he lyes upon the hard, stinking Cot, heavy Irons upon his Legs, and considers the *woeful Plight* wherein he finds himself.

Eyndhoven, accursèd Eyndhoven; is his young Life to end in this by God forsaken Place? Paris would have been preferrable, or London, or Vienna; if the Knot needs be tyed around the Neck, then tyed it should be in a City of *some Importance & Reputation.* Oliver Goldsmith thinks upon those who, perhaps, should be made acquainted with the grave Matter of his impending Gibbetting: his Family, Contarine, Dr Ellis in Leyden. ...

He has much Time in which to dwell upon such Things, for the Day passeth slowly. His Jayler, an Oaf with no French, and surly Manner, brings a Bowl of watery Soup, and a Portion of Black Bread, both of which Delicacies Goldsmith consigns to the Rodents; outside, upon the Square, there are the Comings & Goings of the Brabandters: 'Tis Monday, the Day following upon the Sabbath, and the Populace is abroad; by the Sound of 't, 'tis Market Day; Goldsmith hears the Lowing of Aver, and the Grunting of Swine; a Pyper plays a thin Melody, that is reminiscent of One of the *Irish Airs* he knows; he is Sick at Heart.

The dim Light of Winter fades ere long, and the Undertide settles upon his Cloere; the Cold is *intense*; Goldsmith's Coat will not hinder or hamper 't; he strives to beg a Blanket of his oafish Jayler, but the Ruffian does Nought but spit in his Face. The Hours pass; Goldsmith tells them by the striking of the Campanile: Eight, Nine, Ten. ...

Upon the Stroke of Eleven, there is a Commotion in the Prison; Goldsmith waits, expecting the Worst; Moments later, the Jayler approaches his Cell, carrying in his Hand the Ring of Lock Keys; he opens the Cell; he strikes the Irons from Goldsmith.

'*Eruit!*' he says.

What Terror awaits our Hero? He is pushed roughly through the Passage that leads to the Guards' Quarters; they stare at him, and make indecorous Remarks in the barbarous Tongue that are not complaisant upon the Ear; there is uncouth Laughter. Is it to be the Gallows so soon?

The Jayler unlocks the outer Door, and Goldsmith feels the cold Air upon his Face; the Jayler holds an unwasht Finger to his Lips. Goldsmith is mystify'd: what can this *strange Behaviour* portend? The Man makes known, by Gestures, that Goldsmith must follow him.

The Two set off through the darken'd Streets of Eyndhoven; again, there is no Moon, and Goldsmith must be watchfull of where he treads; on and on they journey, past the great Church, through the Poort in the Seventeenth Century Wall of the City, over the Bridge that spans the Dommel. Here, the Jayler stops; he will go no farther; without a Word, he turns upon his Heel, and steals back the Way they have come.

Goldsmith stands now *without the Walls* of Eyndhoven; he is Free. Yet can he be certain of this? Perhaps, thinks he, this is *one more Trick*, one more Jape of the mad Apothecary, Rogier van Aerdenhoudt. Will he run? By the poor Light of the Stars, he sees the River Dommel, sparkling behither; bethither, there is the dim Shape of the Road to Maestricht; he will run.

Sounds! The Snorting of an Horse, the Champing upon a Bit, the Clomping of sho'd Hooves; Our Hero turns in the Direction of the Sounds; there are Buildings visible at Hand: Cottages, Stalls, Out-houses; no Lights show at their Windows; Goldsmith strains his Eyes, in order to pierce the Shadows; there is Movement.

'Monsieur Goldsmith ...?'

'Tis a Stranger, a Man, whose Voice he does not recognize; he approaches, leading a large Horse; 'tis Gray of Colour, ghostly in the Star Light.

'Pray, who are you, Sir?' asks Goldsmith with tremulous Voice, for he fears a Misschief; the Stranger draws nearer; Goldsmith sees that he is dress'd in the Outdoor Livery of a Foot-man: there are gay Buckles upon his Shoes; he wears a dark Coat, and his Face is almost hidden by a wide Hat.

'My Mistress—', begins the Stranger, but an other Voice cuts through his Words: 'Tis a female Voice, and Goldsmith marks now this *Second dark Figure* that has emerged from the dark Concealment of the Out-house; the Woman is clad in a long Capuchin that reaches to her Ankle, and its Hood umbreres her Face.

''Tis I: Maedeliefje, Monsieur Goldsmith.'

Maedeliefje! Can this really be?

She throws back the Hood, and Goldsmith seeth the Golden Tresses, drawn up under a Lace Bonnet; even in the Blackness of the moonless Night, there is no mistaking the *sweet Form* of that angelick Countenance.

'I am asham'd, Monsieur Goldsmith; o, so asham'd for the ill Deeds of my Father. I know all. He is given to great Boasting, Monsieur, and this Morning he did confide the Details of his foul Trick. That I should Live 'neath the Roof of a Man so inscrupulous—and a Mother so ... so ...'

She stops, o'ercome by a great Emotion. 'You were beguil'd, Monsieur Goldsmith,' she continues, presently. 'First, by the Marking of the Cards, and Second, by the *nefarious Witchery* of the Schnapps, concocted by my Father's own Hand, and season'd with a Philter of Cinnamon, Ginseng Root, and Carduus Benedictus.'

She reaches into a Fold of her Cloak, draws out a Purse, and presses it into Goldsmith's Hand; 'tis heavy with Coin.

'I am here to make Amends, Monsieur,' says Maedeliefje. 'Tonight, whilst my Father slept the *sound Sleep of the Wicked*, I spirited away his Purse, the Contents of which are yours by Right. Here, Monsieur, here are the Moneys due to you, less the Fifty Guilders, with which I have purchas'd your Release from the Jaylers;

here is your Knap-sack, too. Take them, Monsieur, and fly. See: I have procur'd, also, a fleet Mount from my Father's Stall; 'twill carry you swiftly away from this Place. Go now, I urge you, before the Alarum is rais'd.'

Goldsmith is *fill'd with Love* for this Lady, who has risk'd so much for him, a poor Travelling Flautist.

'Fair Maedeliefje,' he says softly, ''tis I who must be asham'd; I vow to Gad, you make me blush. I came to your Father's House, and accepted his Hospitality; I drank and supt with him, and lay'd a Card; I wager'd, sweet Maedeliefje, *upon your Virginity*, and 't fell to me. 'Tis true, that your Father play'd me false, but I ask you: Am I not so base as he, for have I not sacrific'd every Consideration to Commerce alone?

'I will go now, but I will take neither the Purse nor the Horse, for I am not a Thief. Here, I will have *One Guilder*, for that is rightfully mine.'

'You can not! Accept, at least, the Horse that will carry you to Safety.'

'Nay, sweet Maedeliefje, my Resolution is fixt. To shew you how far my Resolution can go, I can now speak with Calmness of my former Follies, my Vanity, my Dissipation, my Weakness; I will even confess, that, among the Number of my other Presumptions, I had the Insolence to think of loving you. I leave you to Happiness, to One who deserves your Love; to One who has Power to procure you Affluence, and Generosity to improve your Enjoyment of 't. Adieu, sweet Maedeliefje.'

Oliver Goldsmith sets his Knap-sack upon his Shoulder, and doffs his Hat to the Lady and the Lacquey. The Road to the East is a faint Thread, creeping as a *Chinese Silk Worm* into the Blackness. He walks Twenty Paces, and turns; the dark Figures still stand motionless. Goldsmith heaves a Sigh, and pulls his Coat tight; he turns once more, and resumes the first Leg of his Journey *away* from Eyndhoven, upon the Silk Road to the East.

The Brown Hat upon his Head, the Brown Coat upon his Back, the Brown Breeches upon his Arse, the Stockings upon his Calfs, the Shoes upon his Feet: this is the only Raiment that Goldsmith possesses. There is, yet, a Golden Guilder in his Purse, and, in his Knap-sack, the *Systema Naturæ per Regna Tria* of

Linnæus; and a fine German Flute, that will procure for him Lodgings & Board.

Oliver Goldsmith: this Scholar, Rake, Christian, Dupe, Gamester, and Poet; tho' a Mixture so odd, he shall merit great Fame, this strange Meteor, this *Noteable Man*.

Firstly, tho', dear Freinds, he must follow the Track that leads *beyond* the Holle Berg, the Hollow Mountain; firstly, he must enter the Door in an other Rock. He *must* explore the Candle-lit Caverns of Maestricht!

Johnny and the Tall Lady

JOHNNY'S STICK MADE a rhythmic sound as he pulled it along the railings of Trinity College in Nassau Street. If he walked slowly, and held the long stick as high as he could, he imagined he could hear the notes of the bells of St Laurence O'Toole's Church: *ding-dong, dong-dong* they went. When he ran, as he did now, he could make the sound of the Northern Express as it rushed out over the North Strand on its way to Belfast. This was harder to do: you had to hold the stick low, right down near the bottom of the railings, an' then sweep your arm up an' down as you ran, so that the stick performed a series of graceful, broad curves along a stretch of the black iron railings: *chichi-chum, chuchu-chi, chichi-chum, chuchu-chi.* ...

Johnny saw the tall lady being helped down from the hackney cab on the far side of the street. He signalled to the guard to stop the train—which he did at once, Johnny being the driver, after all.

There was something about the lady that attracted Johnny's attention; and he wasn't the only one to have noticed her. A group of men who had just come out of the National Library stopped on the pavement to stare.

She was very tall, the tallest lady that Johnny had ever seen; she musta been about seven foot tall. She wasn't an oul' wan either, though old enough: more than twenty, at any rate. She had light brown hair with a reddish tinge to it, tucked up under a wide, blue hat with a crown of eighteenth-century quillings of valenciennes. She held the hem of her white skirt in one hand, so that it would not be soiled by the dust of the pavement. There was a lot of dust that year, in the early summer of 1889; there had not been rain for weeks, and that suited Johnny, whose boots coulda done with a new pair of soles and heels.

The men outside the library continued to stare at the tall lady and talk amongst themselves. But Johnny wasn't so much interested in *her* now, as in the things that the cab-driver was handing out to her. They were white and gold bird cages; he counted five of them. Johnny's eyesight was very poor, so he crossed over the street to get a better look.

Two little raggedy girls—they were about Johnny's age: eight or nine—were bent over the cages an' makin' cooing noises at the birds in their white and golden cages. He wished he knew something about birds, but he didn't. He knew well the kinda birds sparrows were; not worth a tuppenny damn, for even Jesus said that two of them were sold in Jerusalem for a farthing; indeed you wouldn't get even that for a dozen of them in Dublin. He had seen a redpoll, a green linnet, a thrush, a blackbird, and a goldfinch, all in cages; they were all the birds he had seen so far.

These birds weren't like that. They were all great singers; there was, in particular, a little yellow one that hopped from one bar of its cage to another, singing its little heart out to beat the band. There was another that looked like a sparrow to Johnny, except that it had a great voice on it, very melodious. A high cage with a rounded top held a pair of snow-white birds that huddled together, humming to each other and cocking their little heads sideways to look at the passers-by.

'Oh do be careful,' said the tall lady to the cab-driver, in a very hoity-toity voice. 'The poor little dears are frightened enough as it stands.'

The lady's voice was awful loud, Johnny thought; it rose above the din of the horses and the rattle of a tram passing down Nassau Street. It was very clear, slightly theatrical, and full of authority, a bit like Miss Valentine's when she made Ecret read the whole of St Paul's First Epistle to the Corinthians in front of the class. The cab-driver had a bird cage in each hand; he put these down very gently on the step of Morrow's bookshop and returned for the others. Mr Morrow called for one of his assistants to help with the cages, while he himself opened the lady's hall-door with a big, shiny key. At last the birds were safely inside, and the cab-driver turned his attention to the rest of the lady's belongings on the roof of the hackney, whilst the lady herself opened the cab door. Johnny was startled to see a dog as big as a pony emerge. He and the two little girls drew back in terror from the monster, with Johnny holding his stick at the ready, in case he had to defend himself and the girls; but the tall lady just stroked the beast's head and gave its chain to the shop assistant. The boy looked, goggle-eyed and frightened, at the dog.

'Don't worry,' said the lady, 'he's as gentle as a lamb,' and she stroked the dog's head just to prove it. 'A big boy like you ought not to be afraid.'

'Are you sure now he won't bite, Missus?' said the boy. 'I do be afraid o' dogs. I got bit by wan once an' me da had to take me to Jervis Street to get stitches.'

'Oh very well,' said the tall lady, taking the chain back from the shop assistant; 'I shall just have to bring him upstairs myself.' The boy looked very relieved, as dog and mistress disappeared into the darkness of the hall.

They were gone only a minute, by which time the cab-driver had taken down the lady's travelling-bags and hatboxes and arranged them neatly in front of her door. Then he went back to the cab to have a last look inside. No sooner had he opened the door, than Johnny saw a tiny figure scurry out through the window and race up the side of the hackney. It wasn't more than a foot long, but it had a tail on it that was even longer. It took up a position on the roof of the cab and waved its little hands about, chattering away in a high-pitched voice. Its fur was brown and it had a face on it the like of a wizened old man—except for the teeth, which were, Johnny noticed, sharp and pointy. One of the young girls let out a scream.

'It's a monkey!' she cried; 'sacred heart o' Jesus, it's a little monkey!'

An omnibus drove slowly by, and heads craned over the rail on the upper deck, to see this wonder. The 'wonder', grown excited by the calls of the people, jumped up and down on the roof of the cab, waving its tiny hands and its long tail in the air. Then, to Johnny's amazement, it lepped from the roof in one bound and darted across the road, right in front of another cab. The horse reared and let out an unmerciful whinny, and it was off down the street like greased lightning, with the driver hauling on the reins for all he was worth, and shouting 'whoa, whoa', as cab and horse thundered in the direction of the Turkish baths in Leinster Street. People jumped out of the way, fearing for their lives: wasn't it only last week that a man had been trampled to death in Fitzwilliam Square when trying to stop a runaway horse and van.

'What is the cause of all the excitement?' called a voice behind Johnny. He turned around, to see that the tall lady had come out again.

'It's that monkey o' yours, Miss,' the cab-driver told her; 'it's after runnin' across the sthreet an' frightenin' the horses.'

'Oh my poor little Chaperoni,' said the tall lady; 'he'll be killed for certain.'

'There he is!' said the cab-driver, pointing. 'He's climbin' up the railings o' Thrinity.'

'Gracious me,' said the tall lady, 'can someone do something? The poor little thing.'

Sure enough, Johnny, when he strained his eyes, could make out the tiny figure hopping along between the spikes. A small knot of people had gathered by then, and were following its progress. Johnny saw the tall helmet of a policeman who was advancing to the spot.

Johnny was across the street in a flash, stick in hand. The monkey stopped its acrobatics, and remained now in one place atop the railing, looking down on the people and screeching fit to burst.

Johnny acted without thinking; he dropped his stick and clambered up the railings. The monkey eyed him with suspicion, and bared its little white teeth.

'G'wan,' somebody shouted; 'it takes wan monkey to catch another!' There was laughter and more cat-calls. Johnny ignored the taunts and, wrapping his bare legs around the iron bars, he hooshed himself up higher. The monkey glared at him, its eyes appearing almost human, with their bushy brows and quick, darting movements. The laughter and gibing increased; Johnny inched himself higher. He had come this far and he wasn't going to let them bowseys think he was afraid.

Suddenly he heard a familiar voice, one that stood out from the rest.

'Brave lad! That's the way; gently now.' Even without looking, Johnny knew that it was the tall lady. At the sound of her words, the hubbub around him ceased, because there was something about her voice that commanded respect, something that made people stop an' listen an' obey.

Upon hearing the woman call him a 'brave lad', Johnny really was emboldened. He levered himself up until he was only inches away from the monkey. The little animal screeched a warning at him but did not budge.

'Chaperoni! Naughty fellow, come down here at once,' called the tall lady. The monkey looked down past Johnny and seemed to grin. 'Come now, Chaperoni,' the lady called once more. Very cautiously, Johnny stretched out his hand. The monkey blinked.

Keeping a good hold on the railing, Johnny grabbed the monkey. It emitted a dreadful shriek that was like a knife being scraped across a pan, and bit Johnny in the hand. But he held his grip on the animal's fur, and slid down the railings. The crowd parted to make room for the young rescuer. Towering above him was the lady in the blue hat, smiling sweetly at him; at these close quarters, Johnny saw that she was indeed worthy of the admiring looks that the men from the library had thrown her.

'Oh do give him here,' she said, holding out her hands. Johnny released the monkey and it lepped up on the lady's shoulder, where it sat chattering and making funny little faces at the onlookers.

'You *are* a brave boy!' said the tall lady. 'But oh dear, your poor hand is bleeding.' Johnny looked down and saw that this was indeed so; in the excitement he had barely noticed the pain in his right hand, but the monkey's sharp little teeth had broken the skin, and a thin trickle of blood had flowed down his wrist, leaving a red stain on the frayed cuff of his shirt. His ma was going to murther him!

'We shall have to have that seen to,' said the lady; 'it could turn septic.'

Johnny knew what 'septic' meant; all those visits to St Mark's Ophthalmic Hospital for Diseases of the Eye and Ear had given him a thorough grounding in the language of sickness and disease. Words the like of septic, infected, inflammation, ulcer, discharge, pus, festering, were as common to him as the words of the Psalms; if he didn't learn them from Mr Story, then he learnt them from the other patients in the long waiting hall.

Johnny followed the tall lady across the road to Morrow's bookshop. By this time, the cab-driver had carried all her things upstairs, and he waited on her with an ingratiating smile. But she tipped him generously, and he went on his way well satisfied. Mr Morrow and his assistant looked at Johnny in his worn clothes with disapproval; when it became clear to them that he was about to accompany the lady upstairs, their disapproval turned graver. Yet such was the lady's powerful air of authority, that Mr Morrow actually nodded pleasantly to Johnny when bidding her good-day.

Johnny followed the lady up the stairs, feeling the nervousness that boys like him must feel when in the house of a stranger of the upper classes. He noticed that the house smelt the same as the Reverend Hunter's: clean but with hints of age and decay. The walls were bare and washed with a pale green distemper of the type you'd see in hospitals. The lady marched on ahead of him with the little monkey still on her shoulder; it showed its teeth but was silent now. It eyed Johnny with malice.

'Well, here we are,' said the tall lady, ushering him into a set of rooms. 'I'll fetch some soap and water.'

Left alone, Johnny had the opportunity to look around. He had expected the room in which he found himself to be as full as the Reverend Hunter's, but it was surprisingly bare of furniture. There was only a suite of armchairs and a couch with coloured cushions, a writing desk and a small table. The carpet on the floor was worn, which led Johnny to think that the tall lady was not as rich as he had supposed. There was a huge basket in one corner, probably for the enormous dog, and he was relieved that the brute was nowhere to be seen. The five bird cages hung suspended from curved iron stands close to the two windows, one of which was partially open. He could make out the little shapes of the cages' occupants, as they flitted to and fro in their confined spaces; the yellow one was in fine voice. What caught Johnny's eye, however, were two very tall vases which stood at each side of the chimney. They were filled with green fronds of a type he hadn't seen before, and some dried blooms with long stalks. But pride of place had been given to eight strange and beautiful flowers. Johnny used his old trick for seeing better in the distance: he pulled back the skin at the corner of one eye—Massey had caught him doing it once and had told him he looked like a bleedin' Chinaman with a bad squint—and the unusual flowers came a little better into focus. He sauntered over to take a closer look at them, sucking the blood from his hand to stop it dripping on the floor and staining the rug.

 Yet when he got really close to one of the vases, he discovered that what he had taken for flowers weren't flowers at all. Their fronds, or leaves, were very dark, almost black. What he had mistaken for petals were queer ovals, each about two inches wide, which had the appearance of eyes. They had the most marvellous colours and, when he turned his head, the colours shimmered and changed like the rainbow colours you saw in a puddle of oil. He reached out a finger and touched one. It was soft like down, and Johnny knew then for certain that these weren't flowers, but feathers. Jasus, he thought, what kinda bird would have feathers like that? They musta come from a bird-o'-paradise.

 He was still stroking the strange feathers when the lady came back into the room. She was carrying a white enamelled bowl and had a towel draped over her arm. The little monkey sat on her shoulder as before, but when she went to Johnny's chair it made a giant leap that carried it all the way to the chimney-piece, where it sat on its haunches and licked one of its forepaws, throwing nasty looks at Johnny all the while.

 'Now, let us see to that bite, shall we?' said the tall lady.

She was very gentle, just like a nurse. She bathed the wound with soap and water, and he watched in fascination as the water in the white bowl turned slowly pink. It was a dirty pink, however, and Johnny felt a flush of embarrassment when he realized that the lady was scrubbing off more than the spilt blood: he wasn't due a bath until the following week. But the lady didn't seem to mind a bit, and she continued to wash the hand until it was so clean that Johnny could clearly see the four little holes—no bigger than pinpricks—that the monkey's teeth had made.

'That was a very brave thing you did,' she said, 'rescuing little Chaperoni. What's your name?'

'Johnny,' he told her; 'Johnny Casside.'

'You're a very brave lad, Johnny,' she repeated, and that made him feel on top of the world.

He liked the touch of the tall lady's hands on his skin; they were very white and smooth, with long, tapered fingers, and nails so translucent and shiny, you'd think she polished them or something. She dabbed away the last of the blood and wound the towel around his hand.

'Hold that there,' she told him, 'while I fetch a bandage.' As soon as she stood up, the monkey took its cue, sprang from the chimney-piece, bounced on the back of a chair and landed neatly on her shoulder.

Johnny was again left by himself in the big, airy room, listening to the sounds of Nassau Street coming through the partly opened window. He heard the sudden cheering of a crowd from somewhere across the way, and it was only then he realized that the figures in white he'd seen in the grounds of Trinity had been playing a cricket match. From below on the street came the voices of shoppers and the rattle of passing cabs and carriages. He heard birds calling out in the treetops opposite; their songs were answered by some of the caged birds in the room. Johnny felt a little bit sad for them.

'Now then,' said the tall lady, coming back in with a strip of white linen, 'let us bandage that up, shall we?'

The monkey again took up sentry duty on the chimney-piece. Johnny removed the towel, noticed how it was flecked with blood, and wondered whether he should offer to bring it home with him and get his mother to wash it. But the tall lady was busy already, sprinkling some white powder on the bite, and wrapping the linen around his hand, criss-crossing it this way and that. So fascinated was he by the way she performed the operation, that he forgot all about the towel.

'Are you a nurse, Miss?'

She smiled at that and told him 'no', but that she'd trained for a while as a nurse at the City of Dublin Hospital.

'I think all Irishwomen should know the basics of nursing,' she said; 'it will be useful when the time comes.'

'I don't understand, Miss,' said Johnny.

'I shouldn't think so; you are much too young to understand such things.'

'I'm nine!' said Johnny in a very hurt voice, and that made the lady smile again. She had a lovely way of smiling, he thought—not at all like some of the nurses he could mention. When the lady smiled that way, you could forgive her for anything; you could even forgive her for thinking that you were just a child, instead of being almost a grown-up.

'There!' she said, tying the bandage. 'Try not to get it dirty; you can take it off in a day or two.'

'Thanks very much, Miss,' said Johnny. 'I better be goin' now. Me ma 'll be wondherin' where I am, an' she'll kill me if I'm late for me tea.'

'Oh, but you can't go without taking tea with *me*!' said the lady in her hoity-toity voice. 'Just you wait there while I put the kettle on; I shan't be a minute.'

Well, what was Johnny to do? At that moment, the huge dog ambled in from the other room, went to where Johnny sat and began to sniff at his legs. Johnny remained stock-still, too terrified to move. He heard the sound of running water and the rattle of crockery from somewhere in the house.

When the lady returned, she was carrying a silver tray, which she placed on the low table close to Johnny's chair. There was a silver teapot and delicate, bone-china cups and saucers and plates, and a silver stand piled high with luscious-looking cakes that made Johnny's mouth water. The dog lumbered over to investigate.

'No, Ferdia!' said the lady. The dog looked at her with big sad eyes and dhrippin' jowls. 'To your basket!' she ordered, and sure enough the cr'ature went to the basket in the corner, stepped in, turned around twice, and settled with a great heave of a sigh, its head resting on the rim and eyes wandering slowly to Johnny and the lady in turn.

But Johnny's eyes were on the cakes on the silver stand. Jasus, but he'd never seen cakes like them before! There were long chocolate wans wi' cream oozin' outta them, an' wans wi' cherries an' icin' on top, an' big thick slices o' fruitcake burstin' wi' raisins an' sultanas an' nuts an' orange peel.

'One lump or two?' the lady asked.

'Two please,' said Johnny; then he saw that the sugar wasn't like the sugar at home, but had been cut up into lumps so tiny they wouldn't satisfy a sparrow. So Johnny, gauging the size and relative sweetness, asked for eight.

'Do help yourself to the cakes,' said the tall lady. He did, and within three minutes there remained only a sprinkling of crumbs on the white lace doilies on the silver stand.

'You have a good healthy appetite,' said the lady, and Johnny took that as a compliment. She stirred her tea and inspected him; he felt a bit nervous about that, him sitting there in his grimy jacket and trousers on the lady's lovely chair with the coloured cushions. He hoped he didn't smell. Not only that, but he felt a fart coming on; he'd eaten too many cakes too quickly. He shifted his bum on the chair to prevent the fart escaping.

'Do you live around here, Johnny?' she asked him.

'No Miss, in Hawthorn Terrace.'

'Oh, where is that?'

'It's near St Barnabas' Church, Miss.'

'St Barnabas'?; I don't believe I know it.'

'It's near the North Strand, Miss.'

'Goodness me, but you are a long way from home; won't your mother wonder where you are?'

'I don't think so, Miss; an' it's not that far reely. I don't—'

Suddenly the lady exploded in a fit of coughing. Her face turned bright red. Her cup rattled on its saucer and fell to the floor, throwing a dark stain across the rug. She let the saucer follow it. The dog jumped out of its basket and ran to her, baying like a wolf, as the lady clutched her chest and let out great whoops of coughs, so savage that Johnny was sure that at any moment she'd get sick or faint or even die. Her eyes were wild. Johnny was so shocked by the violence and suddenness of the attack, that he lost control and felt the fart creep silently out. He stood up and waved his hands frantically to disperse the fumes. The lady continued to cough and the dog continued to howl; the little monkey had sought refuge on the pelmet of a curtain; the caged birds flapped around in confusion.

'Are you all right, Miss?' he asked her nervously. She lay halfway back on the sofa, and pointed across the room. Johnny didn't understand. The lady was trying to say something, but the coughing made her impossible to understand. She pointed again.

'Bohll!' she said.

'What?'

'Th' bohll!'

'I don't folly you, Miss.'

'The bottle!' she cried at last. 'On the desk!'

It was then that he saw the tiny green bottle. It stood next to a stack of books and a newspaper. Johnny went and fetched it.

The lady's coughing had not improved. Nervously, he passed the little bottle to her. She took it hungrily and uncorked it. He saw her put it under a nostril and inhale sharply. She coughed again, and some of the liquid in the bottle spilled out. Johnny smelt something very odd, the kind of smell he remembered from the hospital. She replaced the cork, and lay back on the sofa, eyes closed. The coughing lessened.

'Will I get someone, Miss?' Johnny asked. She shook her head and waved a hand at him, very slowly and languidly. It was some time before she spoke again.

'I'm fine now,' she said. 'It is just a cough; nothing to be concerned about.'

'I'll go then, Miss, in that case.'

'No, please stay, Johnny; I am perfectly well.' But he noticed that her talk was lazy now and her words were slurred. She shut her eyes again, and he heard her sigh gently. She murmured something that he didn't catch.

'Please stay, Johnny,' she said in a dreamy sort o' voice; 'please stay and keep me company. Will you do that?'

'If you want me to,' he told her. She was fully reclined now on the sofa; the coughing had stopped, and her face bore a look of gentleness and serenity. Johnny saw her then in profile, and noticed for the first time the set of her jaw. It was surprisingly firm for a woman as gracious as she was; he thought it was the jaw of somebody who was used to getting her own way; it was a bit like Ella's, only nicer.

To Johnny's great surprise, the tall lady began to hum a tune. He didn't recognize it; it sounded very foreign. The lady hummed as though he wasn't there at all, as though she shared the room with only her birds an' dog an' monkey. But presently she spoke again, and Johnny knew that he hadn't been forgotten.

'It is a lovely melody, is it not?' she said.

'Yes, Miss, it's very nice.'

'It is French; I do not suppose you've ever heard it before?'

'No Miss.'

'A very pretty melody.' Her voice sounded as if it came from very far away; he couldn't understand her at all now. Then he realized that she was speaking in a foreign language; it wasn't Latin, so it must be French, he decided. Why would she be talking to me in French? he wondered. Johnny was at a loss.

'Oh … the French … are … on the sea. …'

Was she goin' mad? Johnny thought. He began to panic a bit; he couldn't follow this at all. The lady's lips moved slowly; she seemed to be reciting poetry, but her words were very indistinct.

'Oh, the French are on the sea, says the Shan Van Vocht; the French are on the sea, says the Shan Van Vocht. …'

The lady's eyes closed again and her lips continued to move; Johnny heard some words the lady spoke; others were mouthed silently: '… are in the Bay, they'll be here without delay … Orange will decay, says the Shan Van Vocht.'

'Are you still there, young Johnny Casside?' she asked.

'Yes, Miss.'

'Do they teach you that poem at school?'

'I don't think so, Miss, no.'

'No, of course they do not!' she said. 'If they did, then young men like you might get notions, and what should become then of this fine nation of ours?'

She opened her eyes again and stared at Johnny. Her eyes had a glazed look to them; they made him uneasy; he wanted to leave. The big dog lay now at the foot of the sofa; the birds were silent; the monkey was nowhere to be seen.

'Would you like to be a soldier, Johnny?' she asked him. He brightened at this.

'I would, Miss; me brothers are soldiers, Miss.'

'Really?'

'Me brother Tom is in the Royal Dublin Fusiliers an' me brother Mick is in the Royal Engineers.'

'Have they killed many people?' she asked.

'God no, Miss!'

'What is the point in being a soldier,' she said, 'if one doesn't kill people? A soldier should go to war; it is his only duty in life. To die in battle is the most noble death imaginable; do you know that?'

'No Miss.'

The lady fumbled around and found her little green bottle again. She uncorked it and inhaled. She shut her eyes.

'There are no more heroes left, Johnny,' she said drowsily. 'Ireland has no more heroes. Talk, that is all men do these days; they talk. Ireland has grown weak; the heroes have left and have gone to France.' She turned to him again. '*You* will fight, won't you, Johnny, when the time comes?' He did not understand her, but he said 'yes' all the same. She was beginning to frighten him; he felt another fart massing in his bowels.

'You're a good boy, Johnny,' she told him. 'You don't talk overmuch; that's a good thing.' She sighed. 'I am cursed with friends who talk too much, and *do* so little. They are not like you, Johnny; they do not accept me for what I am; they put me on a pedestal and call me Ireland personified and other such nonsense; they flatter me with their talk, thinking that this is what I want to hear. They write love letters to me, and poems. Can you imagine that, Johnny, someone writing a poem to you?'

'No Miss,' he told her truthfully.

She laughed, and it was a lunatic laugh. Then she began to hum once more the tune he had heard earlier. But suddenly she stopped and opened her eyes, as if a new thought had occurred to her. She raised herself on the couch.

'Yes, a poem!' she cried; 'you must read a poem for me; I should like so much to hear one from your lips; how different it will sound, the voice of young Ireland!' She pointed at the desk again. 'Over there, under the red book; do you see the sheaf of papers?' He went to the desk. 'Yes, yes, that's the one. Bring them to me.'

Johnny handed her the papers and she studied the topmost sheet with that strange, distant look in her eyes. Johnny smelt the medicinal odour again.

The lady handed him the sheet of paper. 'Here,' she said, 'do read this one.'

Johnny stared hard and long at the handwritten words, trying to make some sense of them. He hadn't the courage to tell the tall lady the truth: that he couldn't read at all. He felt his cheeks redden, and the fart that was close to evacuation. He looked at her in desperation, and she smiled warmly.

'Oh, of course,' she said, 'you cannot read the handwriting! Silly me, I should have realized that. Give it here, and I shall read it for you.'

Much relieved, Johnny returned the sheet. The tall lady lay back once again on her cushions, the paper held high to catch the light from the windows. She began to read:

> 'I am haunted by numberless islands, and many a
>   Danaan shore,
> Where Time would surely forget us, and Sorrow
>   come near us no more,
> Soon far from the rose and the lily, and fret of
>   the flames would we be,
> Were we only white birds, my beloved, buoyed out
>   on the foam of the sea.'

When she had finished reading, she let the paper drop from her hands and it spiralled to the floor, where it fell on the tea stain on the rug. Johnny saw a faint yellow blotch form on the paper.

'We are only white birds, my beloved,' the lady said very quietly and languorously; 'we are only white birds. ...' She shut her eyes again and said no more.

'Are you asleep, Miss?' Johnny enquired.

'Almost.'

He was silent, watching her breast rise and fall; an oval brooch with a French miniature was pinned to her blouse, just below the throat, and it caught the light from the ceiling. There was a temporary lull in the noise of the traffic in Nassau Street; even the birds had gone quiet. Johnny's gaze was fixed on the lady's bosom, as it rose and fell, rose and fell, alternately tautening and loosening the white starched blouse.

'I liked the pome, Miss,' he said at last, and she smiled at that. 'But I think I should be goin' home now.' She nodded without opening her eyes. Johnny stood up and made for the door. 'Goodbye, Miss, an' thanks very much for the cakes.'

'Johnny,' she said, so quietly he barely heard her, 'you cannot leave without some little reward for the kindness that you showed to my Chaperoni.'

'No no, that's all right, Miss,' he protested; 'I wouldn't feel right about that.' The lady laughed.

'Brave *and* proud,' she said. 'But you must have *some*thing—a token.' She gestured towards one of the tall vases. 'Do take one of those; I saw that you liked them so much. So very much. ...'

Her eyes shut again and her breathing became shallower. Johnny stood over her, watching with interest the motion of her breast as it pushed out the stiff fabric of her blouse. Her face, with its thrusting, proud jaw, was serene now, almost like the face of a sleeping child. Johnny tiptoed to the vase.

Minutes later, he opened the front door and went out into the noise and bustle of Nassau Street. Two maids carrying shopping baskets looked at him with curiosity as he emerged from the house. So, too, did Mr Morrow, the bookseller. Evidently he had just made an important sale to the lady whom he was now escorting to a waiting carriage; an assistant was bringing up the rear with an armful of paper parcels tied with twine. Mr Morrow's professional smile vanished when he saw what Johnny held clutched in his hand. He excused himself to the lady customer.

'Here, you!' he shouted; 'where do you think you're going with that, you thievin' little blackguard!'

But Johnny was already halfway across the street, dodging a

hackney cab and baker's dray; the confined wind finally escaped with a loud report. When he reached the Trinity side, his poor eyes picked out something familiar lying on the pavement where he had left it all those hours before—it seemed like hours, but the sun still shone brightly upon the little white blurs that moved against the green. A cheer went up as Johnny retrieved his favourite stick. Twenty minutes later he was skippin' across Butt Bridge as there sounded, in the distance, the welcoming tolling of the bell in the Pro-Cathedral.

'IN THE NAME o' god, Johnny, what have you got there at all?' said his mother when he got home again. She was standin' gassin' to an oul' wan outside the door.

'Nothin', Ma,' he told her, but her hand was already swoopin inside his jacket and pulling out the long feather.

'Where did you feck that thing?'

'I didn't feck it at all, Ma,' he protested; 'a lady give it to me; honest to God, Ma, she did.'

'God, it's lovely, isn't it?' said the oul' wan. 'I seen Lady Aberdeen wearin' a hat full o' them wance. Would you look at the colours of it, aren't they only *gorr*juss.'

But his mother wasn't having any of it.

'He has me heart scalded, Missus,' she told the oul' wan. 'I can't let him outta me sight or he's feckin' somethin'.'

'I know, Mrs. Casside. Sure me own chiselur's the same; if I told him wance, I told him a thousand times, you'll be sent to the reformatory, you mark my words.'

'I didn't feck it, Ma, reely.' Johnny was near to tears. 'The lady in Nassau Street give it to me for savin' her monkey. He was after climbin' up the railin's.'

'You young scut, tellin' lies like that; may the Lord look down on you. An' what's that on your hand?'

'I keep tellin' you, Ma. I climbed up after the monkey an' 'e bit me, so the lady wi' the birds an' the big dog brought me in an' put a bandage on it.'

'Get into that house this minute,' said his mother, 'before I lose me temper! Here, an' take that thing with you.'

'What'll I do with him at all, Missus?' said his mother when Johnny was indoors, though not out of earshot. 'He has me mortified. Ah, what's the pains I suffered bringin' him into the world to carry him to his cradle, to the pains I have to suffer now? If his poor father was alive, God rest his soul, he might learn a bit of discipline. Reverend Hunter can't do a thing with him neither. Birds an' monkeys! What'll he think o' next?'

'I wondher what happened to his hand, all the same,' said the oul' wan. 'Maybe the chiselur was tellin' the thruth afther all.'

Johnny's mother sighed. 'An' hell might freeze over, Missus. Sure gaw telp him, he lives in a dhream world, it's not Johnny's fault; he jus' makes things up. The stories he does be comin' out wi'! Where he gets them from, *I* don't know. Las' week it was Johnny and the Viceroy. Yesterday it was Johnny and the Queen. Today it's Johnny and the Paycock. I'm tellin' you, Missus, he has me heart scalded.'

An Hibernian Tale, Taken from Facts

'THAT REBEL IS bleeding like a stuck pig, Lieutenant. What is to be done?'

'Damn him and blast him! He was perfectly all right when in Longford.'

''Tis the road, Sir; all that pounding and shaking has opened the wound again. If we dinnae let a doctor look at him, then I fear we're going to lose him—Sir.'

'Can nothing more be done, Sergeant?'

'I dinnae believe so, Sir. His bowels are half hanging out, as 't stands, and no amount of bandaging will staunch the blood. The cart is awash with 't.'

'Pray, don't exaggerate, Sergeant. But, ay, you're right; we cannot have him dying. The man must stand trial, and there's no more to be said. 'Twould be pointless to bring a corpse to the Provost; we might just as well dump the bugger in a ditch.'

'We could, perhaps, go back to Longford. ...'

'Hmm. We could, but we will not. If the blasted road has done the prisoner no good thus far, then 'twill kill him for certain if he has to undertake the journey back. How far to the nearest town, Sergeant?'

'That would be Mullingar, Sir; but that is upward of thirty miles, by my reckoning.'

'Damn! And there's little likelihood of finding a doctor sooner; not in this part of the country. Moore made certain that all the best surgeons went him to Moate, curse him, and the others went with Trench to Castlebar. But who are we to question our great generals in their infinite wisdom, eh, Sergeant? ... Noakes!'

'Sir!'

'Let me have that map.'

'Sir!'

'Ecod, Noakes; that horse of yours ought to be gelded! Cannot you control the blessed animal?'

'Sorry, Sir.'

'Well, fall back in, man. There's *something* here, Sergeant. 'Tis a village at the crossroads, called Edgeworthstown; does the name mean anything to you?'

'It does not, Sir.'

'Well, there would appear to be a manor house—here: at the end of the village street—though we cannot take that for gospel; I've known these maps to be wrong before.

'Edgeworthstown. ... Look you, Sergeant; take Noakes and his riggish stallion—and two more troopers, to be on the safe side of prudence; this part of the country is probably still swarming with damned rebels and Frenchies. Ride on ahead, and reconnoitre this Edgeworthstown.

'And for Christ's sake, Sergeant, let us have none of your Scotch heroics. If there be trouble, do not, on any account, attempt to deal with 't yourself, but return here instead.'

'Will you be stopping the train then, Sir?'

'Ay. Rebel or no, the man's an officer, and I will not be responsible for his death in these circumstances. He'll die by the musket-ball or by the rope, but not by bleeding to death in the middle of some godforgotten bog.

'Find out whether there's a doctor in Edgeworthstown—a veterinary surgeon will do, if we're pinched. If so, have him ride back here with you. That will be all, Sergeant.'

'Yes, Sir.'

'THE SITUATION', SAID Richard Lovell Edgeworth, 'may be summarized as follows. A company of the King's cavalry has forced itself upon us, and shall be billeted here for one night, perhaps two. 'Tis a situation that is not to my liking, as you must all appreciate. Nevertheless, we must do our utmost to accommodate them.'

Frances Edgeworth sat with her ten stepchildren and the Sneyd sisters, Charlotte and Mary, at the big library table. The servants of the house—Englishmen and -women all, with but two exceptions—had arranged themselves in ragged order in front of one of the book-lined walls. Their master's words filled them with disquiet; nervous looks were exchanged.

'What of the prisoners, Father?' Maria Edgeworth asked. 'What of the wounded officer?'

'I shall not sleep soundly with rebels under this roof,' said the housekeeper. There were mutterings of agreement from some of the senior staff.

'You have no choice in the matter!' Edgeworth said. He spoke rather harshly, causing the woman to lower her head. 'Look at me when I am speaking to you, Mrs Billamore. That is better.

'Now, need I remind you—all of you—that we are fortunate in having a roof over our heads at all. Every Protestant house between here and Roscommon was broken into and plundered, whilst the owners were away fighting the rebels. Yet Edgeworthstown House was spared. This, taken together with the fact that some of my yeomen are Catholics, has served to cast suspicion upon this household.'

Edgeworth walked to the little desk in the corner of the library and glanced idly at his daughter's papers, arranged in neat piles upon its top. There were notebooks and a diary, and a tall, ledger-like book in maroon binding. A handmade label was affixed to its cover; written in an elegant, slanted hand were the words *Castle Rackrent*.

'These are dangerous days,' Edgeworth continued. 'The fighting is far from over. Lake and Cornwallis may have carried the day at Ballinamuck, yet I have no doubt that every town, village and farm in the midlands harbours insurgents, bent on further slaughter and reprisals.

'Our situation, then, is a delicate one. On the one hand, we are mistrusted by the loyalists, who doubt our allegiance to the government forces. On the other hand, should we be seen to come out too strongly for the suppression of all those who have risen against His Majesty, then we shall be thought not a hair better than Lake's Dragoons, who cut down all those Irishmen in cold blood after they had surrendered. Our work here shall be undone; we shall not be trusted again by the people of Edgeworthstown, whose respect we won hard.' He picked up his daughter's unfinished manuscript and flourished it at the room. 'All shall revert to the circumstances preceding 1782, the year of Grattan's Parliament: the Rackrents shall rule once more.'

His wife Frances, silent until now, cast her hazel eyes around the room. She was well aware that the matriarchate that she held in the Edgeworth house was a nominal one; at twenty-nine she was a year younger than Maria, the eldest daughter. Frances knew that decisions of importance rested with her husband and Maria, and she accepted this.

'If Maria is in agreement,' she said, 'then I should welcome the presence of the military here. I am in no doubt that the rebellion will be speedily quashed. When order is restored, then those who have demonstrated their loyalty to the King will have nothing to fear.'

Maria squeezed her stepmother's hand.

THE OFFICER STILL wore his battle uniform. Stained though it was from combat, it was an impressive affair. The coat was of the rich blue used in the tricoloured banner of the French Revolution; the lining was the scarlet of the same flag. The plastron front was buttoned back on the chest; the coat was also fastened back at the knee, for ease of walking. The red standing collar had two bars of silver embroidery; the epaulettes were silver, too, and laced with heavy bullion fringes. Red, also, was the colour of the barrel sash.

The waistcoat, adorned with silver *passementerie* buttons, had once been white; it was badly soiled now, as were the breeches, with the dust of Longford (and was that blood on the left leg?). You could tell that the officer thought most highly of his boots, because these were polished to a high lustre, and someone had cleaned their silver piping and tassels with great diligence. The soldier carried his cocked hat in the crook of his arm. It was of black felt, edged in the ubiquitous silver lace. In all but one small detail, the uniform was that of a high-ranking French officer: the cockade in the hat was green.

'Oh,' said Maria, 'I did not hear you come in.'

'I apologize, Miss Edgeworth, for the intrusion, but I was given to understand that I am at liberty to peruse the shelves of your excellent library.'

Maria lowered the blotter onto the page and replaced the stopper in the ink-horn. She smoothed her house-dress with her palms, and turned in the chair to take a better look at the visitor.

It was the splendid uniform which lent colour to an otherwise plain young man. He was not quite thirty, Maria decided; indeed, there was something very boyish about him. He was short in build, and his hair, cropped in the fashion of the revolutionaries, emphasized this boyishness. Maria thought him rather charming.

'I am Matthew Tone, Miss Edgeworth,' he said, bowing.

'Tone ... Tone ... I had supposed you and the other prisoner to be Irish, Sir. Tone is surely a French name?'

'Of Gascony, Miss Edgeworth; my forebears settled in Ireland in the last century. I am a Dublin man.'

'And a rebel.'

'I am not ashamed of that fact, Miss Edgeworth. On the contrary, I am proud of the modest part that I have played in the rebellion.'

'And the slaughter ... and the burning, the wanton destruction. Are you proud of those, too, Mr Tone?'

The officer paused before replying. During the two hours that followed his arrival, shortly after noon, he had been bemused to hear Maria's name fall so frequently in conversation at Edgeworthstown House; daughters very rarely held a position of importance in Irish country families. That the Edgeworth household was an unorthodox one had been evident to him from the moment the company entered the estate. Matthew Tone was not a man well-versed in mechanics and design, yet the bewildering collection of strange machines had quite taken his breath away, and he recognized genius when he saw it. The gravel sweep had been lined with fantastic carriages of peculiar shapes and proportions; there was even a phaeton with a single wheel, and a curious contraption of reticulated runners and arcane machinery that was designed, he learnt on enquiry, to climb walls.

Their host, a middle-aged man of quick gestures, great energy and a ceaseless flow of talk, was clearly a most unusual and gifted individual and Tone had, from the outset, observed that Richard Lovell Edgeworth's eccentricity had touched his offspring, too. He was not surprised, therefore, by Maria's forthright—if not to say blunt—manner.

'As in every desperate struggle, Miss Edgeworth,' he said, 'those acts of barbarism have not been the province of one party only. I do not deny that there is blame well earned by the Citizen Army, yet I think you may find that, when the history of this particular revolution comes to be chronicled, 'twill be shown that the greatest number of heinous acts were perpetrated by His Majesty's men.'

Tone went to the library table and set down his cocked hat upon it. When he turned to Maria, she saw that his face was suffused with blood. Gone suddenly was the boyishness and easy charm; she was now in the presence of a soldier, a warrior. A phrase she had heard, or read, somewhere, flashed through her mind: *battle fury*, the demonic passion that can seize control of a civilized man in the heat of combat, and induce him to commit acts of unspeakable barbarity. Maria was afraid.

She looked upon the gaudy uniform, that peacock confection of lace and silver, that frothy tinselry, that *laissez-passer* to murder, whose awful hypocrisy lay in its pretence to chivalry. Scarlet or blue, its claim to defender of decency and order rang as hollow as drill-orders on the parade-ground; hollow, because its *true* purpose revealed itself when the drums of war were beaten.

But Matthew Tone's anger subsided as abruptly as it had risen. When he spoke again, his voice was cold and impassive, as he detailed crimes that sent revulsion through Maria.

'The forces of the Crown, Miss Edgeworth, do not discriminate between the guilty and the innocent. In Carnew in County Carlow, they had arrested and imprisoned all those whom they considered to be rebels. As a reprisal for the shooting of a trooper, they marched twenty-eight of these men from the town gaol, and paraded them in the handball alley. Then, one by one, they were shot in cold blood by a squad of yeomen and militia, and their bodies thrown in a quicklime grave.

'At New Ross, a company of Lake's troopers happened upon a wandering hermit, a gentle and devout soul who had never, 'twas said, raised a finger to harm either man or beast. They discovered that the wretch had in his pocket a Catholic prayer-book, so of course 'twas assumed that he had sworn a rebel oath. What do you think they did, Miss Edgeworth, those brave soldiers? Why, they brought him to the barracks yard and half-hanged him—not once, mark, but three times. When he still did not disclose where a cache of pikes might be hidden, they flogged him with a cat o' nails. They flogged him so viciously that the intestines could be seen protruding from his wounds. Then, for good measure, they hanged him again—properly this time—until he was dead.'

'Yes, Soldier Tone!' Maria exclaimed. 'Yes, yes; I do not doubt the veracity of such reports; news of these and similar outrages has reached even our ears, here in Edgeworthstown, and I blush in shame, when contemplating such base cruelty. And yet, I put 't to you that your but recent return to our heretofore peaceful and smiling land has acquainted you with one side of this desperate struggle only. You, Soldier Tone, cannot have read the newspaper accounts of the atrocities and unboundedly wicked deeds, such as those perpetrated in County Meath.' The young woman's face darkened. She rose from her chair and crossed to a bureau. She took out a slim book, looked through it briefly and placed it, opened, upon the table. Tone saw that it was a scrapbook containing newspaper cuttings. Maria jabbed a shaking finger at an entry.

'There, Soldier Tone! Read about the brave exploits of your so-called Citizen Army. An army that broke into the house of the Reverend Nelson, a schoolmaster in Dunshaughlin, and slaughtered him and his gardener, and mutilated the bodies beyond recognition. And why? Because they were Protestants. Another unfortunate in that same village was taken, and cast, living, into a barrel of burning pitch. He, too, was a Protestant.

'You see, Soldier Tone, this is not a revolution such as that which took place in France; this is not a class struggle, but *sectarian* warfare. My good friend Dorothea Herbert has told me what happened in Tipperary. She is the daughter of a clergyman in Knockgrafton —you will not know the place; 'tis of importance to few. Now, some of the good people of Knockgrafton entered the rectory in the Reverend Herbert's absence, riddled the children's nurse with musket-balls, and hacked the sexton to death with a cleaver. When Dorothea returned and saw the bloodstains on the rectory carpet, she went quite insane.'

Those eyes! Those clear, brown, accusing eyes. Tone had seen their like before; caught and uncomfortable in Maria's unblinking stare, he could not at once bring the circumstances to mind. Then he remembered: Danton on the final day of his trial for treason. Georges Jacques Danton, the architect of the Tribunal, hauled before his own invention, the engineer hoist; Danton in the outer office of the court, delivering his final and most eloquent speech, while the official pronounced the inevitable sentence of death upon him and his fellow accused; Danton ignoring contemptuously the droning words, and the whoops and bay of the mob, intruding most audibly from the court proper; Danton addressing his noble and damning lines to a young, foreign soldier, whose straining to follow the *soigné* French, Danton had mistaken for compassion and humanity. Tone had never thought to see eyes such as those in a woman.

'You spoke of burning pitch, Miss Edgeworth,' he said evenly, 'yet 'tis clear that you do not know whence this novel method of torture came. I will tell you. It began with Captain Swayne's treatment of the people of Prosperous; his favourite instrument was a cap filled with blazing pitch which he had placed upon the victim's head. If the wretched fellow survived at all, then his poor brain was so damaged that he was much worse off than your beloved Dorothea.

'Oh, the King's men like to burn, Miss Edgeworth! Do you know of the events that took place in Enniscorthy? Our people had taken over one of the town houses there, and converted 't into a hospital for the treatment of the wounded insurgents, as well as the ordinary people who had become ensnarled in the fighting. Lake's men succeeded in capturing this makeshift hospital, and then they set fire to 't, with the wounded men, women and children still inside. 'Twas told to me that the men who visited the site the next morning found the bodies still hissing in the embers.'

The eyes flashed coldly. 'Fire is fought with fire, Soldier Tone. Consider the massacre at Scullabogue. You have not heard of 't—or perhaps you choose not to remember?' She picked up the grim scrapbook and turned to an entry. She read it aloud.

'"Whereas on the eve of the thirtieth of May, Captain King, a local gentleman, and the proprietor of Scullabogue, was advised to abandon his house; he made his escape next day, and the rebels took possession of the property. When the insurgents encamped on Carricksbyrne-hill marched towards Ross, on the fourth of June, the Protestant prisoners were left at Scullabogue, under a guard of three hundred rebels, commanded by Captain John Murphy of Loughnageer, Nicholas Sweetman and Walter Devereux, who both had the same rank.

'"When the rebel army began to give way at Ross, an express was sent to Captain Murphy, to put the Protestant prisoners to death, as the King's troops were gaining the day; but Murphy refused to comply without a direct order from the general. He soon after received another message to the same purpose, with this addition, that the prisoners, if released, would become very furious and vindictive. Shortly after, a third express arrived, wherein Father Brien Murphy, parish priest of Taghmon, gave orders that the prisoners, more than two hundred men, and about thirty women and children, should be put to death at once. The rebels, on hearing the sanction of the Romanist priest, became outrageous, and began to pull off their clothes, the better to perform the bloody deed.

'"The prisoners were led out in fours in front of the dwelling-house to be shot; the rebels who pierced them when they fell, took pleasure in licking their spears. Whenever a body fell on being shot, the rebel guards shouted, and pierced it with their pikes. While the prisoners were being shot, a party of men and women were engaged in stripping and rifling the dead bodies. All told, thirty-seven men were shot in front of the house.

"'The barn at Scullabogue had been converted into a prison for the confinement of about an hundred and eighty prisoners; some twenty-four of them had been taken from the village of Tintern, about eight miles distant, many of them old and feeble. The daemonic rebels endeavoured to set fire to the barn, while the poor prisoners, shrieking and crying out for mercy, crowded to the back door of the building, which they forced open for the purpose of admitting air. For some time, they continued to put the door between them and the rebels, who were piking or shooting them; in attempting to do so, their hands or fingers were cut off. The rebels continued to force into the barn bundles of straw to increase the fire. At last, the prisoners, having been overcome by the flame and smoke, their moans and cries gradually died away in the silence of death.

"'Thomas Shee and Patrick Prendergast were burnt in the barn, both Romanists, because they would not consent to the massacre of their past masters. William Johnson, a very old man, though of the same persuasion, shared a similar fate. He gained a livelihood by playing on the bagpipes, and was so unfortunate as to incur the vengeance of the rebels by playing the tune of 'Croppies, Lie Down'.

"'During this dreadful scene, a child, who got under the door, and was likely to escape, but much hurt and bruised, when a rebel perceiving it, darted his pike through it, and threw it into the flames.

"'The barn was thirty-four feet long and fifteen wide, and the walls were but twelve feet high. Suffocation then must have soon taken place, so great a number of people were compressed in so small a space; and besides the burning of the thatched roof of the barn, the rebels threw into it, on their pikes, a great number of faggots on fire. In the ruins of the barn, charred corpses were found, families huddled together and still standing upright for want of space. The rebels were occupied for several days in turning over the bodies to look for coins or other valuables.

"'Not only every honest individual, but whole bodies of men must feel impatient to rescue themselves from any imputation, even by their silence, of abetting the horrible monster that has started up in our island, that now scatters anarchy, confusion, and death, in its progress.'"

Maria shut the damning ledger and placed it gently on the table. 'Now 'tis your turn, Soldier Tone,' she said. 'What barbarous deeds can you recount that can compare with those? Do tell one; one should like to know!'

The officer was silent.

'Nothing? Truly you disappoint me. The newspapers had given one the assurance that our generals and their men have acted impeccably during the course of this uprising, that they have demonstrated great gallantry and exemplary conduct, as befits the finest army in the world.' Still Tone was silent. 'You are the man of action, Sir; you, in your gorgeous uniform and green cockade! Will you tell me now that you have seen nothing in the course of your honourable campaign to rid us of foreign tyranny? Tell me what that action is *truly* like, Soldier Tone; give me an officer's eyewitness account of glorious battle!'

Those Dantonesque eyes again; he found that he could not meet them.

'Do you really wish to know?' he said at last. He crossed to the window, turning his back to her. His hands were clasped behind him and she could see his knuckles whiten as he kneaded a clenched fist. 'Very well, then.'

'On the twenty-seventh of August,' he began, voice low, shorn of emotion, 'we marched on Castlebar, under the command of General Humbert. We had met no resistance whatever since we had landed at Killala five days before.

'But Castlebar was defended by ten curricle guns and a howitzer, and we had with us but a single cannon. Lake had arrived the previous night, d'you see, otherwise we could quickly have o'ermastered General Hutchinson's garrison. Now the troops and artillery guarding the town were deployed in three lines on the hills, greatly outnumbering us in men and field-pieces. We thought to be done, yet Humbert gave the order to advance.

'Colonel Sarrazin led the charge. 'Twas all over within minutes, for Lake's army fled, abandoning their guns, and did not stop running until they reached the town of Tuam.'

'They called 't the Races of Castlebar,' Maria said.

'Ay, they did; a pretty name indeed. I took a company of Grenadiers in order to pursue the retreating army. 'Twas thought that they would regroup and launch a counter-attack. They did not. We followed their progress for some of the way to Tuam, and saw how they had treated the people of the villages through which they had passed. There were the corpses of men, hung between the shafts of upturned carts. Another man had been flogged so much that 'twas as though an animal had been slaughtered on the spot, so copious was the blood and severed flesh we found there. The soldiers had gone from village to village, burning every house and shooting, bayoneting or hacking to death men, women and children. There was scarce a soul left breathing.

'The corpses lay in the streets, surrounded by broken glass and earthenware. Some of the bodies were perforated over and over with musket-balls, or the bayonet, and some were hacked beyond recognition with sabres. *Such* is the fury of a defeated enemy.

'But worst of all were the pigs. They wandered amongst the carnage, snuffling blood. I came upon some of them eating the brains out of the cloven skulls, and gnawing the flesh of the raw wounds. Flames and smoke were everywhere. Many people were reduced to ashes, and many were partly burnt and partly roasted. The soldiers had shot some of the pigs, too, and I was hard put to distinguish between them and the roasted bodies of the villagers.'

He turned round to face her. 'Glorious battle? Ay, Miss Edgeworth, that was the glory I saw on the road to Tuam, in the wake of the Races of Castlebar.'

The colour had drained from Maria Edgeworth's cheeks. She sat down again at her desk, and her breathing was difficult in the tight bodice she wore. She could not look at the soldier.

'The century draws to a close,' she said softly. 'A mere fifteen months more and 'tis done; though my father,'—she managed a weak smile—'who is sometimes prone to pedantry, insists that 'twill end upon the final day of 1800. This century draws to a close, and what of the coming one? I had thought to know.' Maria reached across the desk and picked up the maroon-covered book. She opened it and leafed slowly through the pages of manuscript.

'It is a novel,' she told the soldier. ''Tis the first fiction of length that I have attempted for adult readers. It gives an account of this country in the bad old days, when the buckeens and squireens ruled. I had hoped to portray Irish country life as 'twas lived before 1782, when the Edgeworths came to stay for good in Edgeworthstown.' The officer saw Maria's brown eyes skim over some lines; he saw her frown, and hurriedly turn the page.

'I need hardly tell you, Soldier Tone, what life was like in those times; the evils perpetrated were, after all, those same evils that you and your brother rebels imagine still exist. In some respects, you are correct. I choose to think of Edgeworthstown as an oasis of civilization in a wilderness of inequity. My father differs from the great majority of landlords, inasmuch as he believes—as I do—in education as the means whereby this country can prosper. He devotes his life to this ideal, and has, almost single-handedly, propounded a system of schooling which will exhalt the consciousness of the country people. What he is building here in Edgeworthstown shall serve as an example to all.

'Yet this can be achieved for the whole country only when order rules, only when the enlightened men of the aristocracy turn their backs upon the past, and endeavour to purge themselves of the sins of their fathers.'

'They will never do so,' Tone said. 'France and her Revolution have taught me as much; the aristocracy will never alter by so much as an hair—unless they be o'erthrown.'

'I do not believe that!' Maria cried. 'Change will take place; gradually, perhaps, but take place 't will. We are making such progress, and I had such hopes for the coming era. I pray that the Union of Ireland and Great Britain will soon be a fact; only then can we achieve *true* progress.'

Tone snorted. 'Progress?! There can be no progress for a people under foreign rule. And your enlightened aristocracy is a myth. People learn from the cruelty of others; 'tis a cycle that never ends. We have talked of cruelty; 't has been with us since the beginning of history, and 'twill be with us always.'

'I do not believe that,' Maria said again. 'I cannot believe 't. Education shall be the saviour of the new century; it shall bring greater learning and greater prosperity; this new age shall be one wherein machines and mechanical contrivances are put to work for the prosperity of all. I see a new society emerging, a civilization such as never was seen before.'

'Listen to me, Miss Edgeworth,' Tone said, taking the book from her hand. She turned her head from him. 'You and your father are awaiting the coming of Utopia. You envisage a world without poverty, wherein the just rule.

'There is no room for cruelty and barbarism in your world, because the people are so educated that they have risen above such beastliness. Wars will be fought between brave soldiers upon set battlefields, preferably bloodlessly; and when one side is the victor, why, they will shake hands and march back home, honour having been satisfied.'

Maria stared intently at the young officer. The still afternoon air outside the house was disturbed by the commands of a sergeant, evidently directing some kind of drill or exercise.

'You must think us very naïve,' she said.

'I would not presume as much, Miss Edgeworth,' he told her. 'Your vision is a laudable one, and I wish sincerely that 't could become a reality. But I do not believe that 't ever shall. The French Revolution gave me hope, ay, and 'tis my fervent wish that 'twill spread to the rest of Europe. When all Ireland rises, England will fall, too. There is a tide sweeping this quarter of the terrestrial globe that is bringing a new order: *Liberté, Egalité, Fraternité.* This is the Utopia of my own brother Theo, whose arrival upon these shores is imminent. The tide is powerful enough to sweep away the inequities to which you refer in your novel. Yet 'twill change nothing of mankind, for we are doomed to repeat those inequities forever. A century hence—*two* centuries hence—men will still burn hospitals and slaughter infants. There is no end to 't.'

'I cannot accept that. What of God's plan—?'

'I do not believe in God.'

'Then I am sorry for you.'

'Do not be, Miss Edgeworth. I have lived my life without God and have not regretted 't. I have fought for that in which I believe, knowing that my efforts could bring but temporary change. 'Twill not matter in the tract of time; yet I am a man who believes that every person has a duty to his race; our duty in life is to leave the world somewhat better than we found it. I am already a dead man; I am resigned to my death.'

Maria's eyes opened wide. 'They are going to execute you?' She was shocked to hear this man, younger than she, talk so calmly about his death; she seldom—if ever—thought of her own.

'You did not know?' Tone laughed without humour and went to the window. He screened his eyes from the sun, the hot sun of September: the sun that had been Humbert's undoing, the sun that had given the country the best harvest in memory, that had kept the peasants in the fields, and dissuaded them from joining the ranks of the insurgency. 'Those men in the yard, Miss Edgeworth,' he said, 'are escorting me and a fellow Irish officer to Dublin; we shall be boarding a barge moored in the Grand Canal at Mullingar, that shall carry us to our court martial. Should that court find me guilty of treason—and there is no doubting that 't will—I shall be sentenced to be hanged, drawn and quartered.' He turned to her. 'Do you know what that means, Miss Edgeworth?'

She shook her head.

''Tis a delightful method of execution that is practised by your enlightened aristocracy: your Lords Cornwallis, Bucky, Longford *et al*, the men who will usher in your Utopia. The method works as follows. Firstly, the prisoner is half-hanged, an experience dreadful enough in itself; he remains conscious whilst he is taken down from the gallows and his clothing is stripped from his body. Secondly, a sharp razor is applied to his lower abdomen, which wound causes his bowels to tumble out in front of his eyes; the prisoner is conscious all the while; that is what is known as "drawing". Lastly, his head is lopped off, and his body is divided by an axe into four parts, each with a limb attached; this is called "quartering". The severed head is skewered upon a long pole and raised up for the rabble to see, a truly edifying spectacle. And the rest of the body, you may ask? Should the executioners be half-genteel men, then this is buried in a grave of quicklime; should they be diligent practitioners of their trade, then the four quarters are fed to the prison pigs which, I am told, are amongst the most saginated in the land in these times.'

He had thought ... what had he thought? That Maria Edgeworth would fall faint upon hearing his lurid description? She had not done so. Maria sat motionless, and her expression betrayed anger rather than shock.

'You must escape,' she said urgently. 'I can arrange for a cart to be—'

'No! No, I shall not escape, for I have given my word of honour.'

She did not understand. He joined his fists and held them up in front of her, displaying the soiled lace on the wrists.

'Why d'you think that I am not manacled hand and foot? 'Tis because I am an officer, and my rank is higher than the lieutenant under whose command I was brought here. He salutes me in the same way as he would salute his own commanding officer. This is the way of things; a soldier salutes the uniform, not the man who wears 't.' He studied the silver lace on his cuff. 'If you wish to talk of civilizing influences, well then, you might include this uniform amongst them.

'Humbert surrendered at Granard and, when he did, he left the Irish troops to the mercy of Lake and his Dragoons. I knew what was about to ensue, as did Humbert, Sarrazin and the other staff officers. The "boys" did not. One of Lake's officers rode up to where they had assembled after they had thrown down their arms, and cried, "Run away, boys, otherwise you'll all be cut down!" He was too late, and that is precisely what happened: hundreds of defenceless men were hacked to pieces. The Dragoons had had a good day.

'Yet I and my fellow officers—French and Irish—were spared. Not only spared, but treated with the utmost respect. They shall hang me, 'tis true, but they respect the uniform I wear.

'You wonder why I do not attempt to run, to escape the gruesome and ignoble death that I have outlined. 'Tis because I, too, respect my uniform. I have given my word as an officer and a gentleman, and the honour attached to this uniform forbids that I should break my word. And when I go to the gallows, I will go there with my head high, as befits the wearer of this uniform. That, Miss Edgeworth, is civilization.'

'SERGEANT!'

'Sir!'

'Why is 't taking so damned long to load that cart?'

''Tis Mr Edgeworth, Lieutenant. He insisted that the wounded prisoner should be made as comfortable as possible. His words, Sir, not mine.'

'Ay, well, we cannot argue with that. We owe a debt of gratitude to Mr Edgeworth and his household. I, for one, will be glad when we reach Mullingar; then 'tis someone else's responsibility. Is Captain Tone ready to travel?'

'I could not say, Sir. I left him in the library, where he's taking his leave of Miss Edgeworth—the eldest daughter.'

''Sblood and guts! I suppose the woman's fallen in love with him, has she? Women who write books are too romantic, Sergeant. They should not be left alone with young officers.'

'No, Sir. But I dinnae believe 'tis as you see it. When I left, she was saluting him, d'you see.'

'Lord save us! What is the world coming to?'

'She said a strange thing, too, Lieutenant, when she thought I was out of earshot. I heard her say these words to the rebel: "I am not saluting the uniform, Soldier Tone; I am saluting the man."'

Tally Ho and Away We Go!
by Gertrude F. Munroe

IT'S NOT EVERYBODY who can hope to publish a book at the age of ninety-one, yet Miss Edith Somerville has done just that. Very proudly she presents me with the new volume of essays—just off the press—called *Maria and Some Other Dogs*. It's a remarkable achievement for a woman whose writing career spans all of sixty years, from the first novel published in 1889.

Many of us were not even born then, yet how many of us have not been charmed and delighted by those wonderful adventures of the Irish R. M. or indeed by *The Real Charlotte*? I open the book and yes, there—as always—are the two authors: Martin Ross, though she's been dead more than forty years now, and E. Œ. Somerville, Hon. Litt. D.—the honorary degree that Edith Œnone received in 1931 from Trinity College, Dublin.

I'm sure one of the very first things our readers will want to know is: how did Miss Somerville come to acquire that delightful middle name? It's one of the questions I put to her during our very enjoyable talk at Tally Ho house in Castletownshend, Co. Cork, Ireland.

'It *is* an unusual name, is it not?' says Miss Somerville with a smile. 'I do not believe that in all my ninety-one years I have come across more than one other person who shared the name.' (I should point out at this stage that these are Miss Somerville's exact words. I'm using a tape recording machine for the interview, an instrument which she at first found a little off-putting but actually grew to enjoy after a while! Miss Somerville speaks in perfectly formed sentences, an art that is dying out I'm afraid.)

'My parents were living in Corfu at the time of my birth,' she continues. 'My father, Colonel Thomas Somerville, was in command of the 3rd Buffs there. I expect it was inevitable that they should choose a Greek name for me.' She laughs. 'I am so very glad they didn't call me Nausicaa—you remember that Ulysses and she met on the island of Corfu?'

'I should but I don't, I'm afraid,' I confess.

'Oh, yes. Ulysses was shipwrecked off the coast,' she reminds me, 'and Nausicaa and her maidens were playing ball on the beach. The poor fellow was quite naked and must hide his private parts behind a fig-leaf or some such covering. The Greeks were rather prudish in those days—though you would not think it to look at their statues. I remember seeing one in that lovely museum they have in Athens. It was of the god Priapus. Goodness, it quite made me blush!'

A WONDERFUL TALKER

ACTUALLY I FIND it hard to imagine Miss Somerville blushing at anything. Our conversation has been extremely frank, I can tell you, and I won't embarrass our readers (or Miss Somerville for that matter) by telling all! She is a wonderful talker and needs no more than a cup of tea at regular intervals to sustain her conversation. I have to rein her in, though, because she tends to go off at all kinds of tangents.

'About the name ... Œnone ...?' I prompt.

'Oh yes, the name. I think Nausicaa sounds a lot like "nausea", don't you? Nausea Somerville; Martin would have enjoyed that! No, Œnone was far, far better. She was the wife of Paris, did you know that?'

'Wasn't he the one who fell in love with Helen of Troy?' At least I remember *that* much!

Miss Somerville tosses her head and inclines it to one side. It's a habit of hers I notice from the very beginning. She gestures a good deal, throwing her hands about with abandon. I suspect that this exuberance is a 'cover' for a lady who's basically quite shy.

'Œnone was a nymph, the daughter of the river god Cabren and the wife of Paris,' she tells me. 'He deserted her when he saw how beautiful Helen was. Sad, very sad. ...'

'I see. While we're on the subject of names, you mentioned Martin a moment ago. I don't think many of our readers know that that was not her real name.'

I almost regret bringing up the subject of Miss Somerville's writing partner because it seems to upset her. Miss Ross died in 1915, yet to hear Miss Somerville talk about her you'd imagine it was only yesterday. I don't believe two other writers in history were ever as close as Somerville and Ross. They did everything together. They were tied by such a strong bond that even when apart the one usually knew what the other was doing. It's said that their 'rapport' was so great that they merged their consciousnesses in order to write the novels. Edith was completely heartbroken when Martin died.

'Well, we wanted pen-names, didn't we?' Miss Somerville says. 'I called myself Geilles Herring, after an ancestor of mine, but the silly gommawns called me Grilled Herring; can you imagine? In the end, I used my real name; this was after we had written *An Irish Cousin*.'

'That was your first book, wasn't it?'

'Yes. Violet went to no trouble whatever when choosing her pen-name; she simply used her surname as a Christian name. She was extremely proud of her family, d'you see.'

'I thought perhaps that in those days a woman writer might be more successful if she used a man's name,' I remark. 'I'm thinking of George Eliot, for example.'

Miss Somerville finds this very amusing. 'No doubt that was

the case in *your* country,' she says, 'but not here. Oh, no. We were fortunate, d'you see, in having had Maria Edgeworth pave the way for us; by the time our turn came 'round it was quite acceptable to be a woman novelist.'

'Mind you,' she says, 'I remember how the reviewer in *The Bookseller* was fooled into thinking that both Martin and I were men. He called me *Mister* Somerville, if you please!' She smiles at the memory. 'Martin said at the time that the poor fellow must have supposed that the 'Œ' stood for Œdipus! Men can be such dears.'

We're interrupted at this point by Miss Somerville's nurse who comes into the room with the lame excuse of asking the elderly lady whether she's taken her pills. Really she wants to know whether I'm not tiring Miss Somerville out. She's sent away with a flea in her ear.

FROM MECCA TO MEDINA

IT'S CLEAR WHO rules the roost at Tally Ho. The household, I'm told, is a lot smaller than it used to be in its heyday. Now there are only four servants, a gardener and an old groom—Mike—whom Edith is very fond of. He's really an odd-jobman, since there's just one pony left in the stables.

Dogs and horses have always figured very prominently in Miss Somerville's life. She hasn't been able to ride in almost four decades and that is a great regret for her. In fact, she's a semi-invalid now, beset by rheumatism, sciatica and other ailments that confine her to a bath chair. She has lost most of her eyesight too and I get the impression that this is a more bitter blow to her than anything else. She can't write as much as she'd like to.

Her sister Hildegarde, whom I judge to be nine or ten years younger, lives here also. They have frequent visitors to the house, Irish gentry mostly. The current guest is Miss Geraldine Cummins, whom I shall meet later today. She is, Miss Somerville assures me, a most remarkable woman, but does not explain why. I am to learn. ...

Castletownshend is an unusual village by Irish standards, having no less than ten great houses all contained within a square mile or so. The castle that the village is named after is at the eastern end, overlooking the harbor and the church. Drishane House, where the Misses Somerville were born, is at the other end. Edith had to leave it when her nephew Desmond and his wife came to live there in 1946. The move hurt her deeply, she tells me. She compares it with Mohammed's flight from Mecca to Medina. Yet she had no choice but to go because it was Desmond, not she, who had inherited the property.

We're sitting in Miss Somerville's big parlor in her own wing of Tally Ho house. It lies just off the main street that climbs steeply up from the Drishane end of the village. This unusual thoroughfare is dominated by two very ancient and spreading sycamores that grow in the middle of the street. One of the maids has thrown open the French windows. We're looking out over the lovely sloping garden and there's a fine view of the ocean beyond the trees. It's a delicious August afternoon, almost tropical in fact, unusually close. I'm told that the country has been experiencing a heat wave this summer, the like of which hasn't been known for years. The lawns are well tended and the flowers are still in full bloom: red and yellow roses, hydrangeas, pansies, heliotropes and the red and purple fuchsias you see in just about every Irish garden. The scents of the flowers blend gaily with the salty air of the sea. It's an idyllic place, this Castletownshend.

FAMILY TREES

MISS SOMERVILLE'S PARLOR is cluttered. She explains that most of the things I see once occupied two or three rooms at Drishane. Her library is here—in fact the books are spilling off the shelves and onto the floor and tables. The walls are hung with her own paintings and drawings as well as portraits and old photographs of her family and ancestors. Pride of place has been given to two beautifully hand-lettered family trees: the Somervilles and the Rosses.

There are also paintings and photographs of horses and hounds in abundance. I recognize a younger Edith posing very smartly in her hunting costume and riding crop. The date on the photograph is 1905, when she must have been in her late forties. There isn't space for some of the bigger paintings and they are propped here and there against the walls.

The furnishings of the room are how I imagine they must have been at the turn of the century. The wallpaper is heavy and embossed with a dark red fleur-de-lis pattern. The rug is brown and has a floral design. It is very worn now; many generations have trodden on it. There are three over-stuffed armchairs. The side of the upholstery of one of them is in tatters, chewed away by Miss Somerville's only surviving fox terrier, Porgy II, who lies fast asleep at his mistress's feet. There is a strong 'doggie' smell in the room which I find quite charming, having four dogs of my own.

'Was there ever a Bess?' I ask. 'You know, Porgy ...?'

Miss Somerville gesticulates impatiently. 'You must speak up, my dear!' she chides me. 'My hearing is simply dreadful these days.' I have already been told by the nurse of Edith's accident two years ago when she tripped over Porgy and suffered a bad fall. It affected her sight, hearing and power of movement. I repeat the question more loudly.

'Bessie! Oh, yes.' Miss Somerville's old eyes light up. 'Bessie was a dear; quite, quite wonderful ... oh, and so independent. She was Porgy's mother, you know. He was absolutely devoted to her. Poor old Bessie; Mike buried her at the end of the garden in ... in ... well, whenever it was.'

I must say Miss Somerville looks rather spruce. She's wearing a dark blue pants suit, an immaculately laundered white shirt and a necktie with red and purple stripes. A tartan rug keeps her legs warm—despite the exceptionally fine summer weather she is often cold and her rheumatism causes her a great deal of distress.

Yet, ailments aside, she looks far younger than her ninety-one years even though her hair is snow-white. It's cropped quite short and tied severely at the nape of her neck. Hers is the face of a strong, determined woman. She has the habit of thrusting her jaw out, giving the impression of fierceness to those who do not know her well. Her mind seems as keen now as it was when I first met her in Dover, Massachusetts in 1936. And of course she still retains her wonderful sense of humor.

We have had a small table placed near the French windows and it supports my tape recording machine. Miss Somerville's fountain pens are here too, and two diaries. Last year's looks to have been much used but this year's has not been opened at all. Hildegarde has told me that Edith hasn't made an entry now in almost a year; her eyes can no longer manage it. This must be a blow to her also because she'd kept a diary every year since 1872, writing on average a hundred words each day. It's been calculated that Miss Somerville's diaries run to almost three million words—more words than you'll find in all her books combined!

ANIMAL IMPRESSIONS

I'M THINKING ABOUT this huge production when Edith startles me a little. She puckers her lips and allows the air to escape through them in short and rapid bursts, sounding just like a dog! Porgy II wakes up at once and cocks a floppy ear in her direction. Then my hostess begins to whine. I think my ears must surely be deceiving me—but no, Miss E. Œ. Somerville is doing the greatest animal impression I've ever heard.

She must sense rather than see the dumbfounded expression on my face because she turns to me and says: 'Martin could do it much better, you know. My goodness, she used to fool even me!

'I remember one night—we were very young at the time—when she played a prank on some puppies we had at Drishane. They were about four weeks old, the dears, and of course still very dependent upon their mother. There were three of them and one evening when mother and puppies were fast asleep in their basket, all curled up together in a corner of the scullery, Martin ever so gently lifted the mother out and carried her upstairs to her bedroom and shut the door. Then she went downstairs and hid herself in a broom cupboard under the stairs. She'd wedged a broom handle against the door, so it could not be opened from the outside. Then she began to howl.'

Miss Somerville laughs loudly and there are tears of mirth in her eyes. 'Well, my dear!' she says, 'those puppies woke up at once, thinking that their mother had deserted them, and scampered to the broom cupboard. The little ones began to yelp and scratch at the door, thinking that their mother was trapped inside. The more noise they made, the more loudly Martin howled.

'By this time, half the household had been alerted. The Chimp [*Edith's oldest brother Cameron—Ed.*] and I led the way to the broom cupboard. Two of the servants had brought lamps. The Chimp tried to force the door but of course it wouldn't open. The din those puppies kicked up! They were joined by the other dogs —six or seven as I recall—all barking to wake the dead. And all the while Martin was howling like a she-devil and squealing and scratching on the other side!

'Eventually one of the grooms fetched a crowbar and managed to prise the door open. Imagine our surprise when we found Martin in there in her night dress, clutching her sides and laughing. Well, Papa was so angry about the disruption of his night's sleep that he "fined" Martin for the damage caused to the door and debarred her from Drishane for a month.'

Miss Somerville smiles at the memory. But there is more.

'I remember one occasion we stayed in Oxford; *when* I cannot recollect, but we were guests of Herbert Greene, who was dean at Magdalen by then. He proposed to me once, did you know that? No, I expect you didn't, but no matter. ... One day Herbert was giving us a tour of the Bodleian Library. A magnificent building— do you know it?' I shake my head. 'It is well worth a visit; the collection is quite superb.

'In any event Herbert brought us to an upper room that housed the manuscripts. Martin thought the whole place rather boring, I'm afraid—until she found a ventilating shaft that was covered by a big brass grille. When Herbert's back was turned she whipped it off and did her famous party-piece: the blood-curdling squeal of a terrier that's had its tail caught in a door! Quite authentic, I can assure you.

'Can you imagine how the grave students below us in that home of learning must have felt, upon hearing this unearthly cry from the heavens? I'm afraid Martin quite upset our host.'

'Martin and dogs,' she says. 'She loved them as much as I do— and still does, of course.'

This is the first overt reference to Edith's spiritualistic relationship with her dead partner, a relationship that began at Martin's death in 1915 and has continued up to the present. I know I must tread carefully—I don't want to offend Miss Somerville in any way. I'm skeptical about these things. Besides which, I was brought up in the belief that communication with the dead is unnatural and wrong. But I switch off the recording machine for the time being because the maid appears again with a fresh pot of tea, a plateful of cake and Miss Somerville's afternoon medicine. The nurse has gone shopping in the village.

Edith urges me to fetch a photo album from the shelf and while we sip our tea I leaf through it. All the pictures were taken in the last century when Somerville and Ross were young women. They are mainly of Edith and her sister Hildegarde. It's a curious thing: most people think of Edith and Martin as tomboyish but seeing Hildegarde riding, shooting, rowing and sailing it seems to me that the younger sister was far more the tomboy. Yet she married and neither Edith nor Martin ever did.

NUDE PHOTOS

I PAUSE FOR a long time when I come upon two photographs affixed side by side in the scrapbook. Miss Somerville leans closer to see them and I know she can recognize them by their shapes. They are studies of two young women basking nude at the sea. They're lovely; they could be water nymphs and I think of Edith's story of Œnone. I switch the machine on again.

'I'm the one on the left,' Miss Somerville tells me. 'Wasn't I pretty?'

She certainly was. Hildegarde took the picture, she tells me. A wasp-waisted Edith is photographed from behind, looking out to sea. Her own photo shows Hildegarde reclining like an enchanting mermaid on the rocks and seaweed. The pictures remind me of the 'art' books that Victorian gentlemen purchased in Paris during the Naughty Nineties. I am not far wrong. Miss Somerville assures me that she submitted prints to a French publisher but cannot say whether they were ever published. She is proud of the photographs.

'When you reach my age,' she says, 'it's comforting to know that this old bag-o'-bones you see was once a fine figure of a woman! Have you ever posed in the nude yourself, my dear?' she asks me. I blush slightly, assure her that I have not and quickly change the subject. I lay the photo album aside.

'The new book,' I say; 'can you explain the title to our readers?' Miss Somerville tosses her head.

'I should have thought it obvious,' she says rather impatiently. 'It is a collection of little biographies and my sketches of some of the many, many dogs we've known down through the years. Maria I'm sure you know from the R.M. stories; we based her on Pastel, a delightful water spaniel that Egerton had at one time. Dear, dear things.' She reaches down and strokes the hound's ear. 'All gone ... all except old Porgy. The house isn't the same without the dogs. A house never is.'

'You're not eating, my dear!' she says suddenly. 'And you look much too thin to me. You young people nowadays don't eat half enough. I expect you're concerned about your *figure*—I believe that is the expression?' She points imperiously in the direction of the cake-stand. 'Do help yourself to the carrot cake. Hildegarde had it baked specially.'

The cake *is* rather good, though a bit too sweet for my liking. Irish people I notice tend to be over-generous with sugar. I suspect it's because it was rationed here during the war and everyone seems keen on making up for the shortage.

'DOGS HAVE SOULS, YOU SEE'

'YOU WERE VERY attached to your dogs, weren't you?' I say.

'Oh, yes. Well, they were part of the family, after all. Did you know that dogs are the closest creatures to human beings—more so than horses?'

I continue eating my cake. Miss Somerville closes her eyes and turns her face to the ceiling. I imagine she's seeing some of her former pets with her mind's eye. Her next words, however, cause me some astonishment.

'Dogs have souls, you see—just as we do. Oh, yes. Martin will bear me out on this. They're up there with her, you know.' She gestures toward the ceiling. 'She often tells me about them, and how they're getting on. Dear little Taspy in particular—you can read all about him in the book—and Patsey and Candy and Sheila. Sometimes I hear one of them at night, scratching on my bedroom door, trying to get in. Is that not a comforting thought—that we shall be reunited with our loved ones at death?'

I nod. 'I feel sometimes that my own dogs and I have a special bond,' I tell her, 'almost as if they understand every word I say.' This is not strictly true, but I feel it's what Miss Somerville wants to hear. She becomes very excited, tossing her head and spreading her old hands wide.

'Oh, but dogs *do* understand!' she exclaims. 'Why, I remember once when Martin and I were at a meet of the West Carberys [*the hunt which Miss Somerville founded—Ed.*]; somehow or other I had got separated from the field but could hear the 'view halloo' quite clearly in the distance announcing that the fox had been started. I did not know it at the time, but I had contrived to position myself ahead of the fox and the pack.'

Miss Somerville wrings her hands together in agitation, causing bright blue veins to stand out against the white skin. 'Imagine my surprise when suddenly the fox burst from cover—directly in my path! You could have knocked me down with a feather. I don't know which of us was the more startled—I or the fox. However, my mare—dear old Bridget—proved the most startled of all, for she reared up at the sight of Reynard and I lost my balance in the saddle.

'You must remember that we ladies rode side-saddle in those days.' She shuts her eyes again. 'One got used to it, I suppose, but it was hard going, I can tell you. Your right leg was jammed up against the saddle for hours at a stretch—most uncomfortable. Worst of all was the night of the Hunt Ball when the men expected you to dance out your card when your legs were still stiff and numb from the day's ride. But they never gave it a moment's thought, bless 'em.'

'Do you ride yourself?' she asks. I confess to never having done so. The nearest I've ever been to a horse was in the jockeys' enclosure at Saratoga Springs.

I almost feel the acute pain and discomfort as Miss Somerville describes how it felt to ride side-saddle. How fortunate we modern women are to have escaped the tortures of this dreadful practise dictated by Victorian prudery! My heart goes out to Edith and her generation.

'It was totally unnatural,' she says. 'One's body was twisted in the saddle, everything squashed together, one could hardly breathe properly at times. Don't forget we all wore tight girdles too in those days, which were constraining enough. Men could use their whole weight to stay in the saddle: feet firmly in the stirrups, rising and falling with the trot, standing at the gallop. But we women had to rely only on our hands and our sense of balance. And woe betide the girl who got her long skirt caught in the saddle if she was thrown! It happened so frequently—especially during the hunt, when one took a fence wrongly. I have known girls to be dragged to their deaths in this way. What we must endure in the cause of propriety!'

She says this without a trace of bitterness. I coax her slowly back to the hunting incident.

PULLET TO THE RESCUE

'YES. AS I say, Bridget reared up and threw me. Very heavily too, because all I remember is waking up to find myself lying under a hedge with a shocking pain in my head. I'd probably hit it on a stone or something. Bridget was nowhere to be seen—she must have bolted for some reason.

'I could not have been "out" for long, though, because I heard the baying of the hounds very close by and I knew from what they were saying that they were in hot pursuit of Old Reynard. Sure enough, the leaders suddenly burst through the hedge I lay under, scampering right over me as if I wasn't there at all. I attempted to crawl out of their path and it was then I realized that I must have sprained my left ankle in the fall. Not only that, but my right leg was absolutely numb. Would you mind pouring some more tea, my dear? My throat is quite parched. Thank you. I'm not boring you, am I?'

I assure Miss Somerville that she most certainly is not. It has struck me that I'm hearing an authentic hunting tale—and one, I might add, that the creators of the famous 'Irish R.M.' didn't include in any of the books.

'Where was I?' she says. 'Oh, yes. Just as the stragglers were running off I heard the sound of hoofs approaching. Good heavens, I thought, the field are right behind! They'd never see me in time. I'd be trampled for certain.

'There was no time to lose. I raised myself somehow and barked at the top of my voice. I'm surprised they heard me above their own baying, but they did. The little fellow at the tail end—dear Pullet, he was always the slowest; we called him Pullet because a chicken could run faster, d'you see. He heard me calling to him and stopped dead in his tracks.

'"Head them off, Pullet!" I yelled at him in doggie talk. "Head them off!" And d'you know he did. He saw my predicament in a trice and called out to the other stragglers. About six of them turned and rushed back through the hedge, just as the leaders of the field were getting set to take it. The pounding of the hoofs seemed so close that I thought I was surely done for. But no, I heard the baying of Pullet and the rest of them, as he led the hunt off in an entirely different direction.'

'That's remarkable,' I say.

Miss Somerville tosses her head as if in irritation. 'It is just what I'm telling you,' she says. 'Dogs know these things. They are the most wonderful, intelligent creatures. Martin speaks to them, you know—on the other side—in the same way we are talking to one another now. It is perfectly true. When we pass over, our souls can communicate with their souls exactly as if they were human beings. And they remember their lives here on earth. They remember the little kindnesses one has shown them.'

I remain silent.

'Pullet remembers that incident very well, Martin says. He asks about me and wishes to know whether I am going to join him soon.' Miss Somerville sighs heavily. 'People ask me if I'm afraid of death. How could I be, I tell them, when so many good friends await me on the other side? So many ... so many. ...'

Edith Somerville has shut her eyes again. I wait patiently for her to continue but she does not do so. I hear that her breathing has become slow and rhythmic. She has fallen asleep. I get up, switch off the tape recording machine and softly close the French windows.

Dinner is at seven o'clock in the big dining-room in the main part of Tally Ho house. Miss Somerville has bathed and had a change of shirt and tie. She looks so well rested and gay that I no longer feel guilty about tiring her out in the afternoon—her nurse has spoken to me very sternly about that.

There are five of us at table. Edith sits at the head, as befits the matriarch of the house. I sit facing her. Hildegarde sits across from the two guests to whom I've just been introduced: Mr Townshend of the Castle, a man who looks to be as old as Edith and who shares her wit and ready laughter, and Miss Cummins, the lady whom Edith spoke about earlier.

I see nothing unusual in Miss Cummins. She is an elderly lady, but a good deal younger than Edith. She is very thin with one of those 'lived in' faces. She speaks slowly and very decisively with a soft country accent. Sometimes she makes a pronouncement upon an everyday matter such as the weather with all the gravity of an undertaker or a venerable cardinal. At other times she tells an anecdote about one of the local people that has us all in stitches, while keeping an absolutely straight face. I can see why Miss Somerville enjoys her company so much. In ways they are alike.

COUNTRY FARE AT TALLY HO

MR TOWNSHEND DOES his best to assert his position as male in this predominantly female company, yet I can tell he's finding it an uphill struggle. Seldom have I shared a dinner table with such forceful personalities as the Somerville sisters and Miss Cummins.

The meal is surprisingly plain, even frugal. Two servants bring up the first course, a clear and very bland chicken soup that we eat with some home-baked brown bread. I notice that none of the others uses condiments so I resist the temptation to fortify my own soup. The main course is a bit better: a huge side of smoked bacon that Mr Townshend carves for us—no doubt it gives him a welcome opportunity to prove his manhood—served with floury potatoes and green cabbage which has been boiled beyond recognition. Fortunately Edith has had the good sense to order a fine bottle of claret to be served with the meal and this makes the whole quite palatable.

Our conversation consists of amusing tidbits of local gossip and who has won what at the Limerick Show. Horses are the favorite topic. Mr Townshend speaks with much pride about his stock-breeding activities which appear to be very successful.

The war years had not been kind to Miss Somerville in this

respect. Her income had been derived from her books and the sale of horses to the USA. During the Blitz on London a bomb had fallen upon the building occupied by Longmans, Edith's publishers, destroying their entire stock of her books. They refused to reprint them on the grounds that paper was scarce. Meanwhile the German U-boats in the Atlantic put paid to her horse exporting. I had wondered before why Miss Somerville had continued writing at such a great age. Now I know. It was—and is—simply a question of financial necessity.

How gracious they are, these Irish country people! I am quizzed on America, my family and my work. They inquire about President Truman, whether his second term in office will be as successful as the first and his attitude to the communist advance on Hong Kong. I have to confess that I haven't been following these topics as well as I should have been.

They speak flatteringly about the USA—whether in deference to me I don't know. Mr Townshend is all for having a federal Europe based on the American model. He thinks it's 'just around the corner'. He's read an item in today's newspaper about the Council of Europe. Apparently a British Labor MP, Ronald Mackay, has asked for all national European moneys to be wiped out and replaced by a single currency from the Bank of Europe operating under the Council's wing. Mr Townshend thinks it's a good idea. The Somerville sisters and Miss Cummins are appalled by the suggestion.

When the meal ends Mr Townshend and Hildegarde go together to the drawing-room while Miss Cummins, Miss Somerville and I return to Edith's wing of the house. I sense some mystery in the air because Miss Cummins whispers to Edith as she assists her into the parlor.

The maid has lighted the fire in the big grate and the room is already very warm. The light from a standing lamp in the corner is the only illumination. Porgy II is nowhere to be seen. I consider switching on my recording machine but no, I decide against it. I have the feeling that this meeting will be less formal than that of this afternoon. Miss Cummins clears a small table and draws it closer to the fire.

'I want you to see this before you go, my dear,' Miss Somerville tells me. She throws Miss Cummins a conspiratorial look. 'We're highly psychic, you know, Martin and I. We sensed your skepticism right from the word go.'

I start to protest but Miss Somerville waves it aside. 'Nothing to be ashamed of,' she says. 'The proof of the pudding, you know.' I don't quite follow her but Miss Cummins explains.

'If you've no objection,' she says, 'we should like to try a little automatic writing.'

'EXTRA-MUNDANE' COMMUNICATION

I AM FLATTERED and honored. I am to be a spectator—a participant even—at one of the legendary 'extra-mundane' communication sessions held by E. Œ. Somerville and Martin Ross! I don't know what to say. Miss Cummins invites me to pull up a chair. Edith is already seated in her bath chair at the round table, hands held loosely in her lap. Miss Cummins takes a book and a pen from Edith's work table and joins us. She opens the book I see that its blank pages are lined in blue.

How can I describe the scene? I feel I'm catapulted back in time to the late nineteenth century when seances were all the rage in society. There is dead silence in the big room cluttered with Victorian furniture, pictures and bric-a-brac, a silence broken only by the slow ticking of a clock.

The two women are of that past age and I sense the gap of generations yawning between us. I am far, far away from the canyons of Manhattan and the neon lights of Times Square, the hooting of yellow cabs on Fifth Avenue. This is another world, another time.

'Will you be so good as to assist me, Miss Munroe?' Miss Cummins asks.

'It's quite easy, my dear,' Miss Somerville tells me. 'All you have to do is hold Geraldine's hand lightly at the top of the page. When each line is completed then you simply guide her hand on down to the beginning of the next line.'

I hope *my* hand doesn't shake too much. I don't want to spoil the ladies' 'entertainment'. I take Miss Cummins's hand as bidden. It's very bony but surprisingly warm to the touch. She shuts her eyes as I hold her hand with the pen between thumb and forefinger poised over the blank page.

'It always takes a little time,' Miss Somerville tells me. 'First she must enter into a trance.' She says it as though it's the most natural thing in the world—as though she's discussing the finer points of fox-hunting. I feel I want to laugh.

Minutes later my laughter is forgotten. I feel Miss Cummins's hand jerk suddenly under mine. I relax my grip and the hand moves quickly across the page—far more quickly than I'd have thought possible. And yes, words are forming.

ASTOR COMES!

THEY ARE JOINED together in one continuous flow but if I crane my neck I can read them without difficulty. This is how they begin:

Astor-comes-I-see-a-stranger-with-you-today. ...

'Geraldine's control,' Miss Somerville whispers. I imagine she's referring to me until I remember that 'control' means something like 'spirit guide' in the parlance of the spiritualists. 'Astor' has reached across from the Other Side.

Now Miss Cummins's pen is writing so fast that it's hard to follow the words. It's all I can do to make sure the pen is at the right place when each line is finished. We fill one page, then another. I'm so astounded by the whole affair that I almost miss my 'cue' at one point. We're halfway through page number five when the writing breaks off as suddenly as it began. Miss Cummins's hand goes limp and her head falls on her shoulder. I take the pen from her hand and screw the cap back on.

'Give her a little time to recover, my dear,' Miss Somerville says quietly. 'It takes a lot out of her, you know, and she's not getting any younger.'

It has taken a lot out of me too. I've had only one glass of wine to drink but I feel heady and rather disorientated. Miss Somerville on the other hand looks as cool as a cucumber. What an astonishing woman she is.

'There you are, Geraldine!' she says heartily as Miss Cummins appears to awaken from a deep sleep. Our medium puts a thin hand to her mouth and yawns noisily. She looks at the scrawled pages and nods in satisfaction.

'Martin sends her love as always,' she tells us. 'Boyle [*Miss*

Somerville's brother, murdered in mysterious circumstances in *1936*—Ed.] is with her. He misses his old friends in the Admiralty but appears to be quite happy.'

'I'm so glad,' says Miss Somerville. 'Poor Boyle.' All said in the matter-of-fact voice of someone commenting on a postcard just received from overseas! I regret not having switched on the machine.

'Martin has written a little poem for you,' says Miss Cummins. 'Oh, isn't this lovely! "When one abides here, where a day is all eternity, then one could long to be in that place again, where, tho' a day would pass with fell alacrity, its fleeting hours were joyous for we twain."'

To be honest I don't think much of the 'poem' but it evokes a heartbreaking bout of sobbing from Miss Somerville. Evidently the dead Miss Martin is not often given to versification in her communications. I offer her my handkerchief.

THE PINK LARKSPUR

THERE IS MORE. Neither of the old ladies knows what to make of the following lines and I of course am at a loss too. I give them more or less as I remember they were written:

... *for-the-pink-larkspur-in-Blandford-with-the-yank-up-and-Cameron-insists-it's-her-day-well-who-knows* ...

Miss Somerville shakes her head. Cameron was the last of her brothers to pass away. His death in 1942 came as a relief to Edith because his fatal illness had been long and painful. Now there is just her and Hildegarde.

Miss Cummins reads the rest of the communication aloud. There is little else that excites interest. Miss Somerville seems disappointed that she could not arrange a better 'show' for me. Miss Cummins shuts the book.

Miss Somerville offers me a drink but I decline. I want to get back to my hotel before dark. She rings for Mike to bring the car round. I thank the ladies for their generous hospitality and Mr Townshend promises to 'look you up' on his next visit to the United States—the optimism of these octo- and nonagenerians! On the rocky road to Skibbereen I have time to ponder the strange events of the evening.

Am I convinced that Miss E. Œ. Somerville has received a message from beyond the veil? I do not think so—though I must admit that the experience has touched me in a profound way. Edith believes, Miss Cummins believes, and who am I to question the faith of these two charming old women? We all need faith in something; heaven knows the world has seen so much suffering during this decade. If Miss Somerville's faith lies not only in the survival of our own souls after death but those of our beloved pets too then I believe that her world is a better place for it. Yet her world—the old Anglo-Irish world of the R.M. and the West Carbery Hunt—is a dying one. I doubt whether we'll see the like of it again. Or indeed the like of Miss Edith Œ. Somerville.

G.F.M.

POSTSCRIPT: THE DAY after the interview with Miss Somerville, having returned to my hotel in Skibbereen, I was flicking through the local newspaper *The Cork Examiner* when my eye was drawn to a racing fixture: the Blandford Stakes were due to be run at the Curragh race track that afternoon. Beau Sabreur was the favorite in the four o'clock race but it was another horse that drew my attention, a horse ridden by the champion American jockey Johnny Longden. The horse was Pink Larkspur! Could it be possible ...? Casting all discretion to the winds, I immediately rang for the bell captain and had him place ten shillings to win on Pink Larkspur. Imagine my astonishment when the horse romped home!

I ask you, dear readers, was this luck? Or had I really achieved the unthinkable: had I interviewed *both* authors of the Irish R.M. stories in August 1949? I leave it up to you to decide. ...

G.F.M.

The Drowned Man Fished out of the Drink

> All art must be—by definition—illusion. That much-repeated phrase, 'holding a mirror up to nature' contains a fundamental error that is seldom perceived by [those] who employ it as the touchstone by which they measure an artist's success in his striving to reproduce that which he sees before him. They fail to understand that this 'success' is, in fact, an admission of the artist's failure. ...
>
> JOHN SINGER SARGENT

HAVING BREAKFASTED WELL on coffee, bread rolls and some lightly grilled strips of lean Normandy bacon, George Moore presented himself at the studio in the rue Mansard, Paris, at the appointed hour of ten o'clock. Sargent, he was gratified to note, was already at the easel and working his palette knife expertly over a section of the canvas. Moore's gratification turned, however, to chagrin, on his observing that the artist was not applying paint, but removing it. Not for George Moore *une toile virginale*, but a scraped canvas. This should not have surprised Moore: the

American painter was not at that time a wealthy man; besides, Moore was to get the finished portrait gratis; that was the arrangement. Why such generosity on Sargent's part? The answer lies in the fact that George Augustus Moore was, at the age of twenty-four, a young man of striking appearance, a fitting model for the honing of the art of the portrait-painter.

He was tall, this Moore, and had the leanness of the athlete, though this hardly chimed with his mode of living. Moore was an aesthete, a truth easily deduced from his appearance: the hair was worn long, parted in the middle and allowed to fall in gold and brown curls over the ears and the nape of the neck. The curls were, to a large extent, the work of a barber, whose shop was within a short stroll of Moore's apartment in the rue de la Tour des Dames. The moustache and imperial likewise received their twice-weekly coaching in the wiles of appearing nonchalant, whilst being, in reality, the careful creations of Moore's expensive *friseur*.

The clothing, because of its subdued colourings, might have led a less observant man towards the belief that Moore's purse did not stretch far, that he could safely be compartmentalized alongside the literary *ratés* and struggling artists of the Café Guerbois; but Sargent—who had a keener eye than most for such things—was not fooled. He was quick to catch the perfect fit of the bowler hat and the equally flawless cut of the topcoat, before his visitor removed these items, together with a pair of soft pigskin gloves, tossing them carelessly onto one of the window-sills. Moore went to the big gas stove that hissed in the centre of the studio and rubbed his hands briskly in its warmth. A light vapour rose from his trousers.

'How abominably cold and wet it is!' he muttered in disgust.

Chantal, Sargent's current model and bedmate, took stock of Moore's rear from a divan where she sat sipping coffee. She, too, noticed the fineness of Moore's tailoring—if for reasons that differed from those of her employer. When Moore turned in her direction, she observed that the suit, like the coat, did not advertise its wearer's wealth loudly from the rooftops; in truth, it was rather drab. Only one who had sweated long and hard at the sewing machine could have appreciated the harsh discipline of the seamed edges of the revers and the almost pinched economy of the scyes.

Chantal was such a one. She noted, too, the softness of the shirt, whose high collar would never punish its wearer's neck, and the exquisite match of the frond motif of the tie to that which was cunningly, almost invisibly, woven into the waistcoat.

Moore caught her smile and, Moore being Moore, assumed, mistakenly, that it was intended for his person. Mistakenly, for Chantal's eye, as we have seen, was a professional one; her own dress was less decorative than functional: it was a bright, silk tea-gown that could be shrugged off for her employer's benefit at a moment's notice. Moore knew that it covered *only* her natural beauty. He savoured the jiggle of her round breasts when she rose.

'A coffee, Mr Moore?' she asked him.

'Thank you,' he said. 'Make it a strong one, please.' He followed the movement of her hips beneath the gown as she left for the kitchen. Sargent had now completed his scraping of the canvas; he ran a hand over its surface to test the smoothness. On finding a last irregularity, he began to saw at it.

'Manet tells me that he ran into you at the Athènes the other evening,' he said to Moore without looking up. 'He spoke highly of you, too—I can't imagine way.'

'How could you?' Moore countered. 'The French know about literature; that is one of the many attributes which set them apart from the Anglo-Saxon races.'

Sargent's lip curled in a little smile. He was Moore's junior by two years but already a painter of reputation, and one who commanded respect in a city noted for its distinguished artists. He wore success easily, as though it was no more than the anticipated and natural reward for the application of his talent and ability. Perhaps it was; most men known to Sargent and Moore laboured at their art, hardly believing that success—if and when it came—was their due. Sargent had never entertained doubts about his future, and he admired a similar confidence in others.

'I hope you didn't discuss your work-in-progress with him,' he remarked. 'They say that brings bad luck to a poet.'

'That is easily said by a painter. Painting is the most indiscreet of all the arts.'

Sargent let that go and lapsed into silence. He squinted at the window whose light fell most favourably into the room and altered slightly the angle of the easel. It was good light today, Moore's comment on the weather notwithstanding.

All things considered, John Singer Sargent was blessed with a very decent studio. He had northern light and southern light, and could choose at will that which better suited the work in hand. The rent was not high, and had remained the same ever since Sargent had taken the studio, shortly after his return from Brussels. The house had the luxury, too, of a *heated* staircase, a modern convenience that made Sargent's premises popular among the models —the Italian girls in particular—who, after climbing the four steep flights to the studio, arrived there pleasantly glowing, and quite willing to shed those articles of clothing which Sargent considered superfluous for the subject.

The studio furnishings always delighted Moore, who was himself a fond admirer and collector of the bizarre. Sargent had never revealed the method by which he had achieved the feat, but somehow a swordfish, measuring at least fifteen feet from tail to tip, hung suspended from the ceiling. Moore was uncertain whether the fish was a stuffed specimen, or a wooden replica of a fisherman's superior catch (or *near*-catch); the point was, surely, that the cramped staircase and landings must have presented formidable barriers to the conveyance of the fish up from the street; Moore had seen with his own eyes Sargent's difficulty in manoeuvring a particularly large canvas down those very stairs—in the end, he had had to detach it from the stretcher, and it had never regained its original, drumlike tautness.

Moore was especially fond of the beautiful khaddar hanging that covered the greater part of the east wall. It was clearly a fake: no Indian artist, no matter how great his devotion to the sacred rites of Kama, would have rendered the blue-skinned Krishna disporting himself with *quite* so much abandon. In a collage that was both labyrinthine and libertine, the ubiquitous Hindu avatar was shown entwined and embraided with a splendid selection of kohl-lidded beauties, whose pliancy of limb was truly remarkable.

Positioned flush with the base of the hanging was the old upright Rosenkranz piano with the missing leg (Sargent had countervailed its loss with a stone garden-statuette modelled upon a Caryatid), upon which instrument Chantal sometimes entertained her employer's guests when the day's work was over.

There were seldom pictures other than those upon which the artist was currently engaged; Sargent worked by and large to commission, and rarely—if ever—disappointed his patrons. Moore saw two canvases, draped in cloth, propped against the rear wall.

The chairs, divans and sofas were, perhaps, the most notable items of furniture. There were some twenty examples in all, arranged haphazardly in the six hundred square feet that made up the studio. They came from all corners of Europe, and dated from the time of Louis XI to the present. Together they were worth a fortune, yet Moore had been assured that Sargent had paid next to nothing for most of them, having scoured the flea markets and backstreet shops of Paris, Antwerp, Amsterdam and Copenhagen in search of them, dispatching each foreign purchase ahead by train, to await him upon his return. They were no extravagance, however: they served as period stage property for Sargent's portraiture.

Moore sat now in a comfortable Biedermeier, whose seat fitted almost exactly the length of his thighs and buttocks. Chantal returned with the coffee, nudged a small table with her foot until it was comfortably close to Moore's chair, and placed the cup and saucer upon it. She retired to her own divan, lit a cheroot, and proceeded to ignore Moore. Sargent selected a length of charcoal from his work table.

'How do you wish me,' Moore asked; 'couchant, gardant, statant, sejant or rampant?'

Sargent studied him with the measured look of an undertaker. 'For the moment, *muet*,' he told his sitter. 'Can you turn your head a little more this way? No, your head only ... yes. And keep your hands still.'

For a few seconds only the scratching of Sargent's charcoal on the canvas and the faint drumming of the rain on the roof disturbed the quiet. Moore broke it.

'I have often wondered, Sargent,' he said, 'why you did not choose to throw in your lot with the Impressionists. It seems to me that someone of your temperament should be ideally suited to their manner of working. You are quick to grasp your subject. It is a talent one could well envy.'

These observations caused Sargent some amusement. He was familiar with Moore's habit of pronouncing with the gravity and authority of a savant on subjects with which he had no more than a passing and (Sargent must assume) superficial, acquaintance. Yet Moore, he knew, had studied under Julien. Whether that non-load-bearing pillar of the painting establishment had provided the Irishman with something other than the techniques required in the production of 'mechanical' art, Sargent could not say. Moore was fond of describing himself as a 'poor ignorant boy without preconceived ideas, without prejudice and without ambition', a homily of self-deprecation which Sargent thought ludicrous, in light of Moore's habitual, ponderous statements on art and letters in general.

The Irish dandy, moreover, was talented. Sargent had been shown some samples of what Moore called his 'daubings'; they were, the American thought, not bad at all, youth and inexperience taken into account, and could, in conjunction with the proper training, lead easily to better things. But Moore was impatient; he resented education. This trait was a forgivable one in the sub-genius, the individual who could penetrate to the heart of a matter without the tedious preamble of acquired learning. Sargent thought Moore bright, but by no means a sub-genius.

As for Moore's remark on the Impressionists: was this the same Moore who had rushed to the 'Salon des Réfusés'—the alternative exhibition mounted by some of the Impressionists in Nadar's studio—in order to mock the work of embattled Berthe Morisot and her brothers-in-arms? Sargent had been present, too; he had heard how Moore had eagerly added his voice to those of the bourgeoisie of Paris, who had almost succeeded in strangling the movement at birth.

Was Sargent an Impressionist at heart? Perhaps, he told himself; Monet's and Pissarro's invitation to join their group remained open. Moore's judgement was a perceptive one: Sargent had the facility for exploring a sitter's character at a glance.

'It is not the same thing as Impressionism,' he said aloud.

'Hmm?' said Moore in puzzlement.

Sargent stepped a pace back from his charcoal sketch. He was satisfied with the way his few deft lines delineated Moore's long face, thin nose and slightly bulbous eyes. The chin was wrong, though: it was too firm; he would rectify that in the painting.

'May I see it?' Moore asked eagerly.

'No, you may not. The last thing I require is your advice on how I should further proceed.'

'Oh, very well then,' Moore sniffed. He turned his attention to Chantal, who had kicked off her slippers, and was lounging on her divan, playing with her little cat, a spiteful creature with but a single eye, the other having been lost in the course of a vicious scrap with a neighbouring tabby. Sargent prepared his palette.

'What did you mean a few moments ago,' Moore asked, 'when you remarked that something-or-other is not the same thing as Impressionism?'

'I meant that ...' He threw Moore a serious look. 'This must remain *entre nous*, you understand. ...'

'Of course, my dear fellow!' Moore assured him, while pricking up his ears. 'I am as the narrow house.'

'I like to think', Sargent began, 'that my theories of art go, shall we say, *deeper* than those of Monet and the others. Whereas they are concerned with outward appearance, I wish to explore those aspects of my sitters which are not visible on the surface ... their inner beings.'

'That is scarcely what one might term an original approach,' Moore said. 'Was it not old Rousseau who said, "Let us try in our works to make the manifestation of life our first thought. Let us make a man breathe, a tree really grow."?'

'Forget Rousseau for a moment, Moore!' Sargent snapped. 'The point that I am trying to make is that the Impressionists have overlooked a crucial fact of nature, namely that we perceive the world through our *five* senses. They are concerned with the evidence of our eyes only, the play of light upon a subject. They strive to emulate nature by the control of their colours on the canvas, rather than on the palette. It won't work, Moore! Nature is otherwise; the world is infinitely more complicated than the reflection of pure colour on the retina. Just as there are half-tones—and further subdivisions—in painting, so also are there subdivisions in music, and in those areas of human endeavour that employ our other senses.

'I had a fierce argument with Pissarro about this. He called me a dissembler, would you believe? "Sargent," he said, "every time you draw an outline, or introduce a half-tone, you are simply adding to the pile of lies upon which the Salon is built."'

'To which you responded that he was talking through his hat,' Moore said carefully.

'Please stop fidgeting, Moore.' Sargent applied briskly a muted colour that would serve as a basis for a background. 'I said nothing of the kind, for he was right. Blast it, they are *all* right: Monet and Pissarro, Renoir, Cézanne and Degas and the rest.'

He paused and looked intently at his sitter. 'Do you think that Cabanel or Lefèvre or Bouguereau are the men who will endure? Hah! They know nothing of real art—Goya might never have existed, as far as they are concerned—they are only draughtsmen.'

'Dashed good draughtsmen, though,' Moore said, vexed to hear some of his heroes of the classical school insulted thus.

Chantal flung the one-eyed cat from her in boredom, got up off the divan and padded barefoot to Moore's table, where she scooped up the cup and saucer, without asking whether he might like more coffee. Sargent continued to paint with a near-automatic, fluid rhythm, hardly pausing to consider his next brushstroke.

'I agree,' he said. 'They are splendid draughtsmen, and I have learnt much from them. Damn it, Moore, we simply cannot throw out the baby with the bath-water! Even Degas, that most stubborn and opinionated of men, knows that. Were you aware that he knew Ingres? Head a little higher—yes. According to Degas, Ingres gave him an invaluable lesson: "Draw lines, young man," Ingres told him; "many lines, both from memory and from nature!" Degas has never forgotten that.'

Sargent paused only long enough to clean the three brushes he normally used for portrait work; he did this methodically and at great speed.

'But I have also learnt much from Pissarro and the others,' he went on, '*and* from Manet, of course—perhaps more from him than from anybody else. The man's a genius, you know. Can you look a little more to the left?

'Now, consider this, Moore. How d'you think people might respond if someone were to chance along, someone who should combine the freshness of the Impressionists, the scholarship of the

École, and the conceptual thinking of Manet?'

'I should think they'd jolly well sit up and take notice,' Moore assured him. Sargent grinned in such a boyish way that Moore was reminded with a jolt of how young this precocious artist really was.

'They would, wouldn't they?' He flung a paintbrush down on his table with a violence that startled his sitter. 'And, by God, I will do it!' Chantal was gazing at her employer with interest; the cat was clambering up the side of a settee. Sargent ran a hand through his thick, fair hair. His eyes, Moore noted, were a little wild.

'D'you know what it is, Moore?' he said. 'Being a successful artist is simply a question of economics and steady, forward-looking thinking.'

'Good heavens,' Moore exclaimed, 'but you talk almost like a banker!'

'And what of it?' the painter retorted. 'I'm damned if I'm going to waste the best years of my life beating my head against a stone wall. To blazes with idealism, I say! I have no intention of wrecking my health in the pursuit of an ideal—or my artistic integrity, call it what you will.

'You see, Moore, I know too damned many people in this city who are rotting away in some filthy hovel, unable to put a decent meal on the table once—never you mind twice—a day. And all for what?' Sargent squeezed out a worm of vermilion and stirred it angrily. 'So that they can remain true to themselves, and not have to bother about what the buyers want. Try not to let your chin droop so. It is madness, sheer madness, I tell you.'

'It is the way of things,' Moore said quietly.

'Well, things can damned well change!' Sargent replied. 'And I am the man to change them. Once again, Moore, *entre nous*, eh?'

'Sealing-wax could not secure my lips more effectively.'

'Good. My plan is this. I fully intend to pander to the whims of the establishment, and to accept the patronage of high society with open arms. In other words, Moore, I intend to secure the most lucrative commissions available in this city. And they are there for the taking! My ambition is to have the crowned heads of Europe sit for me—they and their children, and nieces and nephews and uncles and cousins—bastard sons, if need be! And the nobility of

Europe. *And* the captains of American industry, together with their snooty daughters and snot-nosed brats. I don't care. I am interested only in their money.'

'Go on,' said Moore. 'This is most entertaining.'

'In short,' Sargent said, 'I intend upon becoming the most sought-after portraitist in all Christendom. I shall not be required to submit my work to the Salon—the Salon shall call upon *me*! I shall be rich and influential.' Sargent stood back from the portrait and pursed his lips. Moore saw that his brow was beaded with perspiration; it was now close to noon and the gas fire had made the studio exceedingly warm.

'But in the meantime', Moore said drily, 'you will have sold your artistic birthright for a mess of pottage. ...'

Sargent rounded on him. 'I shall have done nothing of the sort! You have heard only the first part of my plan. The other is this: In a few short years from now, my work shall have made me a rich man. But more than wealth, it shall have given me freedom: freedom to do anything whatsoever I choose. And this is the point, Moore. I shall then do just that. I shall follow my own bent; I shall put my theories into practice, painting only for myself.

'Yet, far from being in the position of Pissarro, Degas and the other poor unfortunates, I shall be in one of power; no one may dare ignore me, for my reputation shall be secure.'

Moore reached down to stroke the one-eyed cat, which had ambled over to his chair; the animal raised its tail in a question mark. 'I do believe that you are serious, too,' he told Sargent.

The artist carefully wiped his brushes clean and placed them in a pot. 'Of course I am serious!' he said tartly. 'And to show how serious I am, I shall allow you to buy me luncheon at the Maison d'Or.' He glanced at the canvas. 'We shall finish this tomorrow.'

THIS PROVED TO be the case. Moore again presented himself at the studio the following morning at ten o'clock. The day was less cold than the previous one; the sun gave out a feeble warmth and, when Moore had negotiated the stairs, he found the heat of Sargent's gas fire a little uncomfortable. Chantal was nowhere to be seen—that was a pity—and the cat lay curled up on its mistress's favourite divan. The artist was already smocked, pigment mixed. He nodded curtly to his sitter; there was no invitation to coffee.

'I have thought at some length', Moore said when he was seated, 'about your "plan", as you call it. It is really quite disgraceful, you know.'

'Oh, it is, is it?' Sargent said. His mood, Moore noticed, was not a good one.

'My dear fellow, you know as well as I do that it is. Why, if every artist thought as you do—'

'—and if every sitter *talked* as much as you do, there would be precious little work done in this studio. Can you not keep still for a moment; I am trying to do your eyes.'

'I apologize,' Moore said. 'I shall try to talk only with my lips. I merely meant that it should be the downfall of art if every painter were to follow your lead. None should dare commit himself to tread a fresh road; he should fear failure, poverty and anonymity. Art would *die*, Sargent!:

> 'I gaze upon thy face now changed in death
>   In fear and awe-held breath,
> And ponder if this day-built tenement
>   Be of divine intent;
> If for it God has not conceived a soul
>   And made a perfect whole
> To live transfigured through all change and time,
>   Immutable, sublime.'

Sargent had paused in his work; now he regarded Moore with a look that bordered on the contemptuous.

'And just what was that all about?' he said. 'I wish you poets would leave art alone; you have no understanding of it whatsoever.'

Moore bridled. 'The temple of art is, according to Holland, built of words,' he sniffed. 'Now, as regards my poem, it was not intended to be about art, yet its sentiments could be applied to painting, and the intentions of the painter. You have conceived of an art without a soul, an art that must all be outward show. Such an art cannot endure; it is a dead thing.'

Sargent leaned close to his canvas in order to complete some fine detail. He was smiling; his bad mood seemed to have left him.

'I did not say that my portraiture will endure,' he said, 'yet I do not dismiss the possibility that it may. There will always be a market for beauty, no matter how superficial that beauty is.'

'There you have it!' Moore cried. 'There must be more to art than mere beauty; if a painter thinks otherwise, then he is out of touch with modern thought. You might', he told Sargent mischievously, 'take a leaf from the writer's book: beauty is *passé*; 'tis naturalism that counts nowadays. Take my poem, for example; I intend giving it the title, "Ode To A Dead Body".'

'Good grief!'

Moore ignored the American's scorn. 'You are out of step so far as such matters are concerned,' he told Sargent. 'You remain untouched by *l'esprit de l'âge*, a condition common to most painters.' He sighed. 'I'm afraid it is, as always, the task of us men of letters to show the way. Indeed, only the other week I was discussing morgues and corpses with Zola.'

'How very uplifting,' Sargent said.

'Zola seems to think so, and, indeed, I am inclined towards agreeing with him. It is only the sight of death at close quarters that brings home to one the ephemerality of life:

> 'Or if 'tis nothing but an instant part
>   Of this world's mighty heart,
> Wandering thro' space in every shape and form,
>   Like changing cloud in storm;
> Either may be! two roads to left and right,
>   Unknown, both lost in night.'

Sargent worked with the speed of a machine. He had not looked at his sitter for some time; his concentration was reserved for his canvas.

'I fully intend', he informed Moore, 'to be part of this world's mighty heart, as you put it—but most certainly not an instant one. You and Zola can keep your morbidity; we shall see who wants it in the end.' He nodded to Moore. 'You may relax now; it is finished.'

Moore sprang eagerly from his chair and rushed to the easel. Sargent busied himself with the cleaning of his brushes; he showed no further interest in the canvas. Moore, in contrast, moved from side to side, studying the portrait from every angle. He whistled.

'By heavens, Sargent,' he declared, 'this is splendid stuff! One of your best efforts, if I am any judge. The light alone is superb. Er, what are you doing?'

Sargent was in the process of removing the painting from the easel; he bore it to a corner of the studio and propped it against the wall.

'I am afraid I am going to scrape you,' he told Moore.

The Irishman's bulbous eyes protruberated more than ever. 'You cannot be serious!'

Sargent lit a cigarette and drew slowly on it as he regarded the portrait. 'I have never been more serious,' he told Moore. 'We had agreed that this would be no more than an exercise, and an exercise it has been.

'You it was who said that we artists are out of step with fashion, that we are concerned only with superficialities. Well, Moore, this painting which you admire so much is nothing more than superficiality. I could not possibly let you have it. You should only grow to loathe it—*and* its maker.'

'No, no ...!'

'Think on it in this light, Moore,' Sargent said gently. 'Were it to hang upon your wall, it would remind you every day of our differences. You would find it shallow, and unworthy of you.' He crossed the room for his hat and coat. 'Come,' he said, 'in order to make amends, I shall buy you luncheon today. Then we shall part as friends, owing nothing to one another.'

Sargent was amused at the sight of Moore, who stood with bent knees before the portrait; he was amused by the incomprehension and dismay that were reflected in the Irish dandy's eyes.

'If you so desperately want your portrait done, go to Manet,' he told him. 'You have often hinted that he might like to paint you. Well, then, put him to the test. I think that he will not disappoint you; you and he are alike in many ways.'

The cat opened its single eye and looked at Moore. It seemed to be laughing at him, but it may only have been hungry. ...

> Be not ashamed of anything but to be ashamed.
> Nature is unashamed; one day men shall return,
> naked and unashamed, to Nature.
>
> ÉDOUARD MANET

'*TIENS!*' MOORE SAID in surprise, 'You are not going to make a preliminary sketch?'

'No,'

'That is what I call daredevilry,' Moore said. He watched in wonder as Manet squeezed some viridian from a tube, agitated it briefly with his brush, threw Moore a quick glance, and committed the pigment to the canvas with broad strokes. Moore peeked quickly behind him. There was no green to be seen.

'Daredevilry? It is nothing of the sort,' Manet said. 'I am not concerned at the present moment with form. It is colour, colour, colour ... ' He slashed at the painting with his brush, rocked on his heels and squinted at the result. He threw the brush down, picked up another—two sizes bigger—and used it to pat the viridian with yellow ochre, again applied pure from the tube. 'Nana! Some tea for Mr Moore.'

'I'm sorry,' Moore said; 'I moved.'

'It is of no consequence.'

'Really?'

'Really.'

Moore watched as Manet squeezed out a large dollop of yellow ochre, grabbed a palette knife and attacked the canvas. There followed a further number of assaults, involving liberal quantities of blues, greens, yellows, whites and greys. Moore waited in vain for warmth.

'Still working on the poems?' Manet asked.

'Yes,' Moore said; 'they are progressing most agreeably.'

'I am glad to hear it. Nana! Draw that curtain a fraction. Yes, better. Try not to fall into the trap that Mallarmé set for himself. You have read 'L'Après-midi d'un faune'?'

'Of course, and I think your illustrations most wonderful.'

More green. 'You do not believe that Mallarmé is being too clever, that he uses words for concealment rather than for elucidation?'

'Do *you*?' Moore asked. He received no reply.

'There!' Manet said after not more than two hours had elapsed. It is done.'

'What, already?'

'Yes.'

'Ye gods!' Moore cried. 'You have made me look like a drowned man fished out of the drink!'

The painter laughed and clapped Moore soundly on the back. 'Bravo!' he said. 'A splendid title. That is precisely what I shall call it.' He reached for a rag and wiped his hands.

Moore continued to stare glumly at the canvas. How confusing art is, he thought, in these modern times! Writing is all sham and dissembling; painting is all naked, ugly truth. Yet he knew that Manet was right. *There* was the rub.

'Well, I hate it!' he cried, and, grabbing his hat and coat, he fled outside—out, out, into the sanity of the rue St Petersbourg.

Hanging

WHEN THE DEAN was in his seventy-sixth year he tumbled from the bell-tower of St Patrick's Cathedral. This is how it happened.

Something had taken hold of the Dean that morning: a fit more violent than usual—so thought Brennan, the Dean's loyal servant. It was an upsurge and outpouring of ire and indignation that had the old cleric's brain boiling and seething within seconds.

The deanery was too small to confine this towering rage—too small by far—so the Dean, mindful even in his fury of the dangers that the outside world increasingly held for his person, chose instead to release his passion within the generous confines of the church itself. On seeing him storm in through St Paul's Gate, the Beadle slipped out, unnoticed, by the door leading into the church of St Nicholas, which happened to be open at that hour. The Dean looked about him, ascertained that he was alone, turned his poor tortured face upward and cried: 'LO-O-R-RD GOD!'

A NIGHT IN THE CATACOMBS

That did the trick. The '-od' of the 'God' resounded quite magnificently through the vast and vaulted structure, loud enough for the Dean's defective ears to receive echo after satisfying echo, until they decayed at last in the gloom behind the columns. The Dean felt better for it; a man's cranium could contain with safety only so much wrath—*ira furor brevis est*.

He must, he really must, try to take hold of himself. Sanity is such a delicate thread, to be treated as the spider threads her gossamer. Hmm. Perhaps the simile of the angler and his fishing line was a better one; gently, gently pay it out; gently, gently reel it in; too sharp a tug and the line is broken.

He had already forgotten his purpose in entering the cathedral. Oh, cruel, cruel mind, that it should play these tricks upon him! That it should play into the hands of his enemies—ay, they considered themselves friends, they with their foul petition. Friends! He could not call his friends to mind/Forgot the place where last he din'd. Friends? he longed for enemies; there was sport in enemies. Where were the enemies now? the Queen Annes, the Marlboroughs, the Somersets, the Sharps and the rest? Gone, all gone.

Hmm. The Dean had forgotten his purpose in entering the cathedral at that hour. There could be only one explanation, he thought, looking down at his old shoes: buckles tarnished, heels worn to nothing, uppers caked with the dried evacuation of the unthinking and undiscriminating rabble that squatted over-frequently to bemest his vines of Naboth. Those heaving, perforated ani, those wond'rous boxes! best not to dwell upon them. No! wrong; if he could but dwell upon *some one thing*, rather than suffer this pell-mell, reckless galloping of the brain, its rushing at speed down every blind alley, its ducking in at one door of thought, forgetting the purpose of its visit as it emerged, breathless, at another; the roaring in his head, as though Asmodeus had bent his foul biceps to the bellows, *whoosh-whoosh-whoosh*. It was intolerable.

Hmm. He had already forgotten his purpose. Exercise was the remedy. Walk, walk ... six, eight, ten miles a day. Walk until the coursing of the blood through the body stole a march on the mad tempo of thought. Walk until exhaustion overtook the limbs, that their wasting kept pace at least with the rate of decay of the brain.

Walk up stairs, walk down stairs; keep the blood circulating through the cerebellum.

No, it was not quite right; it required a syllable after 'blood', in order to achieve the left-right, left-right, trochaic effect:

Keep the | blood a- | circu | lating | through the | cere | bellum.

It was, the Dean thought, a quite perfect marching song, and a considerable improvement upon, 'Oh, Sheelah, Sheelah, Sheelah sits/And Celia, Celia, Celia shits!', which had begun to lose its novelty; the Dean was well pleased: *nulla dies sine lineâ.*

He marched from the west door to the rood-screen: sixty-one paces; he marched back down the nave, almost to the west door: sixty-one paces; then he marched the length of the north and south transepts, the *Gedullah* and *Geburah*, the outstretched, crucified arms of the *Corpus Christi*. He did this a half-dozen times. Gradually, the fury ebbed from him; the turbulent priest could think clearly again.

It was not enough, however; the rage still roared within. He needed stairs, that was it; there was exertion in stairs. Besides, the dampness of the floor of St Patrick's repelled him. He loathed that Stygian sewer, also known as the Poddle, that carrier of disease and contagion that could not keep to itself in its recremental depths, but was wont to rise and flood his church with its ordure at every opportunity, conspiring with its ugly sister above ground to desecrate the Dean's holy soil:

> NOW from all Parts the swelling Kennels flow,
> And bear their Trophies with them as they go:
> Filth of all Hues and Odours seem to tell
> What Street they sail'd from, by the Sight and Smell.
> They, as each Torrent drives, with rapid Force
> From *Smithfield*, or St. *Pulchre's* shape their Course,
> And in huge Confluent join at *Snow-Hill* Ridge,
> Fall from the Conduit prone to *Holborn-Bridge*.
> Sweepings from Butchers Stalls, Dung, Guts, and Blood,
> Drown'd Puppies, stinking Sprats, all drench'd in Mud,
> Dead Cats and Turnip-Tops come tumbling down the Flood.

And the bones of his beloved lay ever prey to that sickening flood: there, *there* in that purportedly hallowed ground beneath the flags. Do not talk to me (so raged the Dean's thought) of dust to dust; my Stella, so dear and useful a friend, was become one with the base effluent, slime to slime. That awful prospect was his, too: to die here, or *in domo decani*, like a rat in a sewer.

Up, up, up he must go. The open door to Minot's Tower swam in his vision—swam, because that other enemy, the dweller in the labyrinth, the ophidian denizen of the auricular depths, hissed once more; the Dean rested a hand against a column, and remained so until the vertigo passed. He thought to hear a distant roll of thunder; he fancied that the offensive smell of the Poddle had increased. The light from the clerestory windows seemed to have dulled but, in this observation, he might have been mistaken.

The stone stair wound helically upward within the square, limestone tower, raised by those 'sixty idle straggling fellows'. As the Dean trod its medieval steps, he retained his equilibrium by pressing his right hand against the spine, its face polished to an obsidian-like glaze by the palms of centuries of bell-ringers. He took comfort from the familiar smoothness, cold though the spine was to the touch, its stone always exposed to the circulating draughts. His giddiness was even welcome now, an adversary to be challenged head-on by the power of his will: *Stat pro ratione voluntas*, he thought grimly; my will stands in place of reason.

He was scarcely out of breath when he reached the door that led to the bells, and this fact dismayed the Dean, for it meant that his body was winning the struggle with his mind: he was truly doomed to die first at the top. *Memento mori*, ay, but there were better deaths than this.

Lightning flashed briefly beyond the crenate windows of the belfry.

Bloody bulb's blown again. Must be the condensation.

The Dean's head jerked up, just as a loud clap of thunder sounded. He imagined that he had heard something *before* the thunder rolled. This was probably a fantasy; these days it was not unknown for his mind to confuse effect with cause, or to misjudge the order of a sequence of events. He placed his hand upon a stout timber transom, and looked admiringly upon his bells.

They were eight in number, and mighty were their voices when rung. When the wind from the south was right, their music sped across Bull Alley; out over the city wall; out over the rooftops of Hoey's Court, the Dean's birthplace in the shadow of the Castle; down Cork Hill and out over Smock Alley; over the waters of the Liffey, to be caught by the ears of the Cistercian monks of St Mary's Abbey, to remind them in their orisons that Protestantism still held the high ground in this country.

The bells were *beings*, each proud of its individual power to summon the laity with loud voice, to work in concert with its fellows for the common good. Each spoke in the serious register of E flat—no natural note could voice the summons of the Supernatural. The Dean ran a finger along the words of the inscription etched into the fifth great bell:

> HENRY PARIS MADE ME WITH GOOD SOVND
> TO BE FIFT IN EIGHT WHEN ALL RINGE ROVND

Henry Paris, where art thou now? the Dean thought. Gone the same way as the incumbent chapter head who had commissioned the bell in 1695: Dean Lindsey; his name, too, was incised in the metal. With a pang of sadness, the present Dean reflected that no bell would, after his passing, toll in remembrance of him. A dark and narrow plot in the fetid earth below: no more than that would be his lot.

The thunder rolled again, unaccompanied by lightning. The belfry was strangely dark.

The Dean liked the Seventh Bell best, not for its tone but for its quaint legend, a relic of a time when monarchs were revered with just a shade less piety than was due the Almighty. A dead hand had inscribed:

> FEARE GOD AND HONNOR THE KING,
> FOR OBEDIENC IS A VERTVOVS THING
> ANNO DOMINI 1670. W. P. — R. P. — I. P.

William, Richard and John Purdue: bell-makers to the great. The Dean tapped the Seventh Bell lightly with his middle finger; it gave off the ghost of a peal, which the Dean *felt* rather than heard. He tapped it again, harder. The bell moved slightly. The Dean's mind was starting to race once more; his anger was returning. He swung a fist at the giant bell; such was the diligence with which its society of ringers greased the great headstock, argent and canon, and leather hangings, that the heavy bell began to move in a gentle arc, booming low the while. Greatly elated at that which he had set in motion, the Dean fisted the Seventh Bell again upon its return. Boom! oh, sweet voice; his head reeled; as the bell returned to perigee, he readied his fist for another blow; he could have shouted for joy.

Instead, the Dean toppled from the platform.

He flung out his hands in blind panic, seeing nothing in the blackness into which he plunged. His left hand closed around a stout rope; he grasped it, and it burned the skin as the weight of his body bore him down. He no longer thought rationally; his instinct to survive held sway as his left hand joined his right. The Seventh Bell tolled above him, and would have deafened a man whose hearing was not already impaired. The Dean cried out to his God. He felt the muscles in his shoulders tear, but still he held on. The bell boomed once more, less loudly than before. Still the Dean held on.

He was filled with wonder, not daring to believe that a man as old as he could retain that hold, could cheat death thus. His bony fingers were clutched tightly about the bell-rope, as tenacious as the jaws of a terrier. It was impossible; he must surely fall ere long. Yet there he was:

>hanging.

Not bad for an old pillock like yourself. ...

The Dean turned his head; the voice had sounded close to his ear, yet there was no one to be seen—how could there be? The blood soughed in his head. He was hearing things. Yes, that was it: hearing things.

Well, no, actually—you're not.

What madness was this? The voice reverberated through the tower as deafeningly as the recent tolling of the Seventh Bell. A sense of dread crept over him; he was suddenly aware that this new dementia did not emanate from within; it was as nothing he had ever before experienced; it could, he thought in terror, have but one provenance.

'*Apage, Satana!*' he roared into the darkness. 'Lord Christ, help me!' He was answered by clangorous laughter.

I'm not the Devil, Dean, I assure you.

'Then you are ... you are ...' The Jews did not dare speak His Name; now he thought to understand why. In the Perfect Presence a name was an insult to a power infinitely beyond language.

No, not Himself either.

'Then who—or what—in the name of God *are* you?'

I like to think of myself as a journeyer in strange places, in landscapes of your making and mine.

'Of my making? I do not understand,' the Dean said. Despite his dire predicament, despite his impending death, his enquiring mind took a curious delight in the situation. Did the same thrill, he wondered, go through the wretch who stood at the gallows-foot with a rope about his neck?

A rope. The rope barely moved now; his arms no longer ached; the draught on his face was really rather pleasant. Hmm. The draught seemed to come from below. The Dean forced himself to look down, down to where the sunken floor of the belfry should have been. There was no floor; *there were no floors*: impossibly, the tower's chambers had fallen away, to expose nothing more than the limewashed walls and the flags that reflected their dull whiteness, scores of feet below him. Of course; it should have been obvious! The Dean laughed merrily, comprehension dawning.

'I am dreaming!' he cried, and laughed again. 'If I let go of the rope I shall fall through the blackness and, just before I reach the bottom, why, then I shall awake with a great start in my bed.' Verily it should have been obvious.

If you truly believe that, Dean, then by all means let go of the rope. You'll be doing me a favour. Off you go.

The Dean licked his lips. His fingers twitched; he began to release them, yet once again that instinct for self-preservation gained the upper hand. Even a bed-louse scuttles away from danger.

'I ... I cannot,' he said.

Pity. But I suspected as much. When death is too easy, there's no fun in it, is there? You'd be amazed at the disgusting ways to top themselves some people in here dream up. I'll never understand that; me, I'd go for the least painful method possible: an overdose or something, so that you'd die in your sleep. I knew a lovely girl who hanged herself. They found her in Vanessa's bathroom in the early morning. There was a terrible stink about it. Heads should have rolled, all things being equal. They didn't, of course.

The Dean was dimly aware that, amongst the patent nonsense of the gabbling he had just heard, the name of Vanessa had fallen; Vanessa, dead these long years. Truly this was a most singular dream. The more the Dean thought about it now, the less dreamlike, he decided, was the experience. He tried to recollect the events which had led to this pass; as usual, his memory proved to be dismally poor. He tried another tack. He decided to explore his surroundings with the aid of his five senses, defective though they were: ay, did he not *feel* the rope, his body, the cool air on his face? did he not *hear* the dripping of water, his breathing, and the churning of the blood in his head? did he not *taste* the faint bile of his saliva, the juices of fear released when he had tumbled? did he not *see*—however dimly—the rope, the walls of the tower, the faint sheen of the glistening flags a hundred feet below him? did he not *smell*—?

Dear God, the smell was abominable! The great wonder was that he had not noticed it until now. It was a commingling of human and bestial ordure excreted by every unclean orifice, the stench of putrefaction and feculence, a devilish brew of dung and scum and decay, the like of which had never before assailed the Dean's sensitive nose. hell, he decided now, is not fire; fire is clean and cleansing; hell must be corruption such as this.

And that fact, surely, was proof that he was not dreaming? Never in his recollection had he been conscious of *odours* during the dreaming hours—and verily not of odours so foul as these!

You're right, Dean: it's not a dream—at least, it's not your dream.

The Dean was conscious of the fact that he had not spoken; yet the voice had answered his thought. He did not understand the cryptic words: the dream was not his. If this were so, then whose dream *was* it? I dwell betimes on the fancy (the Dean thought) that we, and the earth and the heavens, are no more than a dream of the Almighty.

Oh dear, you disappoint me, Dean; that's hardly an original thought. Isn't that Aquinas ... or maybe Bruno; it has something heretical about it, don't you think?

There could be no doubt: the Voice, it seemed, had the power to penetrate his mind. Was that truly so? He decided to put this theory to the test.

'I cannot understand why I do not fall,' the Dean thought.

It's the stodge they give you here. Time and time again I've asked for fresh fruit for dessert—you know, peaches and things. I'm not what you'd call fastidious about food but I do believe in the truth of mens sana in corpore sano. D'you imagine that anybody here takes the slightest notice of that? Fresh peaches, you must be joking; if the Old Man of the Mountain hasn't given it his imprimatur, then you won't find it in your doggie dish. You appreciate my difficulty? Or, rather, our difficulty?

Those alien words: what could they mean? Yet he could understand a little of what the Voice said. There was, for instance, the matter of he and the owner of the Voice sharing some difficulty. The Dean could not conceive of an explanation for this; his mind framed a question; the reply came swiftly.

Sometimes, late at night, when I can't sleep, and they've increased my medication, I go and explore my cranium. Have you ever tried that, Dean?

The concept was an interesting one. 'Nay, I do not think so.'

You'd be surprised at the things you can do when you set your mind to them. Sometimes I can compress my whole personality into a line, just a line that extends from the crown of my head to the balls of my feet. Imagine: all that you are, simply a non-Euclidean line, no breadth, only length, and your whole being is passing up and down the length of that line.

At other times I can expand my consciousness in all directions. I can become a cathedral.

'A cathedral?' the Dean asked warily. A thought, a wild notion, had begun to take tenuous hold (or: 'hold tenure' ... one to remember).

A cathedral, certainly. Think, if you will, of the consciousness, as it occupies every nook and cranny of the cranium. Now shrink it down to the size of a pea. Bene; this 'pea' does not float freely somewhere in the middle of one's skull; no, it clings firmly to the rear, and the eyes become as distant, twin rose windows, set in the west wall; the mouth has become the west door ... are you with me so far?

The Dean no longer had feeling in his arms.

You are still aware of your mind as a sentient entity, yet it has become a fly on the east wall of the cathedral.

'I thought you said 'twas a pea,' the Dean remarked.

Only to offer some indication of relative size; the fly metaphor is better.

'Ah!' the Dean said, 'you are speaking metaphorically.' He was on firm ground here. (Nay, upon consideration, he most certainly was not; this, too, was a metaphor: 'firm ground' swung lazily back and forth at a terrifyingly great remove below.)

The fly metaphor is better, and yet it is deficient. For your mind is no spy, no interloper, in the cathedral of your head; it is a part of the whole. It has retreated back, back into a niche, where it watches. The cathedral is the exponent of the cranium; relative to the size of the cranium, the mind has become the size of—

'—a man?'

That's it. We go through life with a vague notion that the mind has a seat somewhere in the brain. We don't know where this seat is because the mind seems to occupy all the brain. But once you shrink the mind in this way, it enables you to form a better picture of the seat of consciousness. It becomes the watcher in the shadows. Am I making sense?

It was better, the Dean decided, to humour the Voice; if lessons were to be learnt from this, then he should offer encouragement.

'Ay,' he said, 'you make perfect sense.' He felt a knot of fear in his bowels; the fear caused his thoughts to race once more—to race so much that only after the elapse of several seconds was the Dean conscious of the fact that the Voice had been speaking:

... they have these strange ones on the continent Continent— do you like that, Dean: 'continent'?—that have a shelf, or pan, to catch your droppings; I suppose the thinking behind this is that you can inspect them for irregularities before they join the local

Poddle. I knew a girl in Turnhout who invented a new form of fortune-telling; it went a step further than the auguries because she'd examine the fruits of the entrails.

'The Excremental Vision?' the Dean said in some excitement.

The same. She'd noticed that no two evacuations ever convoluted into quite the same pattern. This phenomenon has many causes, and depends upon certain variables: the duration of the sitting, the pressure of expulsion, the constituents of the diet, the state of health of the colon—even the motions of the earth and moon play their roles, as that Whig-lover Isaac Newton might have observed when he had digested his apple. In short, the pattern formed by the deposit in the pan is a cynosure to both the immediate state of mind and body of the sitter and the Umwelt. I always felt it was a little like fortune-telling with tea-leaves—probably a superior method; more personal, you understand.

I used to play with toy soldiers when I was small; well, not so much toy soldiers as toy ships and planes and things; the soldiers were boring because you had to set them up for battle, which was a pain; the only fun part was knocking them down again. I had this little field-gun made of steel and painted army drab; it had a spring you could draw back and a bolt you could cock—you know the ones I mean, Dean? no, I don't suppose you would. You could load it with a miniature shell made of steel, and fire this at the troops. That was good fun but you soon got bored with it. The nice thing about the gun was that you could use it to fire matchsticks as well. Burning ones! The trick was to ignite the loaded matchstick with a cigarette lighter, and fire it just as it flared; that way it wouldn't go out in flight.

I had this toy 5th Cavalry fort made of plastic. It didn't matter what soldiers you used to man the fort: cavalry, cowboys, Second World War soldiers, foreign legionnaires, Wellington's infantry; the point was that you could put little cardboard boxes and things inside the fort and pretend you were the Indians shooting flaming arrows. I had the Indian war-cries off to a tee: you know, things you'd pick up from the films: 'Hokka-hayou, ow-wo-wo-wo!', and I'd fire these flaming arrows over the parapets. The cowboys and soldiers would catch fire and melt; when you blew them out, they'd look like those pictures you saw from the Gulf War of Iraqi soldiers half-burnt away, stumps of arms and things, cauterized by the surgeons. Jesus, the smell of burning plastic was something awful; even if I left my bedroom window open the whole day, the pong would still be in the room when Daddy came home from work.

The ships and planes were great. I'd have spent days making these Airfix models, gluing them together with aeroplane cement. But you got tired of them as soon as they were finished, and destroying them was the best part. I'd have Messerschmidts and Stukas bomb a whole fleet of British warships, or an American Flying Fortress bomb this great model of the Bismarck that took me a week to build. The planes would drop marbles and steel ball-bearings as they flew overhead. The ball-bearings would shatter masts and guns and parts of the superstructure.

But fire, Dean, that was the best of all. My father used to bring home cans of Cow Gum from the office; they used it to paste down the artwork. Highly inflammable it was. You'd take a spoonful from the can and let it dry partially; then you'd spear it on a knitting-needle or something and set fire to it. Black, acrid smoke would billow from it, just like the real thing, and drops of fiery, molten matter would fall. You couldn't use your bedroom floor, of course; you had to bring the ships elsewhere. Flames would fall from the sky on them like Sodom and Gomorrah, or Dresden maybe. In seconds the boats would be blazing from stem to stern. I'd do all the sound-effects, from the drone of the big bombers to the scream of the Stukas. And the voices on each side: 'My God, Captain: the sky's full of bandits; we haven't a prayer!';'Achtung, schnell, schnell!' or whatever jargon you'd pick up from the sixty-fourers. It wasn't the voices that intrigued me, though, so much as the power of life and death that I, a boy of seven or eight, held over the great men of history. They were nothing; I was a god. Exhilarating!

The Dean had understood no more than a tiny portion of this odd monologue. It was the last utterance that convinced him that he had now divined the truth: the Voice belonged to a demon, some base minion of the Lucifer who would be God. This theory fitted well the facts as he knew them; it explained the revolting stench, which, even now, increased; it could not be otherwise but that the fetor which assaulted his nose was nothing other than an emission from the Pit!

Look below you, Dean.

Trepidantly, he cast his eyes downward—and saw the unmistakable swirl and eddying of water: an obscene swill of liquid filth, wherein vile and murky objects moved.

The Poddle.

That which the Dean dreaded and abhorred had come to pass. The thunder and lighting had heralded a deluge of great ferocity; even now he heard the torrent of water fall from the grey sky; he heard faint cries from Patrick Street, the frantic calls of men caught out in the tremendous downpour, the bellowing of beasts seeking shelter. The Poddle had burst its banks again; the meanderer in light had joined forces with its dark, subterranean twin.

The slimy tide was rising: NOW from all Parts the swelling Kennels flow. The Dean shuddered as he thought of the evil it was wreaking in his treasured church: the rot penetrating his varnished timbers, the fourteenth-century glory of the choir; overturning lecterns, dumping the Holy Scriptures into the foulness; scumming Dorset marble, the white wrought stone of Bristol; tainting forever Norman shrines and—worst, perhaps, of all—seeping down into the cold Valhalla of the Viking crypt, staining the bones there, and in the place where his precious Stella slept.

I've often wondered why you and Stella never married. Or did you? Hawkesworth was convinced you did, and that you kept the marriage secret.

'Do not talk of her, demon!' the Dean wailed. 'Her name is too sacred to be uttered by your ungodly voice.' The black water was still rising; he wrapped his legs about the rope, fearful of falling. And yet he knew by then that this was an unnecessary precaution; his numbed hands held him aloft.

Sorry; I only asked. You know what I think, Dean? I think you were afraid of her.

'Afraid? What a nonsense!' All that the Dean feared at that moment purled in black contagion below him. To drown in such muck: Lord God, what a revolting death that should be! Even fire was preferable.

Did you know that in thirty-six African languages the word for hell is the same as that for fire? Just thought I'd mention it. ...

'*Thou* shouldst know, demon,' the Dean said. Ever higher rose the flood.

And shall I tell you why I think you were afraid of Stella—indeed of all your women: Stella, Dorothy and Vanessa? I think you feared their femininity, that you have a revulsion against that which most sets woman apart from man. Do you know that 'man' in Hebrew is adam, *meaning, literally, 'red earth' or 'clay', a symbol of blood congealed as flesh? No doubt you do; but are you aware that the word* adam *derives from the Egyptian* atum *or* tum, *the setting sun, the blood-red dying sun sinking into Amenta, the hidden land—hell?*

'I do not apprehend the relevance of this,' the Dean said.

Life, Dean—and death, and love. Life springing from death. I won't insult your intelligence and learning by belabouring the hackneyed imagery of flowers growing on graves. More important, I feel, is the fungal association known as mycorrhiza, whereby a tree evokes its own, almost self-supporting ecosystem. The tree that we see above ground is but half of the tree proper; in some cases, the root complex is an exact counterpart of the superterranean growth; in other words, for every tree above ground a dark tree prospers in the earth. The roots of the dark twin echo perfectly that which grows in light: they burrow down so deeply as the highest branches of the crown reach heavenward; their lateral extension conforms to the horizontal spread of the branches. Just as that part of the tree above ground produces seeds at its extremities, so, too, do the roots germinate their own dark fruits: the fungi. Each tree has its own fungus, the direct result of putrefaction of superfluous generating material, or those seeds which have been denied procreation. This offal produces life of a different order, which feeds the roots of the tree, ensuring the healthy growth of the light brother. The very life of a tree depends upon its ordure. This is a recondite meaning of 'love'.

'Demon!' the Dean yelled, 'you try my poor brain so!'

I should have thought that the parable was an apt one, and not hard to understand. You of all men should appreciative the use of metaphor and simile. Christ, is this the man who likened women to clouds? who called the Duchess of Somerset a Carrot from

Northumberlond? Hmm. Perhaps we'd better take the scientific approach.

Grant says that, 'Ani, the ego, 61, is also void. Sixty-one is the number of Kali, Goddess of Time and Dissolution. Her colour is black, which equates her on the one hand with the void of space, and on the other with the symbolism of sexual magic typified by the blackness of gestation, the silence and darkness of the womb. Above all, 61 is the number of the 'Negative conceiving itself as a Positive'. This it does through the BTN (61) or womb of Kali. BTN derives from the Egyptian but, the determinative of which is the vagina sign. The womb is the nave or NVH (61) which in metathesis becomes HVN, meaning 'wealth', the nature of which is explained by metonymy. The reference is recondite and pertains to the Goddess of the lunar serpent that appears only when it wishes to drink. It then rests its tail on the ground and thrusts its mouth into the water. It is said that 'he who finds the excrement of this serpent is rich forever'. The excrement to which allusion is made is not anal, but menstrual ... the 'nucleus of impurity'. The substance thus vilified is the water of life, i.e. blood; and because its manifestation in the female determined the period of negation or non-openness to the male, it was execrated by an all-male régime as detestable, noisome, and wholly negative.'

'Demon,' the Dean cried, 'that is not science, but sorcery. I will hear no more of serpents. Return to the Pit from whence thou came!' If he were to die, 'twould be with a prayer upon his lips, and not with nefarious talk ringing in his head. He looked with horror at the rising flood, coming ever closer. Or was it? The Dean turned his eyes upward; the eight bells appeared smaller now. Dear God in heaven, the waters were not rising higher; he was sinking lower!

Yes, Dean; it won't be long now. It's time for you and me to part company. About time. I must say, though I've enjoyed our little chat ... with the man who started it all. Oh, I can echo the words of the poet: 'The Dean haunts me; he is always just round the corner'. You can't go anywhere here without being reminded of the Dean.

Yes, we owe so much to you, you and your time. Did the poet not say that everything great in Ireland and in our character, in *what remains of our architecture, comes from your day? that we've kept its seal longer than England? How does it feel to be the chief representative of the intellect of your epoch? that arrogant intellect free at last from superstition? Tell me, Dean, before you go—confirm this for me—did you really foresee democracy? did you dread the future? did you refuse to beget children because of that dread? If so, then I don't blame you; your seed would have been sucked down into this bog of mediocrity and corruption. Remember how you spoke of the Irish Lords and Commons—how did it go again? 'Biennial Squires, to Market brought—'*

> 'Who sell their Souls and Votes for Naught;
> The Nation stript, go joyful back,
> To rob the Church, their Tenants rack,
> Go Snacks with Thieves and Rapparees,
> And, keep the Peace, to pick up Fees:
> In every Jobb to have a Share,
> A Jayl or Barrack to repair;
> And turn the Tax for publick Roads
> Commodius to their own Abodes.'

Oh, you were right, Dean: the more things change, the more they stay the same. Still, you fought the good fight and I admire you for that. A pity it was for naught; it's of no benefit to me. Your works are my bedside companions, do you know that? They're all I have left to keep me sane. I can quote whole passages verbatim.

'I am flattered, demon.'

No, really.

'I am tired now,' said the Dean. 'I am tired of the struggle; the struggle has been long, and my part has been, *absit dicto invidia*, a not inconsiderable one; how many amongst us can hold up the their pens and cry: verily they are mightier weapons than swords, when the point, not the feather, is used.'

You refer to 'The Conduct of Allies'?

'Ay, tho' that worthy pamphlet served to safeguard physical liberty, there is yet a fairer one: the liberty of conscience and honesty. Let another now take up the cudgels and strike a further blow for this, and let the world remember the Dean thus:

'Fair LIBERTY was all his Cry;
For her he stood prepar'd to die;
For her he boldly stood alone;
For her he oft expos'd his own.'

Liberty: that's the very thing I desperately want to grant you, Dean. Liberty.

Feeling was returning to his hands. The return brought no comfort, though, for now he was reminded of the length of his years: his old hands, when numb, had held him aloft; filled now with the blood of life, they could no longer save him.

'My fingers slip upon this greasy rope,' the Dean wailed. He felt the filthy water touch his ankles. 'I cannot hold longer. I cannot; I am resigned: *de nihilo nihilum, in nihilum nil posse reverti*, from nothing nothing, into nothing nothing can return. I am what I am what I am, Yes.'

'Yes'? Is that your final word on the matter?

'Yes.'

Then here are mine: Talk not to me / Of liberty, / Or Samuel Tuke? / Don't make me puke! / Delaney bolts his door.

Light, lighting, lightning flash, and a most, most satisfied sigh. The long ordeal was ended. But what had/has become of the Dean? Ah, Cicero put it well: *Abiit, excessit, evasit, erupit*—he is gone, he is off, he has escaped, he has broken away:

splash.

1985–1995